The Devil Himself

Steven Duggan

Oyster
Books

Set in Merriweather Light 11

ISBN: 9798770389890

Cover photograph © Christina Hoch

ONE

The man who stole my life is waving at me from across the street, his arm about my wife. He smiles at me. Were you to see that smile, you'd call it sympathetic. Kindly, even. There is no hint there of triumph. Even - to his credit - of pity. He smiles at me and waves. A hesitant thing. An awkward recognition of the broken man outside his home. I am careful. I make no attempt to meet his eye. Instead I bend my head low, allowing what is broken in me to become visible.

In my wife Kate's eyes I see the same pity and confusion I saw as they led me from court to begin my sentence. She would have heard that I am out. No doubt the police, or perhaps the press, informed her. She looks at me as if she barely knows me. It has been eight years, after all. A lifetime ago for her. Hopefully some of her wounds have healed. As much as I hate him, I cannot begrudge her whatever peace she's found.

During those first months, as they broke me and I made myself new, the thought of how it would affect her all but drove me mad. My counsel made it clear that she did not believe in my innocence when advising me against calling her as a character witness. Her absence was damning - but he had argued, convincingly, that it was preferable to her answering in the affirmative when asked whether she believed I had killed the girl. Regardless of everything, I cared for her. And for our daughter, of course. Later on it was my fear of confronting them with the damage done to me which led me to refuse any requests for visits. In the event, of course, there were no requests. From anyone. It seemed people had decided that I was dead. As I was perhaps, to them. I never knew whether Kate stayed away on foot of my wishes or whether she'd simply decided to let me rot. I can only assume that her anger and pain have dissipated. For she feels only pity for me now. I can see it in her eyes. And pity is worse than anger. But I can forgive her all of this, as she is still my wife. No decree can change that. Not even the loss of her love. I vowed once to protect her from harm, and to honour her till the day of my death. I remain a man for whom such things matter.

I look beyond them to the house itself - what had once been our home. The silver birches along the driveway are fifteen or twenty feet high now. The driveway itself has been cobbled - grey pavers with a neat redbrick edge. I can see the tip of an opened skylight at the back of the house. A sunroom? A conservatory? Things must be good for them to be able to afford an extension. I wonder if our daughter still has the same room and whether she is at home now?

I am preparing to turn away and drag my feet toward the cover of the railway bridge, out of their sight, when a sudden movement pulls me back. A girl of five or six bursts between them, pushing them apart and demanding their attention.

And my heart stops.

Kate catches her breath, looking across at me with a mixture of guilt and fear. I see both of them pass across her face, one followed by the other, while my addled brain makes the connection.

No. This is not Laura. Laura — our Laura - is fifteen now. This child is an exact replica of Laura at the age I last saw her, the similarities sufficient to stun my brain. But this is not our child. It is theirs. And another crack appears on the petrified bole of my heart.

I turn away, afraid to meet his eye. As practiced as I have become at hiding my thoughts, he could not help but know my intent if he were to look into my eyes. Instead I crumble, the collapse as real as it is feigned, allowing my shoulders to drop under the weight of this most terrible of betrayals. I walk away knowing that he must be revelling in the moment. In the absolute, the ultimate subjugation of his rival. I am nothing now. Utterly defeated in a way the beatings (even that last one) and the myriad losses of reputation, of family, of friends and of my place in the world, could never have prepared me for.

For he knows me, this man. As Cain knew Abel. He knows that however great my pain and righteous my anger, I could never take this from her. He is safe: and I am ground to dust.

But he is wrong.

Do not look at me, brother. See me as I was. Watch the man you knew walk away as you turn and lead my wife and her daughter back into the home you have built upon the rubble of my life. Though I fear Him no longer and know that He too has abandoned me, I pray God you cannot see past your triumph to the void in me which will bring about your destruction. For I am more terrible now than you can possibly imagine. Whatever evil is in you is as nothing compared to my hate, hard-packed in the space which once contained my soul. What you did was worthy of a demon. But I am the Devil himself.

Two

They hate me here. Each and every one of them. Every young mother outside the organic café on main street pushing a crumb of flourless brownie into her mouth with a finger. Each old soak propping up the counter in McDaid's, a tarn of sour spit gathering in his mouth. Each pretentious twat sitting in the window of one of the dozen coffeeshops scribbling his magnum opus. Every sullen teenager slinking home with a bagful of grudges and resentments old enough to know my name. Every unleashed dog shitting on the sidewalk. Every living thing, in this arsehole of a town.

There was a time when I would have sympathized with them. Empathized, even. A man like that? A crime like that? Who would not feel revulsion? Hatred, even. Burn him at the stake. Cut his balls off. Beat him to a pulp and take a meat tenderizer to what is left. Drag him behind a car across an expanse of gravel and shale, pour acid in his eyes, crush his dick in a vice. Extradite him to a US prison where (so the movies inform us) he will become the plaything to an endless line of enormous rapists. Or something of that nature. Something painful.

Irreversible. And preferably public, of course. The end of public hangings (or hangings, drawings and quarterings!) has been a huge loss to the notion of community. The paving stones of a comfortable suburb like this could do with a little blood.

But as much as I hate this place, I feel nothing. Not after eight years. Eight years of 'paying my dues'. Of late-night attacks from narrow-browed sociopaths eager to vent their rage at someone lower than themselves. Of contempt, both passive and active. Of food that tasted of spit, or semen. Of names that break bones.

Let them think what they want. They'll never do more than tut-tut, or cross the road to avoid me. Maybe one of the braver ones will shout at me from a distance late at night, or stir his Neighbourhood Watch group into making a formal complaint about my presence in their particular corner of suburbia (their neighbours can fend for themselves). He might even come at me one night, with a few of his similarly inclined friends. Let them; or let them try. It's all the same to me. If they have the skills to back up their rage then I'll get another beating. So it goes. And if they lack those skills then it won't be me going to the hospital. Because I have skills too, now. And they were hard earned.

I have a choice to make as I wend my way up the main street past the coffeeshops, the artisan baker's and the four clothes boutiques. I can get some lunch in one of the newer cafes where I'm unlikely to be known, or head to McDaid's by the harbour where the food will be both less palatable and less fresh, and where I am almost certain to be recognised. Naturally, I choose the latter.

Lest you think there is some element of masochistic folly in this, I should make it clear that I do so without wishing any misfortune on myself. It is simpler than that. This is – was – my town, and I will go where I choose. I have served my time, after all, and am regarded in the eyes of the law at least as no less deserving. I am, once more, a Citizen. One who doesn't practice hot yoga or extol the benefits of wheatgrass, mind. Greystones has become a yuppie enclave (though I doubt the term is still in use) and feels deserving of my contempt. As do its inhabitants. I may have suffered fools in the past - if not 'gladly' - but I can't abide the smug self-satisfaction evident here on every pavement. Maybe it's not as smug a town as Dalkey (people in Dalkey have the arrogance of the saved following the Rapture) but the stench of self-regard sits heavy on the breeze. There are more senior executives living in Greystones than in any town in Ireland, apparently. I have done my research. This morning most of their wives (I should say husbands as well, for form's sake) seem to be out and about, drinking coffee at noon or, for the rebels amongst them, an early-afternoon glass of sauvignon blanc.

I leave them to it, and ten minutes later I am walking through the doorway of McDaid's, sizing up the array of taps behind the bar. The place hasn't changed. Irish bars of this kind never do. A lick of paint a few years back perhaps (another refresh long overdue). Some new televisions at the back, determinedly turned off as they are for everything but major sporting occasions. There are new taps behind the counter, some of which I don't recognise. McDaid's has become somewhat gentrified, if the foreign lagers and the overpriced bottles of pilsner in the cooler are an indication. There is even an opened bottle of wine in there. Christ! They're serving glasses of wine in McDaid's now? The elderly alcoholics who kept this place in business during the recession would flip their pickled corpses in their graves.

I order a Guinness from a young barman I do not know and take a seat in a corner far from the window. I sip the bitter stout and gather my thoughts. I have already scanned the room and sit with my back to the wall like a gangster from some bad movie, wary of attack. The picture of the Sacred Heart is still mounted above the door, the votive candle beneath it unlit. Which tells me that old man McDaid must have died since I was last here, otherwise that young barman would be seeking alternative employment.

There is very little faith in prison. Despite the rash of religious conversions. I had no faith as such to lose by the time I left Mountjoy. Mountjoy. My first stop. The first circle in that particular version of hell. From that time on, however, I found it more plausible to imagine Him as present in the world. The God I saw was far removed from the Christian ideal, however. He was the Old God. Cruel. Vengeful. The God who invites fathers to slaughter their children and responds to man's slightest criticism with plagues and devastation. The Supreme Fascist as Dave, one of my early cellmates, used to call him.

"Jack!"

He's there when I turn around. Same ill-fitting blue suit, with the sort of sheen you'd find on a dead fish. Same graveyard pallor. Same aversion to meeting your eye. A little more grey in his hair, but otherwise unchanged. Despite myself, I am glad to see him. Though I do my best to hide it.

"Mick."

He sucks at his teeth, trying to extricate a remnant of food and simultaneously tugging at the zip of his flies. The gesture draw attention to the acne scars on his cheeks, evidence of a miserable adolescence. Some of which I shared with him, when we were teenagers together in the town.

"Heard you were back."

"Naturally."

I wait. I've learnt silence since last we met.

"You look like shite!"

"Thanks for that. I didn't have your advantage of already being an ugly fucker."

"Cheers!"

He pauses, pretending to look about him while giving me a careful once-over. Mick Clancy is a policeman. It's as much a description of his character as his occupation. He could be nothing else. He is also – or was – the only man to believe in my innocence.

"What time do you make it?"

I don't move. I own neither a watch nor a mobile phone, but don't feel the need to share this information with him. I've learnt reticence since last we met.

"Dunno. Late enough?"

"I suppose..." He pretends he's only just been struck by the thought. "I could always join you for a pint?"

"As long as you're buying it yourself."

"Buying – and claiming it back! Sure, this is work."

"Then I'm happy to assist you with your enquiries, Guard."

He gives me a gap-toothed grin - the poster-boy for Irish dentistry, circa 1966 - and pulls up a chair opposite me.

"Two pints Martin, like a good lad," Mick shouts across the bar, gesturing as he does so at the twelve-foot hoardings surrounding the stalled construction work on the old harbour. The view obviously offends Mick's sense of the beautiful. He scowls through the glass, tucking the tail of his jacket beneath him as he sits.

"Bastard planners! Let the place fall to rack and ruin for ten years before handing it over to the property developers, just before the crash - and all we get is an acre of tarmac and those feckin' hoardings for the next few years, while they pray for house prices to creep up again."

"I thought the foreshore belonged to the people? How'd they manage to sell it off?"

"I'm the wrong branch of law enforcement to ask that question. But it's a good one, Jack, and you're not alone in asking it."

"I used to walk Laura down here. When we had a dog. Let the fat hound off the leash to bark at the waves while we went for chips in Mooney's."

The dog had been old even then. We had inherited her from Kate's mother when she was too elderly to walk her regularly herself. A fat, greying lab crossbreed. Laura loved her to a degree entirely unmerited by the flatulent hound I tripped over five times a day, and who woke me from sleep every morning at 4:00 am for months on end that last summer, as age met incontinence. Harry Hound. Harriett, to give her her full name, though no one ever did. Kate used to laugh at the greeting I'd shout as I walked in the doorway each evening, at a volume loud enough to shock the neighbours. "Get up off that sofa you lazy bitch, or I'll boot you halfway down the garden!" Despite myself, I felt a smile tug at the corner of my mouth.

"He's still there, you know."

"Who?"

"Bill Mooney. Wouldn't sell up. Thought he'd hold out until they offered him a king's ransom. Instead of which the old fecker is stuck back there, round the corner of that hoarding with the picture of the girls staring out at the ferry boats, still up to his armpits in grease."

"He always was a miserable fucker. I don't reckon money would have changed that."

"Ye may be right," Mick says. "Though it often has that ability. So I'm told."

"I'm the wrong side of law enforcement to answer that question."

Mick smiled back at me.

"It's good to see you, Jack."

"Is it?"

"You're right. Having you back in town is a pain in my arse. And I'm hoping that it's just a flying visit. But it's good to see you well, in any case."

The term needs no rebuttal. We both know I am not well. Just as we both know I have no intention of leaving Greystones any time soon.

"How long have you been out?"

"You know the answer to that, Mick."

"Took you long enough to get here, then. What do you make of it?"

"The town? Still the same shithole we grew up in. Though with cleaner streets and more expensive houses."

"That's about the size of it. Did you know we now have fourteen coffee shops on or close to the main street? And still only three pubs!"

"A shocking state of affairs, I'm sure."

"People have no sense of priorities!"

I watch as he dispatches a good half of his pint with his first sip and realize that the second pint hasn't been ordered for me. The man has a thirst on him like a desert hound. My tolerance – after years of enforced abstinence – is considerably slighter.

"So. To be serious, Jack. What's the plan? How long are you intending this visit home to be? Just down for the day, I hope?"

"I've booked one of the rooms in Cois Farraige." This is a lie, but one I intend to make good on. Cois Farraige is a refurbished YMCA close to where we sit, with single rooms and family suites available by the day or week, complete with cooking facilities. I'd found it on the internet PC in the lobby of the Dublin hotel I'd stayed in following my release.

"For how long?"

"Not long, I hope. As long as it takes."

"Aghh – Jesus, Jack. Would you not let it go?"

"Would you?"

He looked down at his beer and nodded gently.

"I never stopped looking at it, you know. Been teasing it over in my mind all these years."

"Thanks for that, Mick. I take it you didn't have any dramatic breakthroughs?"

"Nope. Looks like we got the right man."

He raised his glass toward me, and I clinked it against my own.

"He's served his sentence in any case, isn't that it? No need to drag up old wounds."

"That's about the size of it. No one wants to go back there, Jack."

"Except us."

"Except you."

"You couldn't resist it if you tried. And in any case, I have an advantage. I already know who did it."

He grimaced and fixed me with a cold stare.

"Knowing it is one thing, Jack. Saying it around town would be quite another."

"Don't worry. I'm not about to make trouble for myself. Though I can't account for others."

"You're right to worry about that, Jack. There's been a lot of changes here, what with all the new estates and everything. But there's still enough of the older folk around to want you gone, and not be slow in letting you know it."

"I shall count on your protection then, Guard."

"For what it's worth. Seriously, could you not do whatever it is you need to do from Dublin? Or Derry, preferably. Murderers are two a penny up there, I hear."

"You know the answer to that one too, Mick. The answer I need is here somewhere - and if it's here, then I'll find it. I've already spent eight years investigating it. Now I need to do what I never got the chance to do when you arrested me, and see where it all happened."

"People won't like it."

"Fuck 'people'! I promise, I'll leave the day you arrest the fucker, and happily swear never to return. Trust me. I'll miss this place no more than it'll miss me."

He sighed, though I knew he'd never entertained any real hope of things being different.

"Promise me that you'll do it quietly then – will you give me that? The last thing I need is having to rescue you from a hoard of irate locals baying for your blood."

"You'll barely know I'm here," I lied.

THREE

The evening was drawing in when I left McDaid's. Mick was long gone, but with nowhere to go myself I'd stayed by the window staring out toward a distant edge of the sea, watching the light play on subdued waves as the day drew its last breaths. The young saplings planted about the harbour curtsied in the breeze, waving their leaves frantically. It was comfortable here. A quiet corner from which to view the world. I was still having trouble getting used to this - to being in the world. I stepped outside at one point to call the number for Cois Farraige, and booked a room. When I'd asked Martin where the phone was he'd looked at me like I was a crazy man and handed me his mobile. I could have walked the couple of hundred yards between the hostel and the pub and checked in in person, but the pints had made me lazy. I made a booking for a week, with an option to extend it at the same rate. The deposit at check-in would be a hundred euro, which wouldn't be a problem. I was good for it - for all the wrong reasons.

Having no siblings but Tom, and with our mother long dead, I'd held out little expectation of receiving regular family missives in prison. In this at least I wouldn't be disappointed. My father didn't even attend the trial, having convinced himself of my guilt within an hour of my arrest. (No doubt my brother had helped him to overcome any lingering doubts.) For seven years he neither wrote nor phoned me. So it was a surprise to discover that I still had tears for him when news of his death reached me, in the final year of my sentence. They didn't allow me to attend his funeral – which was probably best for all concerned – but there was to be a posthumous surprise in store for me. He had always been a procrastinator, and died without making a will. Which meant that I inherited half of his estate. I found a solicitor in the same law practice as my trial brief and instructed him to sell everything he could, and to deposit the proceeds in a bank account set up under my Irish name. My Dad had never been rich, but he'd always been cheap, and I ended up with a decent five-figure sum. More than enough to 'get me back on my feet', as the solicitor put it. Though I had other plans for it, even then.

When I left the pub the sun was showing off on the horizon, throwing the husks of half-built apartments beyond the hoardings into dark shadow. It was an unlovely sight. I was turning up the hill toward the hostel when the prospect of a walk along the seafront overcame my cynicism, at least temporarily, and I crossed over to where the coastal walk began. The pathway was pitted and worn smooth where generations of dogs and their walkers had traced their way along the coves and buffs from the harbour to the South Beach. It was one of the few places I'd seen since returning which was as it had been before. Indeed, as it had been in my youth. There is nothing a small town hates more than change, and here at any rate that reluctance to embrace any of the doubtful advantages of progress held firm. The old black railings which guarded areas where the walk dropped precipitously towards the rocks were bent and crooked, but pretty much as they had been when the Victorians first installed them. The houses facing the sea were a mixture of Victorian and Edwardian, dating back to a time when this was a holiday destination for the well-heeled, who'd make the arduous twenty-mile journey from Mountjoy or Merrion Square to their summer houses on the coast. Mountjoy! The irony wasn't lost on me. Those old houses had enjoyed many a change of owner in that time, but remained much as they were, the odd kitchen extension or new patio excepted. They were handsome buildings - with wooden eaves and bay windows, and fanlights over the doors. I'd gone out with a girl from one of them, the last-but-one on the southern end of a line of terraced red-bricks. Mary. She had black hair and a crooked smile, I remembered. As if she were guarding a secret. I'd been sufficiently love-struck to write her a poem, which had hastened the process whereby she left me for my best friend.

I heard them before I saw them. I'd rounded the final turn and was heading back up the road parallel to the shore when I passed the back gates of the church carpark. I heard the laughter first. Shrill, and infused with cruelty. It was a sound I knew well. Whenever someone decided to stick a fist in my stomach in the yard, or kicked me in the back as I passed, there'd always be an audience making that sound. Laughter without joy, but with the glee of malice. Perhaps that was why I couldn't pass it by. It was a portentous decision; though I wasn't to know it then.

To my surprise, there was one key difference between the scene I was greeted with on walking through the gates and those I'd seen played out so often in the prison yard. The figures at the centre of the circle of laughing goons were girls. Two girls – one blonde, one dark haired – both of them around the same age as Laura. For a second I thought... but there was no resemblance. Though it did give me pause to realize how carefully I'd had to scrutinize their faces before assuring myself that my own daughter was not amongst them.

The mechanics of these scenes never changed. The aggressor – in this case the blonde girl – always patrols centre stage, keeping their victim in place to emphasise their authority. The audience stands close, but at a sufficient distance to allow room for whatever malevolence the aggressor has in mind. It's nothing to them, after all, what she does. As long as it's entertaining. Just give her space. The difference between girls and boys at this age I'd been told was that girls are more vicious, because they never use force. Apparently, this wasn't always true.

I couldn't hear what was being said but it didn't matter. Everything about the scene spoke volumes. The hungry crowd. The repeated efforts to force their quarry into a corner. To cower. To collapse into tears. As far as I could see she was holding up fairly well, but the marks on her cheeks showed that she hadn't done so well earlier on, and would likely do even worse without my intervention.

"Why don't you all fuck off home and leave her be?" I asked, stepping into the circle.

"And why don't you fuck off and mind your own business?" the blonde girl replied, utterly unfazed. I took a moment to look about me, staring down the less committed.

"Who says it's not my business?"

"Yeah? And who the fuck are you, then? You're not her father! And you're a bit old to be her boyfriend. Unless you like them young, eh?" She smiled a smile of pure malice.

"You don't want to know who I am. Trust me. Let's just call me a concerned citizen, or some shit like that. Either way. I'm not leaving till you and this posse of fuckwits piss off and leave her alone."

I knew only too well how these things worked. I couldn't use my usual approach and take her on directly, so I chose the biggest of the boys instead, walking towards him until I was an inch from his face, with my hands hanging loose by my side.

"What's your name?"

"Mind your own fucking business."

"Oh, but it is my business now. So I'm asking you one more time. What's. Your. Name?"

I smiled and waited.

"John."

"No it's not - but it'll do. Say goodnight 'John'. And make it quick. I've a history of losing patience with little shites like you. And you really, really don't want to try my patience."

Looking around, I realised that kids of this age were not as I remembered them. They were a head taller than me and my friends had been, and bulked up in ways we'd never have imagined. For a second I wondered if I'd be able to hold my own, should they stand their ground or make a move against me. But I needn't have worried. 'John' took a step back, spitting expressively between his feet before turning away in feigned contempt.

"Good boy, John! Now take your asshole friends with you and get out of my face. She might make your life difficult tomorrow for proving such a wimp - but trust me. It's the wise decision."

The blonde girl might indeed have been miffed, but she hid it well.

"Get your kicks from hassling kids, do you mister? Maybe I should tell someone how you came in here and bothered us. In a dark place like this. And how lucky it was that my friends happened to come along just in time, before you tried anything! Don't reckon the police would like that very much. What with me being an innocent young girl and all."

"That's a joke!" the dark-haired girl said. I had misjudged her apparently. She had more grit than most would, in these circumstances.

"Try it!" I said to the blonde. "I think you'll find the police have a pretty low opinion of me already. So you're not going to add anything there. I'm the bogey man, I am, round these parts." I smiled, showing my teeth. "So go on, then. Give it your best shot."

The girl hesitated, then walked up to me and went one better than her sidekick by spitting directly into my face. I held my fists tight against my sides, doing nothing to register what she'd done. Without waiting for a reaction, she turned to the dark-haired girl and gave her a broad smile, saying, "See you tomorrow Sheila, eh?" before walking out the gate with her band of admirers in tow. I waited till they were out of sight before using my sleeve to wipe the spittle from my cheek.

"She seems nice!"

"Believe me, that's as nice as she gets."

"You okay to get home?" I asked.

"Yeah. I'll just give it a few minutes..."

"Good idea."

I suddenly felt awkward, standing alone in the carpark with her. She seemed to sense it too.

"It's fine. I only live round the corner."

"Okay! Well. Goodnight, then."

"Goodnight."

As I walked away, it struck me that she hadn't thanked me. Though once I thought about it, I soon understood why.

FOUR

The room was sparse but clean. Cream carpet. High ceilings. A simple pine bed in the Scandinavian style. Matching wardrobe and desk. There were cooking facilities down the corridor in a communal kitchen, along with a washing machine and dryer.

Two large windows looked out on a square of grass housing a children's playset, with a couple of discarded footballs lying close by. The building itself was L shaped. The wing I was staying in was a modern extension to the old house, which was of a similar height but with a traditional pitched roof rather than the flat roof of the extension, with its copper facia over the guttering. The contrast between old and new was extreme, the old house doing a poor job of hiding its age and general state of repair, notwithstanding a recent coat of paint. The carpark was on the far side of the courtyard formed by the two buildings, two lines of ten spaces on a gravel surface, the stones turned dark by a sudden shower. It was cheap, and considerably more comfortable than I'd imagined. The old youth hostel had been reinvented by someone with an eye on those looking for easy access to the city without the high prices they'd encounter there. At this time of year however such optimism seemed misplaced. As far as I could tell the only other guests were a couple with a young boy of three or four staying on the second floor. I'd watched them come in earlier, the father (lean, balding, several years older than his equally thin wife) pulling the boy past the playset, despite his protestations. Both parents were well-dressed, the man in a three-quarter-length navy coat, the woman in a short leather jacket of the kind favoured by models rather than bikers. Why were they here, I wondered? Visiting relatives in the area? On a business trip to Dublin, and bringing the family along to make a weekend of it?

From what I'd gathered from the noticeboard in the entrance, most of the centre's business came from retreats, religious and otherwise, or group bookings of that type. An evangelical troupe had left some of their literature on the small table beneath the noticeboard. 'Living In Christ'. Not something I could imagine myself signing up for. Before or since.

There were two low armchairs in my room, on either side of a pine coffee table. I pulled one of them over to the window and sat down, watching the rain draw extended beads down the glass. The room was warm, though not uncomfortably so, making me feel drowsy despite the relatively early hour. I wouldn't fall asleep though. The room was too unfamiliar. Years spent in a smaller space than this meant that those dimensions would disturb me, strange as that might sound. When you've fallen asleep every night in a single bed tight against a wall, the opposite wall a mere eight feet away, falling asleep in a double bed in the middle of a large room was a virtual impossibility, the space itself feeling oppressive, and alien.

In the beginning I'd found it hard to get to sleep in prison. Especially during my first months in Sedgefield, when I'd had to share a cell. Sharing a room once you've passed a certain age entails an enormous sacrifice, I discovered. There is something childish about it, somehow. Like it's something you should have outgrown. And that's apart from the difficulties involved in adjusting to another's habits; in accommodating or addressing them. In the beginning, I'd always been the one bending my ways to my roommate's. But that changed once I realized that such things mattered. That there was a hierarchy even in that cramped space, and that living with someone who left dirty socks on the floor and newspaper sheets littering the area - newspaper being something of an exaggeration, The Sun and The Star being closer to picture books - was a recipe for festering resentment, if not dealt with early on. I was fastidiously tidy when I was inside and needed my roommate to reciprocate. In most cases, such an accommodation was easily arrived at. On one or two occasions - once seasoned - I'd had to insist on it. By that time, however, my wishes tended to be respected.

It is a fallacy that prisons make thugs of gentle men. Gentlemen, if you will. Most of those who pass through the system remain essentially as they were when they arrived, be that angry or passive, gregarious or reserved. I'd never quite worked out which prison was harder for, the introverts or the extraverts. For the former, solitude must have been less of a hardship. But the forced bonhomie and incessant chatter in the communal areas must have proved a struggle for them, just as it provided a lifeline for the extraverts. For me, self-reliance was a necessity. Outcasts have no choice but to be solitary. Alone... But not passive. Not cowering. Passivity meant being broken and beaten. Resistance was as necessary as eating, if prison for someone like me was not to become a daily torture. Torture which so often ended in the same sad manner I would witness several times over my eight years inside. Suicide was never an option for me, despite the frequency and viciousness of the beatings that first year. I had to survive. For this. For the chance to set things right. No – that was wrong, wasn't it? I wasn't here to right a wrong. I was here to make my brother pay. I owed him, for each and every blow.

Like most men, violence was a skill in which I was poorly schooled. A few schoolyard 'fights' excepted (none of which I could claim to have won) I had never actually hit someone in anger. But it didn't take me long to realise pacifism was not an option there. And so, I studied. With complete commitment, and guided by logic. Learning how to take care of myself was a problem to be solved, like any other. I started with the Tai Chi classes they organised on Thursday evening alongside the literacy classes, for the inflexible and uneducated in turn. The intention might have been to teach us inner calm, but I knew enough about what the art offered in terms of self-defence to seek out those additional benefits. The rest I learnt from YouTube in the computer room, where a lax regime accompanied by a surfeit of technical know-how meant that inmates had pretty much unfettered access to the internet, in direct contravention of the guidelines pasted on the side of each of the elderly monitors. I studied, and I practiced. Once they locked us down for the evening I'd roll my mattress into a tube, tie it tight with the sleeve of a jumper and spend hours punching, kicking and striking it on every side. What this failed to do in terms of honing my technique was compensated for in improving my physique: my muscles and sinews growing and stretching by the week.

Knowing any battles I'd have to fight would be down and dirty, and at close quarters, I settled on Krav Maga as the most effective style to adopt - the narrow range of blows and blocks easier to master than more formal styles of karate. Krav Maga was originally designed by Jewish resistance fighters in the Bratislava ghetto, and was developed further by the Israeli armed forces. It prioritized defending against an attack in a lift or a similarly cramped space above combat on some kind of mat with an umpire close by, and advocated defending and attacking at the same time. Soon enough, the theoretical knowledge I acquired online was augmented by the opportunity to practice. Multiple opportunities, in fact. At first, my new-found resistance just led to longer and more severe beatings. But, in time, given the opportunity to hone my skills, I became sufficiently proficient - and uninhibited − to dissuade all but the most foolhardy from attacking me. Knowing how to hit back it turned out was only part of it. Being able to take their blows and remain standing was more intimidating to them. I had no fear. What could they do to me, after all, that hadn't been done already? Sometimes I'd let them get the first blow in just to make that point, responding with a smile before I laid into them.

Those beatings originated here, in Greystones. In what the locals had been so happy to say about me and - following my trial - in the label they pinned to me. Child-killers are the very lowest form of life in a prison. You know this already, and I'm sure you understand why. I may not have been a child-rapist (these were persecuted to an even greater extent, and were difficult for even the most charitable to pity) but nearly everybody in a prison has a daughter or a sister to provide them with a convenient excuse to make someone like me's life a misery. If they needed an excuse, that is.

The problem with violence is that it is enjoyable. Many of those who attacked me did so out of little more than boredom, or to entertain themselves. It feels good to hit or kick a man. It provides a rush of blood or, at worst, a diversion. Later on I would have to protect myself from just such attractions.

I've gotten into the habit of viewing my history in reverse. From my release and my return to Greystones, all the way back to that first visit from the guards, and the discovery of the girl's body. It is more natural somehow to unpack it in that way. Now, however, I have to go back to the start. To forget everything that happened subsequently, and focus on those first few days. Whatever hope I have of proving my innocence depends upon my recollection of those events, times and places. Which worries me. It was all so long ago, of course. And many of those places have changed as much as I have.

I would have to talk Mick into sharing the case notes with me. As unlikely as that might be. Or at least into giving me the basic details, so I didn't have to rely on memory alone. And there was so much that I didn't know. Stuff that never came out at trial, or from witnesses that they'd never called. It had been so easy to convict me, in the end, that they'd probably held much of the evidence back. To keep things simple for the jury. Or because they didn't need it. Even my own counsel had called it an open and shut case. Forty minutes – that's how long it'd taken the jury to reach a guilty verdict. Barely enough time for the jurors to order some tea and coffee and choose a seat around the table.

The light outside had disappeared now, the playset leaching colour beneath the sodium lights, fire engine red changing to purple, yellow to the subdued beige of a manila envelope. It was a little after eight. I'd sat there, by my reckoning, for about ninety minutes. Doing nothing. Letting time pass. My choice – as had been the case every evening since my release – was to stay in my room alone, or to wander out to find some company. Or if not company, then the noise of it at any rate, in the midst of others' chatter and laughter. I could either sit here - perhaps listening to some of the music I'd downloaded to the smartphone I'd picked up that afternoon in Carphone Warehouse - or risk showing my face in a pub. On a Thursday evening, when most of them would be full. Thursday was pay day and dole day, and for many people marked the real start to the weekend. It wouldn't be quiet, like McDaid's had been earlier in the day. And this was still a small town. I was almost certain to run into someone who knew me. Or knew of me.

The wise thing to do was to stretch out on the bed, queue up The Blue Nile or Bon Iver on my phone, and try to drift off to sleep. Definitely the smart thing, I thought, as I took my jacket from the back of the chair and walked out into the corridor.

FIVE

The arrival of a new bar in town had passed me by unnoticed. As you'd expect. For generations, two pubs had controlled the bar trade in the town, both run by the same family. The new pub, Molly Riley's, was a boutique bar – a long, narrow space occupying a terraced building which had housed a butcher's shop back when I'd last lived here. I supposed it had been driven out of business by the supermarkets. People no longer bought their sausages in a butcher's, any more than they bought their fruit and veg from a grocer. Those old stores were gone or making a twee return as artisan stores, flogging bread loafs as luxury items.

As I'd anticipated, the place was packed. They even had a bouncer on the door. I met his stare with the same cold glare I used to give the wardens. Fuck you, pal. I'm going in and try and stop me. He was a sorry looking fucker in any case. He wouldn't have lasted a day in The Joy.

The counter ran the full length of the bar, the mismatched stools arrayed along it occupied by a relatively young clientele, though none still in their twenties as far as I could see. No doubt they had their own place to go, and left this place to people they regarded as hopelessly old. At forty-one I fit within their target demographic; if only just.

Opposite the bar was an assortment of equally mismatched chairs and tables – it was as if someone had raided a terrace of houses in Ringsend sometime in the mid-seventies and grabbed what they could, regardless of colour or style. Corduroy, flowery linens and cracked leather sat uneasily side by side. The walls - dotted with bric-a-brac - were papered in patterns of the era, the design changing every few feet or as a corner dictated. Some spaces were decorated with collages of magazine covers, and full-page advertisements from forties and fifties magazines. The news stories told of Victory in the Suez and Rex Harrison's latest virtuoso performance. And there were clocks everywhere. Pendulum clocks, mantel clocks set at incongruous angles, even some grandfather clocks, all of them set to different times - or right twice a day, as they have it. Somehow, it worked. I could imagine it becoming a regular haunt, if I dared to entertain such a notion.

I stood at the bar long enough for the barman to spot me, and ordered a Guinness. The inflation in the price of a pint still took me aback; but I was hardly stuck for it. Spotting an alcove further in, beneath a television showing rugby highlights, I took my pint and started to walk towards it. I was halfway there when the contents of a glass arced through the air and sluiced down my righthand side.

I knew better than to think it was an accident. I stopped and looked over at the stools to my right. The years had been unkind to them - time having deposited several stones on each of them in its passage, and one of them rapidly losing his hair. But I recognised them, well enough. Ronan O'Neill and Francis Carson.

O'Neill was a study in disappointment - his shoulders sagging, his mouth set in what looked like a permanent sneer. At the world in general, I suspected, rather than just those unfortunate enough to be in his company. He wore his hair combed back from his forehead at a length designed to hide the bald spot peeking through at his crown. He had the nose of a rugby player who'd been caught on the wrong side one too many times, and the bags under his eyes were little pouches of dark flesh, the colour of kidney beans. Carson had borne the years better but still looked as if he spent too much time in the pub - his complexion so washed out that it exposed every blemish, and what appeared to be razor burn on the lower slopes of his neck. I'd known them since our schooldays, though we'd never been friends. And they were clearly not looking to correct that now. I decided to walk on and would have been prepared to ignore it (the bar was dark, and my shirt and jeans would dry out soon enough) had Carson not stuck a foot out in front of me. I looked down at it, as if puzzled by what was impeding my passage.

"The exit's in that direction," he said, jabbing a thumb toward the door.

I said nothing, and took a moment to size them up. I had no wish to start a fight, knowing the bouncer would be on the scene the moment the first blow was struck. And that taking out a bouncer would pretty much extinguish any hope I might have of making this my local.

"Thanks for the geography lesson. Now, are you going to move your foot, or do you want me to snap it off and hand it to you?"

"Jack Finch! So - this a flying visit, is it?" O'Neill said.

"Strange. You're the second person to ask me that question today. I'll let you both know the moment I give a fuck what you think."

Carson lowered himself from his stool and squared up to me. We were of a height, both of us a little shy of six foot. I reckoned I was a good fifty-pounds lighter, though. He must have spent a lot of his evenings perched at bars like this, if the beer belly peeking from beneath his red polo shirt was to be believed. I held my ground. I knew how these things went. Sure enough, a few seconds staring into my eyes were sufficient to encourage him to back off and retake his seat. I'd had time to practice that look. And to back it up. Instinct provides good counsel, and what Carson's instinct told him was that it would be a bad idea to antagonise me any further. O'Neill didn't look happy, but they kept quiet until I moved on and took my seat at the table at the back.

"We know what you are, Finch!" Carson called after me, a few seconds later. "Do yourself a favour and get out of town!"

Get out of town? What did they think this was, some second-rate Western? I decided not to let it go after all. I am sometimes very bad at following my own advice.

Taking a quick sip of my beer, I walked back up to them, standing close in the space between their stools.

"I'll keep it simple for you. You were morons when we were younger, and you're giving me no reason to think that has changed. I'll be in town as long as it takes and there isn't anybody you know capable of changing my mind."

Carson sneered, but made no attempt to follow it up.

"If anyone wants to talk to me about Karen Williams's death, however, tell them I'll be here most evenings."

"Is that the Karen Williams you strangled then?" said O'Neill, a note of genuine outrage in his voice. I hoped he knew how to keep a lid on it. For his sake.

"That's her. Only I didn't strangle her. I didn't kill her."

"Oh, right. Now I remember! You were set up, right?"

"That's right."

"Could've been anyone, is that it? Maybe it was me! Or Ronan!" Carson said, feeling braver now his friend had riled himself up.

"Then you should watch your back," I said. "Because I won't be leaving this fucking dump till I've done what I should have done eight years ago."

"Yeah? And what's that, then?"

"Either prove who did it. Or kill the fucker."

They looked at me for a second, trying to figure out if I meant what I'd said, and quickly concluding that I did. Which was fair enough, given that it was the truth. While we were having this exchange, I spied the barman in quiet conversation with one of the regulars at the far end of the bar and he walked up to us now, rubbing a tea towel between his hands as he approached. No doubt the locals had been filling him in on my history.

"Mr Finch?" Right in one. "We don't want any trouble."

Christ! They all watched way too much television. He was quite an imposing figure though. What hadn't been apparent when he was behind the bar was his height, his slim build masking the fact that he was at least five inches taller than any of us, and he walked with the natural grace of someone used to taking care of themselves. It looked like the bouncer was just for show.

"I won't be causing you any. All I want to do is finish my pint without anyone else throwing theirs at me. If that's okay? I know this is your bar, and you're within your rights to get your bouncer to march me out of here.

But I suspect you're the kind of man who likes to make up his own mind about people, rather than being told what to think. I'm not what they say I am, and I won't be causing you any problems. Unless you raise the price of a pint any higher than it already is, that is."

Despite himself, he gave a little smile. I suspected he received more than his fair share of 'advice' from the clientele.

"I would - if I could get away with it," he replied. "But people tend to be a little touchy about things like that round here."

"They're a little touchy, full stop. Just so's you know."

"I'd figured that out."

"I'll bet it didn't take long, either. Look – I just want to finish my pint in peace, and I'll head off afterwards. Is that okay with you?"

"I'd rather you had two or three more. I have to consider my profits. If I can't raise my prices, then I need people to drink more instead."

"Sounds like a perfectly reasonable request. I'll do my best to comply."

"Appreciated."

I turned away and walked back to my seat, feeling more relieved than I was letting on. I needed a base while I was here, and Molly's was just about perfect for my purpose. It also seemed that I could have a new ally - which meant more than he could possibly imagine. I just hoped our relationship would survive the evening, once I'd left and Carson and O'Neill jumped me.

Six

I short-changed the barman – Len Dickens, known to his younger patrons as Lemony Snickets – by having two pints instead of three. But the place was filling up by the time I'd finished my second, and crowded places really aren't my thing. An Irish pub on a Thursday night is a boisterous place, and Molly's was louder than most. The sound system was pumping out a medley of '80s hits along with some throwbacks from the '70's ('Sylvia's Mother Said' followed by The Southerland Brothers and Quiver with 'The Arms of Mary') and all conversation had to be conducted at a volume higher than the longhairs crooning through the speakers. Some of the clientele had clearly been somewhere else beforehand, and the ratio of drunk to soon-to-be-drunk was rising by the minute. I drained my glass, made a point of returning it to the bar – earning myself an appreciative nod from Len – and walked out the door wondering where exactly they'd make their move.

I'd seen them get up in the mirror of an old hat stand close to the main door – grabbing their jackets from the backs of their stools as they scrambled to get out before I disappeared from sight. They needn't have worried. I had no intention of trying to outrun them.

Once I got outside I paused, giving them a chance to catch up while I puzzled over the best place to lead them. Somewhere down by the South Beach sounded good. Nothing like a nice stroll by the sea last thing in the evening, and there were unlikely to be more than a few late-night dog-walkers to disturb us. Hiking up the collar of my jacket, I buried my hands in my pockets and bent my head low as I made my way down the town, maintaining a brisk pace to ensure they didn't get the chance to launch an attack any earlier than I intended, and trying to give the appearance of being lost in my thoughts. The train tracks ran parallel to the shore from the station, two small tunnels beneath the line providing pedestrian access to the beach. I chose the second of these, and stopped to wait for them as I turned off the pathway and stepped into the dark.

"Was there something you forgot to say to me?" I asked as they scurried around the corner a few moments later.

They pulled up, momentarily confused. As I said, they weren't the brightest of their generation.

"You killed that girl!" O'Neill said, still a little breathless.

"No, I didn't. Do you have a problem with your hearing, or did I use too many long words for you?"

"You're a fucking child killer!" Carson said, bunching his fists as he spoke. It was such an obvious tell.

It also told me all I needed to know about his experience of being in a fight. Experienced fighters keep their hands loose, not balled - ready to block as well as punch, and so as not to telegraph their intentions to an opponent. I kept my arms by my sides, thumbs loosely hitched in my pockets.

"You've got daughters too, is that it? Or are you the self-appointed guardians of the local community? 'Neighbourhood Botch!'"

"Eight and six," O'Neill said.

"Karen Williams was fifteen. I don't think her killer would be interested in your daughters. Though you never can tell with people like that."

"My niece is sixteen," said Carson.

"Congratulations. Though maybe I should be offering her my condolences, for coming from the same gene pool as you."

They paused for a second, before Carson gave a nod as a signal to attack.

O'Neill led, reaching towards my neck with his outstretched arms. I quickly raised my hands, and it was the matter of a moment to pick his wrists downwards and bring my right elbow into his face. As he folded, I grabbed him by the shoulder and pulled him behind me, the distance he travelled foreshortened by the presence of the brick wall of the tunnel. He met it head on, dropping to the ground as I turned to face Carson. Inexperienced fighters always do the same thing in these circumstances. They stop for a second, weighing up whether to bolt and run (always the wise option) or whether their manhood or their friendship could survive their bailing when their friend was most in need of their help. Only the smartest, or most self-interested, ever walk away. Meaning I only had to wait a few seconds while Carson decided which blow to choose.

He decided to go with a kick, and launched his right boot towards me with surprising speed and venom. I stepped into the kick, blocking it with the inside of my forearm and hitting him in the throat with an open hand. He staggered back, his legs failing him as he back-peddled toward the far wall, collapsing against it with a wheezing sound as he sought for air. It's a strange thing, the throat. Even the lightest blow convinces the brain that death is imminent and induces panic in the recipient. Done wrongly, or with too much force, that's exactly the outcome which can result. I'd hit him just right, though. Enough force to put him down and nothing which would show up later, if he saw fit to lodge some kind of complaint. Looking down at O'Neill I was happy to see that he also seemed to have escaped any noticeable injuries from his encounter with the wall, though he was holding his head with both hands, and whimpering in pain. Something you learn quickly, when you've been involved in these situations as often I have, is never to give the other guy a second chance. When someone goes for you, put them down: and do whatever is needed to ensure that they stay there. Krav is particularly clear on this, and it was a lesson I'd taken to heart. Allowing

O'Neill the chance to launch a follow-up would have been careless, if not dangerous. And I am a very careful man. So I kicked him in the balls as he tried to get up off the ground.

"Go home, boys. And don't make the mistake of thinking you can rely on our friendship in the future, because next time I won't hold back. That's if you're stupid enough to try again."

It would take a few minutes before they helped each other to their feet. Which left me plenty of time to enjoy the winking lights of the boats and the sound of the waves offshore which accompanied me on the walk back to Cois Farraige. The night was clear, a trimming of stars scattered across the sky. I was lying across the too-big bed within fifteen minutes, headphones in and Paul Buchanan doing his best to wipe the seventies superhits in Molly's from my memory, as I tried in vain to fall asleep. I'd been in town less than a day and I'd already stopped one fight, gotten into another and spent several hours in two different pubs. Not a bad start, all in all. I shuffled uncomfortably on the bed. It was too soft after the thin mattress I'd grown used to in prison. Hardly a problem, you'd think - but there you are. I felt a little lightheaded, too. Something more than the adrenaline crash which always happens after a fight. Between the pint in McDaid's and the later two in Molly Riley's, I'd drunk more alcohol in one day than I had in close to a decade. Which I hoped might at least help me to pass out.

I gave up after thirty minutes, fetching a notebook and pen from my backpack and taking a seat at the desk in front of the window. I decided to sketch out a timeline, a way of prompting and protecting my memory of events. Just the bare bones. The key details. The 'milestones' if you wish. The story - however I dressed it up - of a fucking patsy.

SEVEN

The police came for me two days after Karen Williams's body was discovered. They found her on Matthew's Hill, a wooded area close to the town given over to forestry. Fledgling firs surrounded her body: miniatures of the Christmas trees they would become in a few more winters. She was fully clothed, the only obvious disturbance being a loosening of her school shirt and tie beneath the red marks at her throat where she'd been strangled. She lay there with her legs outstretched, heels together, arms limp by her sides. Laid out, rather than discarded. It took a few days to confirm that she hadn't been raped. As far as they could determine, she had died a virgin. Speculation was that her assailant had been put off - perhaps killing her earlier than he'd intended, or suffering some belated fit of remorse. With sexual assault ruled out, it seemed a motiveless crime. Karen had no more enemies than might be expected of a fifteen-year-old girl. There was no sign of a beating, or other form of assault, and there didn't appear to have been a struggle. It was as if she'd been put down, Mick Clancy said when he visited the crime scene that first, glorious morning, the sun snatching jewels of light from the dew and the young girl stretched out like the muse in a pre-Raphaelite painting. As if she'd had her neck wrung like a hen, he said. Nothing personal. A simple, almost humane way to end a life. But for reasons nobody could understand.

Speculation in the town, once more of the facts emerged, quickly fell into two camps. Those who believed it had been a rape attempt forestalled, and those convinced it was the work of some mentally disturbed assailant. Some schizophrenic or escapee from a mental hospital, perhaps released as part of the 'care in the community' effort to cut costs in the health service which had returned hundreds of sick people to the streets the previous year. Many of these people ended up homeless and lost, starved of shelter and medication. I was one of those who held to this theory - but by that time it didn't matter what I thought, as I was already sitting in Greystones Garda Station 'helping them with their enquiries'.

No doubt you know this from every police procedural ever shown on television, but always – always – demand a lawyer before opening your mouth, should you ever find yourself in the situation I found myself in on October 12th, 2008. Innocence is not a defence. You have to keep your mouth shut – tightly clasped, your jaws locked tight no matter what they toss at you – or they will stitch you up. It is simply impossible over the course of six or seven hours of questioning not to say something to contradict a comment you made earlier, or avoid falling into some linguistic trap designed to panic you, and catch you unawares. Say. Nothing. Trust me on this.

In my case, the decision to charge me with Karen Williams' murder came down to three things – and even now I have to marvel at my brother's ingenuity. I don't think I'd have trusted the guards to uncover one of them, let alone all three.

My first problem was that I couldn't account for my whereabouts. Kate was away in Cork on a girls' weekend – one of a series of getaways herself and her younger sisters took each year, though normally to somewhere more exotic like Portugal, or the Canaries. Secondly, I had denied knowing the girl, though it later turned out that she had babysat for Laura at least once. Babysitters came and went and I seldom booked them or dropped them home, so I had no recollection of this, even after they'd told me. And lastly – most importantly – there was the evidence found at the scene. Taken on their own either of the other things could have been explained away. But cumulatively - with what they unearthed by the body - it was damning.

They found small deposits of dirt at the back of her shirt collar, which matched potting compost from trays of tomatoes I'd planted for Kate a few days beforehand. Microscopic traces of which they also found in scrapings beneath what I had believed to be my clean fingernails. And - the coup de grace - there was my credit card. Lying barely ten yards from where her body was found.

Game. Set. Match. Throw in the usual narrative about middle-aged men and teenage babysitters, and it was effectively game over.

The credit card was easy to explain - at least as far as I was concerned. I'd maxed it out one too many times, and must have taken it from my wallet and left it lying around for someone to pick up. I hadn't figured out who that person must be, at that point. The card wasn't working anymore (I was still ignoring their letters about "clearing my outstanding balance") so I'd jettisoned it, and forgotten about it.

The potting compost, though, was either inordinately clever, or an extraordinary coincidence. Only someone who'd been to my house immediately prior to the murder could have seen me using it. Which - much later on – would lead me to Tom.

For the guards, however, those three things together formed the basis not just for suspicion, but for absolute certainty.

It was me.

I had done it.

You can't imagine what it is like to be accused of a murder you didn't commit. Of being accused of a murder, full stop! And murders simply didn't happen in Greystones. They happened to gangland enforcers on the 'wrong' side of the city, or between the pages of thrillers in the library or the local bookshop. This wasn't just a breach in reason - it was an absolute impossibility. Nobody got murdered here! Getting my head around the fact of the girl's death was difficult enough, let alone fielding the charge they threw at me that I was somehow responsible.

Through it all, I trusted to the fact that I was innocent to ensure that I'd be released. I didn't do it – therefore they'd have to let me go! Nothing else made sense. How would they find the real killer if they kept wasting their time on me? They could tell by my voice I was telling the truth! I knew it! I could see it in the face of Clancy – the dishevelled cop – even as he kept bombarding me with questions. He knew me, for God's sake! We'd known each other as kids, even though always as acquaintances, rather than friends. He knew I was telling the truth! So why didn't they just let me go? Why was I still there, in that weird little room with its battered wood panelling and crappy old desk, watching the light outside fade through the small window high up in the wall, like the window of a school toilet?

Strangely, what I felt most keenly, as the hours passed, was embarrassment. Knowing that I'd have to tell people that yes, I had been questioned – but only to provide them with some background information. Karen had babysat for us, you see. Just the once or twice. They just wanted to know if I'd heard, or seen anything. God knows I didn't want anyone thinking I was involved!

But I was it. Unbeknownst to me, once the credit card was found they stopped looking at anything, or anyone else. From what Mick told me later, there'd never been any other suspects. Once they had the card, why look elsewhere? And when forensics turned up the traces of the potting compost... well. That was it. Case closed.

I was in denial right up until the moment I stood in Bray Courthouse and heard the charges read aloud. And from that moment on, I was in a state of blind panic. They couldn't seriously think this was true? Where was Kate? Where were Tom and my father? Why were people in the gallery – some of whom I knew – looking at me like that? They knew me! Surely they had to know this was a mistake? That I would never...

But you can guess the rest. A short but horrific spell on remand in Mountjoy, and then tried and convicted. Three days in a courtroom with my face plastered all over the newspapers before being bundled into a prison van and delivered someplace where the inmates take a great interest in current affairs, and your face is already known before you step through the gates.

From that first day on remand, prison was a living hell. A much-overused term, but an accurate one in this case. What is hell like, if not this? To be cursed at, spat on, punched or kicked every time you walked down a corridor - sometimes even when you'd taken what seemed like the logical course and stayed in your cell. Staying in your cell just meant you were alone when they came for you. I hadn't worked out yet that I would always be alone. Child killers don't merit friends.

The temptation is to gloss over this time. To lock it down: to keep it buried. But I needed it, now. To stoke the fury which had brought me back here. To keep it hot, so that I could remain focused on what had to be done.

Two incidents from that time spring to my mind. The first was from my first full day – on the morning I woke up in a prison cell for the very first time. The guards, to their credit, had been scrupulously fair and professional. They'd given me 'the speech' and made sure I was settled in my cell before leaving me, minus my laces and belt, on what would be the first of many nights I'd spend alone over the course of almost eight years.

I was barely awake, shuffling out into the corridor with my unlaced shoes, when the first blow landed. I had my head down, so I never saw who threw it. Don't tell me a punch in the stomach when you're unprepared is not a serious injury. The pain and the panic it created, as I desperately sought for breath, were unlike anything I had experienced before. And while I was there, shell-shocked, leaning against the wall for support, one of the inmates walking past my cell spat on my bent head; a huge globule of spit and snot, carefully cultivated before being launched towards me. I remember the feeling as it ran down the back of my neck. But I couldn't move. I looked beyond the walkway to where two guards stood chatting, but they'd seen nothing, and I immediately understood that asking them to intervene would make matters worse.

This was my life. For months. Until I had that epiphany, and learned to protect myself. And it was seldom just a random punch, like that first Welcome to Mountjoy. My tormentors generally operated in pairs –

sometimes more than that – one of them keeping watch to ensure there were no interruptions. Though most of those who attacked me were amateurs, lashing out from anger or spite, some were well practiced in the art. The ones who knew exactly where to punch you in the kidney, and what point of your cheekbone or eye socket was the most painful. The ones who took their time, and made time itself pass impossibly slow.

It was not every day of course. At least, not after that first week. But the periods between beatings were almost worse, somehow. Despite yourself, you couldn't help but hope that that was it. At least for a while. That the beatings would stop, or at least ease off. The tyranny of hope! They knew this, of course. Not all violence is physical. After a while I gave up begging them to stop, and saved my breath to steel myself against the kicks and punches and the knees to my stomach, balls and head. Fuck pacifism. Gandhi himself would make a shiv if he had to put up with this, day after day, week after week. It was like working your way through the stages of grief. Though instead of starting with anger and ending with acceptance, for me it was the other way around.

By the time I'd been in prison for three months, I was utterly broken. Too many beatings. Too little hope. Knowing that I was completely alone, and all the while tortured by the thought of what he was doing outside... Because I was on to him, by then. The pieces had fallen into place. But knowing brought me no relief – just further torture. Especially when I heard about them.

One of the lags had planted the seed in my brain – probably out of malice rather than as a result of anything he'd actually heard. Your wife, yeah? I hear she's taken up with your brother. And then there was that. Lying on my cot, night after night, imagining him with her. Doing things, with her. Vivid, pornographic dreams in which every moment of intimacy we'd shared was disassembled and replayed, with him in the starring role. There was no greater agony for me than this. I was here. Abandoned. Impotent. While they...

Soon enough, though, I grew numb. And the beatings began to stop. Or at least to became occasional, rather than habitual. There is little satisfaction in hitting someone who caves in without protest. Who neither cries, nor begs. Although it's wrong to say I felt nothing, any sensitivity had left me. I cared about nothing. Registered nothing. Like a fucking zombie, as I heard myself described more than once.

The second 'incident' though... the second one was different. This was in my fourth year inside, when I was no longer an occasional punchbag or the focus of an initiation rite for newcomers. When I felt I was safe - most days, anyway. It was just before Christmas, evidenced by the sad, home-made decorations decorating the walls of most of the cells. Cheap tinsel. Cards for Daddy. A strand of coloured lights wrapped around the window frame or the TV. It started with a story on the television news. A young girl of thirteen had been raped and murdered in Coolock. Battered so badly her parents weren't allowed to identify the body: her face a bloody mess of broken teeth and bone. Two weeks later – Christmas Eve – her rapist still hadn't been found and it seemed clear from press reports that the chances of catching him were growing ever slimmer. He hadn't left a convenient clue behind him, as I had. As Jack Finch had. Finch, upstairs in C wing... Finch, who'd killed a kid of about that age.

There is no need to question the similarities when you're looking for a surrogate. One child killer, after all... So they came for me. Five of them. Enough to give each other a rest between blows before they took their turn, or got their breath back. I spent most of it lying on the floor by my cot with my arms up to my face, trying in vain to block some of the kicks to my head. I genuinely thought that this was the one. That, this time, they wouldn't stop. Especially after the third break - the third time I felt a bone give way, and heard the wet snap before the wave of pain. In the end they broke both my wrists, dislocated my left elbow and kicked chunks out of my scalp, leaving my face a picture in blood, my teeth and ribs similarly ruined. And then they stripped me and carried me out of the cell, throwing me over the barrier to tumble, incapable of breaking my fall, onto a trestle table below. I was in hospital for six days and in the hospital wing for a further two weeks before they returned me to my cell. Even the nurses felt some pity for me. Some. I was, after all, what I was.

But that was later...

Right now, I needed to concentrate on those first few days. After I was arrested, and before I was locked up. To dredge up some detail which could help me to uncover the truth. Because from the time I was imprisoned onwards, it was hopeless. The problem with being locked up was that I saw and heard nothing. No local news. No casual gossip from about the town. No idle speculation. All I knew was what was reported in the newspapers, and what the guards wanted me to hear – all of which was untrustworthy.

I had to begin with the evidence. With the facts, at least as they were known to me. To do what I could to fill in whatever gaps existed. This was the only way I could work out how – and when – he'd done it. Was it an accident, or a murder? Or was the girl's death just some sort of 'necessary end'? Had he really planned to kill Karen Williams just to construct this trap for me? Was she picked out for some especial reason, or chosen at random? And above all... why? Why do this?

We'd never gotten on – but, Christ, we were brothers! If he'd found himself stuck for money, or in some other kind of jam, I'd have helped him out. Not that there was ever much chance of my having more cash than he did! If there was something he needed, though, he would only have to ask. Our mother died when we were both still young, and Dad was next to useless, so we were all we had! Later on, of course, I knew. I knew by the time of that second beating. I had figured out his motive.

The truth is, he didn't want to get me - he wanted to get my wife. My life. Everything that I had, and he lacked.

Tom was two years older than me, but other than a couple of on-off relationships which never seemed to go anywhere, he had nothing of what I had at that time. With Kate. And Laura. I'd agonized and hypothesised about who'd killed the girl, and what their motive might have been, when I had this revelation. That the primary intention mightn't have been to murder her, but to frame me. Because that was where most of the effort had gone. This explained why the girl was left untouched. Why she'd been killed in the way she had, and her body lain out to be discovered. Everything slipped into place. And once I understood this, there was no one else.

I leaned my forehead against the window, the condensation damp against my skin. Despite the fact that I was out, now - despite the fact that it was finally over – he had won. He had both of them. And more. He'd taken my life, and improved upon it. Even the house was better than the one I'd left behind!

How do you go from suspecting your brother, to hating him, to the certainty that he has ruined your life? In truth, once I got over the initial shock and self-pity, he made it easy for me. I'd been so royally stitched up that only someone who knew me well and had easy access to our house could have done it. Who'd been there when I was potting those tomato plants (an activity totally out of character for me)? Who else could have known that it was me rather than Kate who'd had their hands in the compost? Even someone hellbent on framing me couldn't have known that. It could only have been Tom. That was the only conclusion I could come to, and it hadn't wavered since. Though, with luck, he was still unaware that I was on to him.

The central heating pumped out a tepid heat, the window fogging up once more as the warmth inside the room met with the chill night air outside. It was after midnight. My first day back over. Taking stock, I decided that it had been a reasonable success. I'd seen them both and given Tom the impression that I posed him no threat (though that would change if he learned about the altercation with Carson and O'Neill). I'd met Mick Clancy, and thought I had a reasonable chance of getting access to the files from the original investigation, or at least to some of the salient details. I'd even found a new local! Tomorrow, however, would be different. Tomorrow the 'murderer' – as they say all murderers do – would return to the scene of the crime.

EIGHT

Matthew's Hill is a wooded promontory rising about seven hundred feet to the East of the town. Approached by farmland mostly given over to pasture, the upper slopes are the property of Coillte, the national forestry agency. With the aid of generous grants from the government, farmers are encouraged to establish copses to support the timber industry and help to preserve the indigenous landscape. In practice, what most farmers do is to grow Christmas trees. It's a more profitable business than tending native oaks, or planting hardwoods for lumber.

I would have had difficulty locating the place where Karen Williams was found were it not for the tired mementos still marking the spot. I wondered whether I'd have done the same, had she been my daughter? Marked the spot where she died in that way? Better, surely, to remember her in some other way, and to restrict any tributes to the grave where she now lay in peace... rather than where she'd been splayed out, cold and broken, across a hillside.

The memento mori took the shape of a bunch of flowers, browned and brittle, tied with a faded ribbon and looped about with three miraculous medals. I'd no idea which saints these represented, though I recognised the Virgin Mary. Apt, I supposed. Given she'd died without that most terrible of assaults to add to her parents' loss. I knelt and looked about me. What had she been doing here? They'd never been able to find an answer to that. In the end, they determined that the killer must have had lured her here somehow. He, being me. But I thought this unlikely. Even the most unsuspecting young girl would hesitate to meet somebody up here. It was too remote. Too far from any conceivable point of interest. No. She'd been brought here, and against her will.

Which meant what, exactly? They'd always assumed that her killer was unarmed, given the manner of her death. But was that right? How would he have forced her to come up here without a weapon of some kind? And if one existed, might there still be some evidence on it? Some vestigial trace? I quickly dismissed the idea. If Tom had used a knife to coerce her to come up here he'd have disposed of it – or chucked it in the dishwasher – by the following day. And I very much doubted that he'd have used a gun. It was too easy to trace a gun back to the supplier, and almost unheard of for anyone but a gangland drug dealer to get their hands on a firearm without it coming to the guards' notice. The risk of somebody talking, once news of the girl's death hit the news, would have been too great. No. A knife was the most likely weapon. And a more intimidating one, somehow. As well I knew. If somebody pulls a gun on you, you actually have a pretty good chance of disarming them without injuring yourself. If someone comes at you with a knife, however – even if you manage to get it away from them – you will get cut. They teach you this in Krav. There are techniques for disarming someone with a knife, but they always stress the fact that you will not emerge unscathed.

And there is something inherently scary about a knife. About an exposed blade. You can't help but imagine it cutting through your skin. Your arms. Your chest. Your face! He wouldn't even have to hold it against her. One sight of it and the threat of lasting disfigurement would be enough. Walk that way, and don't stop till I tell you. There were no streetlights at the extremities of the town, meaning he could safely march her up here without much danger of being seen. If he took the route they'd suggested – from the back of Alma Road, up across the fields behind St Augustine's, crossing the main road where it was at its darkest – he could have her here within ten minutes of snatching her from the street. Everyone was agreed that she'd been heading home when she was taken. And Alma Road was poorly lit, the footpath in deep shadow for most of its length.

How hard would it have been? A familiar voice calling her name? One of the locals trotting over to her with a smile, and then pulling a knife when he got alongside her? Easy-peasy. And a quarter of an hour later, she was dead – a little compost smeared inside her shirt collar and my credit card dropped a few yards from where her body lay, still warm upon the earth. He would have been back at home, or sitting in the pub with friends to provide him with an alibi, within half an hour of grabbing her.

I needed to know what Tom had said when they questioned him. They would have done so, of course. They'd have approached everyone connected to Karen Williams, or me, for witness statements. Asked them where they'd been. If they'd seen or heard anything, and so on. The answers Tom had offered to those questions would be a good place to start.

It was quite a nice spot, really. At least in daylight. Although there wasn't much of an elevation, the way the town tumbled toward the sea afforded me an unbroken panorama, from the golf club at its Eastern edge to the harbour in the West. Greystones is a place where the rustle of leaves is clearly audible a hundred yards from the centre of town – a place where green fights with grey on the palette, and most often wins. It was possible to make out whole streets from here, including most of Alma Road and, further down to my right, the solemn grey of the Church of the Holy Rosary on Trafalgar Road, tucked in behind the bustle of the town centre. The main street was a gently sloping thoroughfare lined to either side with brick houses of one or two stories in height. A wide pavement ran the length of the stores on the western side, a narrower one to the east. A number of those shops had been residential dwellings in the recent past. Some still retained their low-walled front gardens, the courtyards converted to coffee shop aprons. At the base of the hill stood a bank and the railway station, the town tailing off into parkland and a coastal roadway beyond.

It was quiet. An occasional swish rather than a hum of traffic, as single cars glided along wet roads. A noise which was intermittent, rather than constant: punctuation rather than prose. Though there would be the occasional delay on the main street while someone turned into a car park or attempted to reverse into a space out on the street, the concept of a traffic jam was as alien to the town as drug wars or race riots. It was a dormitory town, heavy with child. There are more families with young children here than anywhere in Dublin's equally salubrious environs, and the streets are busy with buggies and strollers, clip-clapped with children's footfalls, and soundtracked by the clamour of childish voices.

Greystones was originally a fishing village. A little Hamlet tucked in on the coast between the larger towns of Wicklow and Dun Laoghaire (formerly known as Kingstown) thirty miles further North. The townland was originally divided between two families, the La Touches and the Hawkins Whitsheds, the latter dying out following the marriage of the last of the line, Elizabeth, to Frederick Burnaby, whose name still adorns the most expensive estate in the town. Having a house in The

Burnaby was still the denominator used to determine whether you could be listed among the town's well-heeled. People from The Burnaby were regarded with suspicion by the rest of the town, and tended to be precious in defence of their boundaries. The year before I was imprisoned they had banded together to prevent a children's playground being built in the park bordering the estate, lest it intrude upon their leafy-laned demesne.

The town grew over the years - first with the building of a harbour on the north shore which gave the town its name, and later with the coming of the railroad in 1854. The extension of rail services was only possible following the building of a line around the expanse of Bray Head - a track which clung precariously to the crags and had to be relocated twice due to sea erosion. In August of 1867, erosion caused the Wexford train to derail and plunge into the sea. The fireman died, but his passengers escaped with a few minor injuries. The original engineer for the railway extension from Bray to Greystones was Isambard Kingdom Brunel, giving the line something of a claim to fame. The railway station – now part of the DART suburban rail network – was established at the point where the Hawkins Whitshed and La Touche estates met, neatly defusing a long-simmering rivalry, and it still marked the division of the town.

Greystones was unusual in having the largest per capita population of Irish protestants in the country. From where I sat, I could make out the Catholic churches in Blacklion and Greystones, the Presbyterian Hall up the road from the harbour, and the larger Church of Ireland house of worship on the immediate outskirts of the town. Even today you were as likely to meet a Bagnall as a Murphy on the street, and the Church of Ireland primary and secondary schools were filled to capacity with those belonging to that faith (or just striving to save their children from the arcane delights of a traditional Catholic education).

Following a building boom in the nineteen-eighties the population of the town more than doubled, Greystones' new status as a Dublin suburb attracting a generation of urban executives looking for a quieter pace of life and a safe place in which to raise their children. Sprawling modern estates now bookended the town, their neat rows clearly visible from where I sat. The small local shops in the town centre had been joined by three supermarkets, the expanses of their carparks standing out as barren patches amongst the greenery, as they set about putting local concerns out of business. People in Greystones were too ornery to allow that to happen, however – the slogan 'Keep Your Town in Business, Keep Your Business in Town' proudly displayed on every shop window.

Greystones people liked to shop in the small but well-stocked bookstore, where they could chat about the latest releases and order anything currently missing from the shelves. They were happy to wait the couple of days it would take the book to arrive – and besides, how is that any different from Amazon? When you buy a book online, you still have to wait several days to get it into your hands. The only difference is that Amazon takes your money in advance.

They liked to buy their lunches in the local delicatessens, or in the myriad of little cafes dotted about the town, prior to swinging by the recently refurbished library or dropping into the pharmacy to fill a prescription. It was cosy, measured, slow. A well-heeled bubble of a place that had survived the recession of the noughties with its restaurants full and its house prices virtually unchanged.

A tidy little town, then, of just over eighteen-thousand inhabitants: and not one secret. Gossip spread through these streets faster than in a girls' boarding school. I remembered the fevered talk reaching a crescendo within hours of Karen Williams's body being found. The initial view was that someone from out of town was responsible. It had to be. Rumours and half-remembered details about every passenger who'd alighted from a bus or DART that day did the rounds, with many a 'shady character' being conjured from people's remembrances. Anyone whose clothes looked dishevelled or appeared unshaven spawned his own narrative, with ever more colourful details added to the characterization as it did the rounds. A swarthy man. Looked foreign. Gave Jenny in the coffee shop a funny look as he passed. Made her feel uncomfortable. Had a knapsack with him: it could have held anything! I'd been as guilty as any of them of speculating as to the motive and identity of the man who'd murdered the poor young girl from Alma Road. Was it some 'teen' thing gone wrong? A dare? A tiff? She used to go out with John Foley, didn't she? Never liked that boy. Something sullen about him.

And so it went on, until my arrest put paid to all of that and sparked a new conversation, characterized by incredulity and revisionist views of my character. Those who initially thought me innocent were quickly persuaded otherwise: and not just by the evidence which emerged. The consensus was that I must be 'sick', or 'depraved' (many refused to believe she hadn't been raped or held firm to the notion that this had been my intent, even if I'd failed to go through with it). Everyone agreed that it was worse because the killer was 'one of our own'. As if the town itself was somehow implicated in the murder.

I sat there on the silky grass and looked out on 'my' town. I'd moved here with my family when I was ten years old, my Dad having decided to relocate us when he changed job at Shell, and was promoted from an operational to a management role. He wanted somewhere bigger - or somewhere he could appear bigger - which meant selling up in Leopardstown and moving here, where the same money he got in exchange for our modest semi-d bought him an Edwardian redbrick a few streets back from the sea. I can still remember the fall of the waves drifting in my window each night as I fell asleep. It took me months to adjust to their absence when I moved to the centre of Dublin, when I went to university. And I returned here myself in due course. Once Laura was born, we joined the ranks of those prioritizing safe streets and 'good' schools over proximity to the city. And Greystones – which was going through a further expansion at the time – was the ideal location. It helped that I knew the place, and had my father and brother close by. In case we needed a babysitter every now and then to take care of Laura. Irony of ironies!

Greystones was still a genteel little village then, with a grocer's and a butcher's shop on the main street. The new Quinnsworth supermarket had only recently opened. Nowhere else was open on a Sunday, and good luck if you needed milk or bread after six o'clock in the evening! Trains into the city were infrequent and undependable, with long waits outside of the morning and evening rush hours. Some locals could still recall when the only trains stopping at Greystones were the morning train at seven-thirty, and the evening one bringing commuters home at six-fifty each weekday evening.

My father became one of those making that return journey, prior to his retirement. Greystones was a stop on the mainline route to Wexford harbour and the evening train included a bar carriage, usually full on a Friday evening and not much less packed on the other days. There is something quaint now about the idea of having a pint on your way home from work, but it was no more frowned upon then than the smoking carriages, the air within them thick as the mist over a Galway bog. As I remember it was non-smoking carriages which were the exception then – usually tucked away at the very end of the train, and typically the preserve of school children on their way to and from the various private schools along the line. St Andrew's and Sion Hill. Blackrock and St Michael's. Loreto Dalkey, its castellated building by the sea as close an approximation to Hogwarts as might be imagined, though Harry Potter was several decades from publication then.

When Kate and I bought the house on Marine Terrace close to the railway bridge the town centre had developed sufficiently to house a video shop and a small supermarket, but essentially it was the same, insular little town I'd grown up in, where everyone knew everyone else, and their business. But we liked that. It suited a young family. Laura was only two years old when we moved in, and the thought of walks along the seafront and evenings spent in front of the TV with a movie and a bottle of wine sounded just about perfect. Particularly as Laura had only just begun to sleep through the night.

I was working in an advertising agency as a copywriter (brochures and company reports for clients in the agribusiness and banking sectors) and occasionally took the DART into the city – though in general I preferred to drive. There was something about that forty minutes' peace in each direction which proved hard to give up. I'd copy podcasts onto a CD and play them as I drove, or play music louder than I ever could at home, even singing along sometimes providing I wasn't in heavy traffic where I might be seen.

Those first few years of Laura's life went by in a blur, despite two changes of job and the myriad of changes Laura imposed upon us as she changed from a baby in a carry-tot (easy to park on the seat beside you if you ventured out for a meal together) to a toddler (which brought a temporary end to meals out, given Kate's reluctance to leave her behind), to a school-going imp in a red pinafore and runners which lit up as she walked. I watched her grow, every day from her birth until three months after her seventh birthday. And then I missed the next eight years. And almost failed to recognise her when I passed her on the road to the church, the day following my return.

NINE

She must be walking back from school, I thought. The petrol-green uniform told me she went to Loreto Dalkey, so she'd have arrived back on the most recent DART. I could hear it pulling out of the station further down the line, on its way back to Dublin and on out to Malahide at the far side of Dublin Bay.

She was transformed. Not just changed, but utterly different. A child of seven bears no resemblance to a girl of fifteen. There was her height, to begin with. Both myself and Kate were above average height, and she had inherited her mother's upright carriage, the same straight back and shoulders. Kate had always moved like a dancer. When I'd last seen Laura, she was a dervish, running in spurts rather than walking unless I was holding her hand. Now she walked like a woman, carrying her body as a weight like the knapsack on her shoulders. All the essentials were the same. Chocolate-brown hair. Sallow skin (again from her mother). No doubt the same clear blue eyes, though I couldn't see from where I stood. Everything but the broad smile I doubted I would ever see again.

She was a big sister now, I remembered with a start. How would she have taken to that? She had to have been ten or eleven when the new addition came into her life. More than long enough to become used to being an only child. Or a 'lonely child', as she called it when she was young. Did she see the new baby as an intruder? Had she resented having to share her mother's time and attention? I'd known nothing of this, of course. Whenever I imagined Laura, it was as the solitary child I'd known – the self-sufficient little girl, happy to play with her My Little Pony toys inside the sprawling Duplo houses she'd construct for them. It never mattered to her that the toys were of a different size and scale, or that the brick houses were out of proportion. But that solitary child had ceased to exist. When? Judging by the age of the child I'd seen that first day, about three years after I was imprisoned. Which meant that Kate had to have been pregnant – by him! – within little more than two years.

I'd no idea how things developed between them. How long had there been between Tom the brother-in-law - the quiet, supportive presence helping her through the horrors of the trial and its aftermath - and Tom the... something else. I could imagine how it had gone, however. And I wasn't blind to the part I had played in allowing it to happen. By shutting Kate out, I had opened the door for him. And of course he would have been quick, despite his apparent reticence, to cement the narrative of my guilt. I was not just a killer, but a false man. A deceiver. Living a different life unbeknownst to her, filled with unspoken desires, which in turn gave the lie to the life we had had together. Did she even know who I was? How could the man she knew do what he had done, if he were not, really, someone else? Someone other than the loving husband and father she had believed me to be. And how easy would it have been not just to fall in love with him - but to have fallen out of love with me? And I had allowed it to happen, if not actively encouraged it.

Laura was walking away from me. I didn't know what I should do, so I watched her pass, waiting to see if she'd turn around. If she'd see me, and recognise who I was. I was changed too, of course. But the years had done little to alter my appearance, compared to the changes they had wrought upon her. Should I call out? Say her name aloud? Plead for her attention? Had she already spotted me, and was waiting now to see what I would do? Which would be worse, then? To call out to her - or not to do so?

In the end the choice was taken from me, as a friend ran up and Laura wheeled about to greet her. I watched as they walked off together toward the harbour. She obviously hadn't noticed me at all. Which hurt more than I could have imagined, even as I acknowledged the relief I felt. I did however get to see that broad smile blaze, before she passed from my view.

There is no better place to take an addled brain and a bruised heart than a pub. It surprised me in prison how often I'd picture walking in off the street into McDaid's or The Boathouse on a wet evening, when I was most in need of a dream of escape. A pub accommodates troubles like a warehouse stores goods: a safe dry place, secure and familiar. A home from home, as they say.

I took the same table as before at the back of Molly Riley's, with a pint of 'the usual' in front of me. It took me aback how heartening the question had been to hear when Len the barman greeted me. To be met with an hello, and asked if you wanted your usual – after a single visit – felt almost like belonging. I could remember regular Thursday nights in McDaid's with my friends John and Cameron, and Sean. We'd originally met up following a weekly football match - a five-a-side game for equally unfit dads, for which we'd turn out religiously each week, regardless of weather or ability. In time injuries and age put paid to the football, but the ritual of Thursday night pints survived the cessation of our sporting endeavours.

We'd talk about nothing, really. The best kind of conversation. Football. Arseholes at work. What the kids had been up to that week. Jokes and comments we couldn't possibly have shared with our wives at home. It was a comfortable, warm hug of an evening, whose value I did not understand until it was taken from me. I can remember walking home afterwards, on dark paths in sweet-smelling rain, the sense of calm and wellbeing that emptying yourself of a good chat and a bladder filled of Guinness could bring. Of the feeling at peace, with the warmth of home ahead of you. Family and friends: the two things we most often take for granted, and whose prolonged absence tortures the soul.

I didn't expect to run into Mick, though I recalled he had a habit of popping into a pub for his lunch. McDaid's seemed more his speed, though. It was incongruous somehow to see him walk in the door of a 'hip' establishment like this. I had rather less expectation of bumping into Carson or O'Neill. They clearly hadn't reported our little encounter beneath the railway arch, or I'd have heard about it by now. I suspected that they'd avoid this place for a while in favour of somewhere they were less likely to bump into me. Which was a wise move, on their part.

"Did you see the game?" Len asked from across the bar.

The question shook me from my reverie. I was unused to being addressed in this way.

"What? No, sorry. What was the score?" Which seemed a better question than "What game?"

"Four-nil. If you ask me, Morinho's lost it. Chelsea were right to get rid of him. You a ManU fan?"

"No", I replied. "Arsenal."

"They're doing alright, I suppose. But they'll blow it at the end of the season. Like they always do!"

"Typical ManU supporter!" came a voice from the door. "Always fucking moaning!"

"Mick," the barman replied, in acknowledgement.

"Len. You got any of that chicken hotpot left?"

"Coming right up", Len replied, walking to the end of the bar to place the lunch order with the kitchen.

"Better than a mouldy sandwich in McDaid's," Mick said, taking a seat opposite me.

"I have to admit I didn't expect to see you anywhere as trendy as this. I thought they had standards."

"Don't know what you mean," Mick replied, putting a finger into the collar of a shirt that looked like it'd last been ironed when Ireland was part of the Commonwealth, and loosening his tie.

"So - is this a happy coincidence?" I asked him.

"Nope. I saw you walking up the street as I was driving past and followed you in here. Following people is a skill we're known for."

"Not so hard in a town where everybody ends up in the pub."

"True. But it's a skill we're proud of, none the less."

"So, what's up, Detective Sergeant Clancy? Did someone report me for loitering with intent? Or grievous bodily breathing?"

"Somebody beat the shite out of Ronan O'Neill and Franky Carson," he replied, never one to beat about the bush.

"Really? I do hope they're all right. A terrible thing to happen to anybody."

"Not those two pricks! There's no shortage of people happy to hear of their misfortune, believe me. Half the women who come in here, for a start! But, regardless..."

"You have to investigate it. I understand. Any idea who performed this public service?"

"More than an idea, Jack. But no. No name came up. Apparently it was dark, and the assailant took them by surprise. Sure, how else would he have beaten up those two strapping lads?"

"Must have been an out-of-towner, then."

"Sure, who else? We haven't had any serious crime in this town since... I don't know? Eight years now?"

"I'll try not to do anything to impair your statistics," I said.

"I'd appreciate that."

"Pint?" I asked, after a long pause.

"No thanks, Jack. Have to get back on the beat. Just thought I'd have a word while I was passing."

"I thought you said you were following me?"

He smiled, tapping the edge of a beer coaster against the table.

"Good luck now, Jack."

I raised my glass to him in salute.

"I don't suppose you managed to lay your hands on that file, by any chance?"

"Don't push it," he said, a sudden edge to his voice. "There's an inspector in Harcourt Street who'd be only delighted for a reason to toss you back in jail. In case you thought I was the boss around here."

"We all answer to a higher authority, I suppose."

"Is that right? And who's yours?"

"Karen Williams," I replied, keeping my eyes fixed on his. "And her family. They deserve to know the truth."

He gave an exasperated shake of his head.

"I'll be seeing you around, Jack. And don't be seen hanging around by the railway line after dark, okay? For your own good."

"Got it, guard. I wouldn't want to suffer the same fate as those two lads. Even a quiet place like this can be dangerous, late at night."

He left, having picked up his takeaway hotpot from the end of the bar and paying for it with a handful of crumpled notes. We'd both said our piece. He'd told me that he needed me to stay out of trouble. And I'd made it clear that I had no intention of doing so.

TEN

Killing time proved harder than I imagined. Years of minutely scheduled days leaves you unprepared for freedom from the clock. On the Thursday morning – my third day back – I decided to hop the DART into the city, looking for a distraction as much as anything else. I also suspected it might be easier to plan my next move if I was away from Greystones, and had room to think. There's something about the anonymity of a city which is conducive to solitude and reflection.

I got off the train at Pearse Street and walked as far as Nassau Street, tracing the railings of Trinity College before turning up onto Dawson Street. I'd waited until rush hour had passed so the streets were relatively quiet, the first wave of shoppers yet to descend and everybody else happily ensconced in their offices and workplaces. Maybe happily was an exaggeration, I realised. People who genuinely enjoy their job are few and far between. I thought about going into the National Gallery on Merrion Square to view the Turner watercolours, but settled instead for a lengthy browse of the bookshelves in Hodges Figgis. Books were hard to come by in prison - a desperate hardship, given the ever-tightening grip of my reading habit. The printed word rapidly turns into an addiction when you're in need of the escape it offers.

There was a café on the third floor, and I took a small pile of books there to check them out. The few other people seated around the pine tables were doing the same, so the practice didn't seem to be frowned upon. I had the latest John Connolly – an exquisite writer who just happens to write murder mysteries – two true crime anthologies, in the forlorn hope that they might provide clues to my own misfortune, and the latest Richard Ford. I wasn't much of a reader before going to prison. I had read the prescribed novels for my Junior and Leaving Cert exams ('To Kill A Mockingbird'' and 'Lord of the Flies' respectively) along with the set textbooks and source materials at university, and an occasional thriller while on holiday. But that was about it. I read the paper every day, but that doesn't earn you the title of 'reader' somehow. In prison, however, I gobbled them up - often starting and finishing a book on the same day. When I was fortunate enough to come across a book like that, it was as if I'd escaped a day of my sentence.

It was strange, sitting down in a restaurant. In prison most meals are eaten in your cell (the canteen, such as it is, being little more than a hatch at the end of a long line where you queued to fill your tray). I retained the habit immediately following my release, buying my meals in one of the local delicatessens and eating alone in my hotel room. Sitting here now, I felt like I'd somehow been forgotten. That someone would appear at any minute and instruct me to go back to my cell.

Joining me in perusing potential purchases were a couple in their early sixties – either studiously avoiding each other, or completely at ease in each other's company – a bearded young man who looked like a post-grad student, his table heaped high with textbooks, and a bespectacled teenager in a woollen polo neck. Either a precocious reader, or dumped there while her parents looked around the store. We ignored each other, as is the custom. People don't go into bookshops for the company.

I flicked through my books half-heartedly. In truth, I was there more for the headspace than for anything else: to free my mind to cycle through the various options and scenarios. In essence, I had learned nothing. Visiting the site of the murder had provided some perspective, but the reality was that I knew no more about what Tom had done, or how he had done it. Nor had I uncovered a single detail which could help me to unmask him.

The term was an apt one. I wondered how good he was at maintaining the mask he wore, and to what degree it had become real? Had the part he'd played as the concerned friend and brother-in-law morphed into a genuine concern for Kate and Laura – or was he still playing them? Had the mask he'd worn while faking sympathy for our young daughter led to some form of genuine parental bond? At what point does the part you play become the real man? For all I knew, he may well have become the perfect husband and father he'd imitated, as he ingratiated himself into their affections. But so what? When it happened - when I was arrested and charged - I needed him on my side, not on my side of the bed.

Whoever he'd become since, Tom was the same man to me. Siblings never really change in each other's eyes. It's why everyone regresses to the age they were on leaving the family home whenever they return. Wisdom has it that no one changes, really. Though I'm proof that this is not always the case. The man I am now bears almost no resemblance to the man I was eight years ago. Could that man have hurt another man seriously enough to put him in a prison infirmary? Or have endured solitary confinement for months at a time? Or pursue his revenge, regardless of the cost to himself, or the ones he claimed to love? Whoever Tom was now he would pay for what he'd done. I couldn't unmake the years - but I could exact a price for them. I just had to find a way to catch him! And I was no closer to doing that, than before my release.

I needed the files! I needed to know what they'd had on me - what I'd said or done to confirm their suspicions. I needed to know what *he* had said or done to confirm those suspicions. I needed to know who else they'd spoken to, and what those witnesses had seen or heard. It could well be that there was an alibi for me somewhere in those accounts, which had been overlooked once they were convinced they had their man. Leaning on Mick Clancy would be difficult: but I had no choice. No one else would share this information with me, and he was the only person – anywhere – even prepared to consider the possibility that I might be innocent.

Protestations of innocence get you nowhere in prison. Everyone is innocent, and everyone is guilty. You claim the former about yourself, and assume the latter about everyone else. It took me some time to accept this. I revised my earlier view - adjusting to a prison sentence really was like the five stages of grief. At first, you refuse to accept that this can be happening. You can't be here! It is impossible to accept that nobody will realize their mistake at any minute, and let you out. You are innocent, remember? Surely people must see this? Surely everyone you know is doing everything possible to get you out? Once you realize that's not going to happen, you become enraged at the injustice of it all. Not just angry. Really angry. I got into my first fight about that time. Another inmate taunting me at the lunch counter, calling me a child abuser. Until that day, I'd kept my head down. I was on remand. Why do anything to jeopardise my release? And, in truth, what Johnson (a wiry terrier of a man with a pock-marked face and wispy red hair) said to me was no worse than I'd heard every day since my arrival. He just got me on a bad day.

So I hit him. More than that - I hit him with every ounce of the rage I felt at being locked up for what I'd begun to accept would be years of my life. When he hissed his little barb and moved past, I wheeled around, shoving him by the shoulder to force him to turn and then clocking him on the cheekbone with a blow which would have continued through to the wall had he not halted its progress with his face. I broke two bones in my hand, and he needed reconstructive surgery to realign his broken jaw and set a fractured eye socket. It was a ferocious blow. I put everything I had into it. Three inmates using the excuse of being his mates (Johnson had no mates, everyone disliked him equally) jumped me once I was released back into general population following my P19. Thankfully they were a little more restrained than I'd been, because I was in no fit state for it. I had languished in solitary for two weeks, where I'd come face to face with the next stage of the grieving process: depression.

If anyone tells you they know what it's like to be depressed without having suffered it as a clinical condition, do me a favour and tell them to fuck right off. Depression is not "feeling down". It is the absence of light in the world. It is the recognition – with absolute clarity – of the meaningless of everything in your life, and your utter worthlessness as a human being. You become suicidal not out of despair, but as a logical solution to the stain you are making upon the world. I didn't try it, though. My anger was greater than my despair. And revenge is a powerful corrective to any thoughts of bowing out early. But a fortnight in a cell with nothing to do but reflect on my situation was hell.

Being alone meant being without distraction. No matter how solitary you think you are, being alone with yourself is hard to endure for any length of time. And a fortnight is a very, very long time.

In retrospect, I'm glad I dealt with the worst of my depression while I was in solitary. I don't know how I'd have handled the beatings and the bullying while I still thought of myself in that way. Twenty-three-and-a-half hours a day cut off from everyone at least gave me that security. Not that I was through it, by the time I rejoined the rest of them. But I'd had time. Time to wallow in the overwhelming sadness and despair, and to gather and press it – as carbon is pressed into a diamond – into cold, pure hate. I'd get through it, as I did in the end, because of what would come after. Because of now. Because of the time when I could revenge myself, and prove my innocence. If I could just find some way to do it!

Bargaining never happened for me in prison. Who was there to bargain with? And as for acceptance... Sure, I made an accommodation there, as the years passed. But I would never accept this. I was out now, and there was nothing I would not do to set things right. He took my life from me. I wouldn't hesitate to do the same to him.

ELEVEN

I left Dublin in the late afternoon, driven by a renewed sense of purpose. I took the DART back to Greystones and walked through the town to the little garda station nestled between the shoreline and the road toward the harbour. The shutters at the counter in the reception area were closed, but I could hear a hum of activity on the far side. I rang the bell to the left of the hatch and waited.

After a minute or two spent perusing the handbills pinned on the noticeboard (Neighbourhood Watch informationals and warnings about the transmission of farmyard diseases) a young guard snapped back the shutters and asked me if I needed help.

"Is Mick Clancy here?" I asked.

"Who's asking?" he replied, fixing me with a suspicious glare. He was tall – well over six three – and had the ruddy complexion of someone who spent most of his time outdoors. I reckoned he was in his early twenties, but he could have been older. Whatever his age, he'd be an imposing figure should you make the mistake of being on the wrong side of the law, and he turned up to respond.

"A former client," I said.

Puzzled, he gave me another hard stare and went off somewhere to the back of the building while I leaned on the counter and tried to make out what was on the screen of the PC he'd left unmanned.

Two minutes later, he returned.

"He says he'll be out to you when he can," he said, before snapping the shutters closed once more.

It was another fifteen minutes before a door to the right of the counter opened and Clancy emerged.

"Thought it might be you!" he said. "Have you come to confess?"

"Not my style. As well you know."

"So why are you here, Jack? You could easily have grabbed me in McDaid's. It's a Friday, after all."

"I hate to mix business with pleasure, and McDaid's is your office. Besides. What I'm looking for is here."

"Don't ask, Jack."

"I have to, Mick. I need to see those files."

"Out of the question," he replied, emphatically.

"Anything's possible."

"Not that. All our files are confidential - which means we make an actual effort to keep them out of the hands of people like you. These aren't the sort of things the general public want to see. We wouldn't want to be responsible for keeping people up at nights. Or suing us.

Especially members of the public who had murdered other members of the public."

"I think I have a solution," I said, having given the problem some thought on the journey back from Dublin.

"Right?"

"You bring them along to McDaid's and make sure only you can see them, and I'll just ask you questions about what's inside. All you have to do is answer yes or no, as it applies. And seeing as you'll have your hands full, I'll buy the pints."

He gave me a hurt look – did I really think he could be bought with a couple of pints of Guinness - and turned away.

"Wait for me outside," he said.

It was a further twenty minutes before he emerged, his blue coat wrapped about him and a thick manila file beneath his arm.

"Right," he said. "Off with you."

I followed him down the road and ten minutes later we were seated at the back of McDaid's, hidden from view of the bar. There were few people in at that hour, anyway. A couple of the regulars (read alcoholics) sitting at the bar and one besuited man in the window tapping away on his laptop over a late lunch. Mick had overcome his disgruntlement sufficiently to allow me to buy him a pint, but it sat virtually untouched as we did our back and forth, and while I strained to come up with questions which could prove pertinent. It was like trying to steer a remote-control car from the far side of a wall.

Being unable to flick through the file to view the context was maddening. And to make it worse, Mick appeared to be enjoying himself.

"For fuck's sake, Mick! Would you not piss off to the jacks for a few minutes and give me a chance to find what I'm looking for?"

"You don't know what you're looking for!"

Which was true. I had no idea how the police collated the details of an investigation, and would have had no idea where to start. I decided to concentrate on Tom's statement. As I suspected, he had been interviewed - five days after Karen Williams disappeared. Mick told me it had been at his home (Tom was living at the time in a rented three-bed semi within walking distance of the town) and that he was alone in the house when they called.

By this time I was already a person of interest, though this was not noted in the transcript, apparently. In later entries however - once I'd been formally charged - Mick told me that Tom was listed as "suspect's brother". Outside of some general small talk to put him at his ease, they had essentially asked him three questions. Did he know the girl? Answer: No, though he may well have seen her about the town without recognising her. Where had he been at the time of her disappearance? Answer: He was with friends at The Boathouse public house (later corroborated by those others in attendance, vis Misters Emmet McLaughlin and Tony Donald). What was his reaction when he heard his brother had been detained in relation to the girl's murder? Answer... And here's where it got interesting.

Tom had hesitated long enough before he answered for it to be noted. At which stage he appeared "evasive", "though evidencing no apparent shock." When asked if there was anything in his brother's behaviour or history which suggested an interest in girls "of Karen's age" he'd appeared outraged; but gave them the impression that he was hiding something, or was trying to deflect the question. Subsequent efforts to draw him out were described as "unsuccessful". "The subject was perspiring heavily during this round of questioning", the interviewer noted. All of this Mick read to me verbatim, having tired of the rigmarole of restricting his answers to yeses or nos.

So that's how it was. With silences, and a few drops of sweat, my brother reinforced their suspicions and helped to convince them they had the right man. Bravo, Thomas. Nicely done.

"The fucker!" I said.

"There's nothing there, Jack. I warned you."

"But they barely questioned him at all! All they wanted to know about was me. Did they even check out his alibi? What did McLaughlin and Donald say? Is it in there?"

Mick spent a couple of minutes searching through the file to find the interviews with Tom's drinking buddies. And all the while I sat there, seething. I'd hoped Tom would have said something I could disprove –made a slip-up of some sort, or given himself away somehow. But he'd been too clever for that. On the face of it, he had successfully ruled himself out of the investigation, while making an effort to shield his brother from suspicion. As you would expect a brother to do.

What he didn't do, however, was say anything to counter the suggestion that I had an unhealthy interest in fifteen-year-old girls. All it would have taken was a simple "no" to that third question. Yet that "no" was never forthcoming.

"Jack? No! Nothing like that. He's devoted to Kate and Laura. He'd never think of a young girl in that way!" Anything at all to refute the notion. A notion which would see me beaten and terrorised for years to come - a notion which would see me ostracized, isolated, and viewed as fair game for every sadistic bastard to cross my path.

"Found them!" Mick said, snapping me back to the present. Both McLaughlin and Donald had been interviewed on November 17th.

"That's at least a fortnight after it happened!"

"They weren't a priority," Mick said, apologetically. And I knew.

"You interviewed them, didn't you?"

"Yeah. Seriously though, Jack, there was nothing there! It's just like I wrote at the time. They'd been in The Boathouse since three, watching the game between Munster and Harlequins. They stayed on afterwards for a burger and chips – your brother had the fish, it says here – and stayed till closing."

"So they'd have been pissed."

"I'd say that's a reasonable assumption."

"Assumption? Seriously Mick. Pints from three till closing? They must have been hammered! You couldn't trust their recollections of that entire time. He could easily have slipped off on them at some stage."

"Not according to this. Not at the time that matters. They were adamant that he'd been there for the whole time the game was on. Swore blind on it."

"And you believed them?"

Mick said nothing for a moment, making a grimace and shifting his arse in the chair.

"I'd no reason not to."

I knew what he meant. They'd only questioned them to tie things up. To make sure there were no holes in the investigation a defence lawyer could use at trial to raise the spectre of 'reasonable doubt'. They already had their man, so there was no need to push it further. By the time Mick interviewed McLaughlin and Donald, it was done. And so was I.

"I'm sorry, Jack. I don't know what you expected to find here. There was never anyone else."

"Seriously? No other suspects at all?"

"None that we could find. This is a small town, Jack. We'd have known about it if there were any kiddie-fiddlers hanging around the schools, or the like. Sure – you remember when Brian Johnson was done for peeping? And he was just a lad of fourteen trying to get an eyeful of the young wan next door as she got changed for bed. Nothing we wouldn't have wanted to do ourselves, at his age. Though we mightn't have hidden out in her back garden..."

I was depressed. Not depressed enough for Mick to buy me a pint, however. Instead he gave pointed, sad looks at his own empty glass until I got the message and ordered one for each of us.

"Thanks Mick," I said, tipping my glass to him ironically once I got back from the bar.

"Sure, what did you expect? We're not fecking eejits, Jack. Don't you think we'd have spotted something if it hadn't fitted? There was nothing there. In fairness, there was nothing to place you in the frame either, if it wasn't for the stuff at the dump site."

"Dump site?"

"You know. Where we found the body."

My heart jumped in my chest.

"But – doesn't 'dump site' mean she was killed someplace else?"

"It's possible. That's just what some people called it. Most people believed she'd been strangled there, on the hillside."

"But not everyone." I looked straight at him. "Not you?"

He sighed.

"Look Jack. Don't get your hopes up. Just because I suspected she'd been killed elsewhere doesn't change anything. Your stuff was still found there afterwards. Whether you'd dropped it while you were doing it, or when you were laying out the body after, makes no difference."

"The fuck it doesn't! If she'd been killed someplace else then all he'd need was the time to drop off her body - a few minutes at most! Not the time he'd have needed to snatch her from town, and walk her up there and kill her."

"Like I said, there weren't many who agreed with me."

"How many?"

"Altogether? None."

"None?" I said, incredulous.

"A couple of them pretended to consider it - but it wasn't what you might call a popular theory. Especially as we had you unaccounted for, for well over an hour. Loads of time to take her up there... and so on."

I thought for a moment.

"So what made you think she'd been killed somewhere else?"

He looked at me, apparently struggling whether to tell me or not. Or with the danger of feeding me false hope on the back of some idea everybody else had discarded.

"The grass," he said.

"Where they found my card?"

"No. Where they found her."

I stared at him, puzzled.

"It wasn't disturbed, the way you'd expect it to be. If you strangle someone – even a wee girl like Karen

Williams – they kick out. They struggle and thrash about to get you off them, to get some air into their lungs. It's basic instinct. You'll try everything you can to get them off you and get up."

"And the grass around her body? There were no signs of that?"

"Nah. Or at least none that I could see. The coroner said it was because she'd most likely been unconscious when she was strangled - but either way, I'd expect to see some evidence of a struggle. Even if you're out cold your body will react to someone shutting off the flow of oxygen to your brain. It didn't make sense to me."

And now I realised why he'd been prepared to believe I might be innocent, back then. Not because of something he'd seen in me, or because he believed I was an honest man. But because of something he'd seen himself, and his unwillingness to let it go, despite the advice of his colleagues and superiors. It wasn't about me at all. Just his own ego. His own belief that there was something off. Because of something that niggled him.

Perhaps worrying he'd said too much, he stood up abruptly, gathering the file and popping it inside his raincoat to protect it from the showers which had intensified while we sat inside in the gloom. Not wanting to waste good Guinness, however, he took a last sup from his glass and replaced it, as good as empty, on the table.

"I have to get this back. And Jack?"

"Yes, Mick?"

"Don't ask to see this again, all right? I'll be putting it back where it came from. And it'll be staying there."

"Whatever you say, Mick. Sure you can always look it up in there if I think of any other questions."

He raised his eyes to heaven. "Not for a couple of pints I won't! Sure, you didn't even buy me a sandwich, you scabby bastard!"

And with that he was gone, leaving me to finish my own pint and go over the details of what he'd told me. I was certain what he said about Karen Williams being dumped rather than killed on Matthew's Hill was important – but, for now at least, I couldn't explain why.

TWELVE

Those showers had turned into driving rain by the time I left McDaid's, joined by a biting breeze which whipped the young saplings about by the harbour and sent the rain sideways till it soaked my legs as well as my trunk. Mick had helped me out as much as he could - but I was on my own from here on. I needed to talk to McLaughlin and Donald. If I was to poke any holes in Tom's alibi, then I had to find an opening. And I knew now that he must have left The Boathouse at some point that evening: if not twice.

How long did it take to strangle someone, I wondered? Seconds? Minutes? If he'd killed her elsewhere, then where? And when? The last time Karen Williams had been seen was walking down Alma Road at around five o'clock that afternoon. But was that accurate? Had she gone missing earlier? How trustworthy was the witness Mick had mentioned - Ann Boland - who claimed to have seen the girl through her living room window as she passed? She didn't know Karen personally, so could easily have confused her with any of the gaggle of schoolkids in uniform who walked past her house each afternoon. And if she was mistaken, then Karen could have gone anywhere following her arrival at the DART station at half-past three.

They'd worked out it would take a half an hour at least to walk her up to Matthew's Hill. Allowing time for him to subdue her after he'd snatched her, and to kill her once they'd reached the summit, they'd estimated that she must have been abducted shortly after she was spotted at five, which would make the time of death six-thirty or later. But what if they were wrong? No one ever managed to explain what she'd done between the train's arrival at the station, and her appearance outside Ann Boland's window an hour and a half later. It was a ten-minute walk at most from the station to Alma Road. And if he'd snatched her earlier than they'd estimated... According to McLaughlin and Donald, Tom had been with them in The Boathouse for the entire match - but what if he'd arrived late? The guards would only have quizzed them about the period between five and six-thirty, and it was unlikely they'd have volunteered the information if he'd been absent any earlier in case they got him into trouble for no good reason. He could have killed her and stashed the body somewhere before he met up with them at The Boathouse, and laid her out on the hillside sometime later that night.

To prove any of that, however, I'd have to get McLaughlin or Donald to admit that Tom had either arrived late, or left the pub at some stage over the course of the afternoon. And I'd no idea even where I could find them! Or Ann Boland, either.

Tracking down Emmet McLaughlin proved easy enough, in the event. A quick visit to the library to check the online phone directory at one of the public terminals was all that was needed to locate his address. And to reflect on the gulf which exists between a modern library in a well-to-do town and a prison library. What I wouldn't have given for one shelf from the fiction section! There were more books listed under 'A' on those gleaming metal shelves than I'd seen in eight years, despite much pleading and the best efforts of one or two sympathetic custodians.

McLaughlin's address was listed as 171 Arbour Heights - a sprawling, seventies-built estate to the North of the town on the lower slopes of Matthew's Hill, maybe a mile from where Karen Williams' body was found. I walked back up the main street, trying to remain invisible, keeping my head down and avoiding eye contact, as I'd learned to do. The bad weather had helped to keep the pathways clear, anyone I came across more focused on getting out of the rain than on passers-by. I slowed down as I passed The Coffee Bean - the café Kate and I used to visit each weekday morning, once we'd dropped Laura off to school. My hours were pretty flexible (and I regularly exploited the excuse of 'working from home') so we stopped off there three to four mornings each week. I wondered if any of our old acquaintances still frequented it? Orlagh the Arts School lecturer taking a lengthy maternity leave, her one-year-old's buggy blocking the corridor? (He'd be nine or ten by now!) Or Janine from the restaurant next door, grabbing a morning coffee before the breakfast shift? Or Aoife and Colin, meeting up before they headed off to work - she in a crèche in Wicklow and he on some construction site to either side of the city, depending on the contract he had at the time? Ordinary people, living ordinary lives. As we were.

The window of the coffee shop was misted with condensation, a speckling of beads visible where someone had used their sleeve to peer out of the glass. The figures inside were blurred, the window forming a frame around a crayon Caravaggio. There were three women gathered at the table inside talking animatedly, one removing a sodden jacket as she sat, and gesturing toward the weather outside. And behind them, at the very next table, sat Kate. Alone.

She was dressed in black jeans and a matching pair of slim boots, the heels visible beneath the hems. Her hair - shorter than I remembered - sat on her shoulders above a grey cross-over woollen top, held in place with a single button of a darker grey. She looked quietly elegant. As she always had. The apparent lack of effort belying the myriad and often protracted choices she'd make before leaving the house each morning. I'd never known her to be poorly dressed, whether we were out to dinner together, or she was planting seedlings in the garden.

Even her gardening gloves were chosen with care. (Always some shade of pink, I recalled.)

I opened the door and walked past her to the counter, giving her a chance to spot me, and to get up and leave if she wished to. Whether I'd paralysed her with fright or she had some other reason for staying, she was still there when I returned with my coffee.

"Mind if I sit down?" I asked.

She didn't answer, which I took as invitation enough.

"Look, Jack," she said, before I'd managed to fully take my seat. "I'm glad you're out. Really, I am. But you can't stay. Not here. You need to find your own place, and get on with your life. Or begin a new life, if that's what you're looking for. On your own."

"It's not going to happen, Kate. Why do you think I'm back? I did not kill Karen Williams! I'm going to prove it - and I'm not going anywhere till I do!"

She gave me a look as much pitiful as exasperated.

"Jesus, Jack! Jesus! What do you hope to prove? That things could be the same as they were before? They can't. Even if it was true that you hadn't killed that girl - everything is different now. I have a new life. We have a new life. I -"

"I want to see Laura," I said.

"No."

"Does she even know I'm out?"

"Of course she does! She's fifteen, for God's sake!"

"I have a right to see her."

"No, Jack. You don't. You gave up that right long ago!" She paused for a second, as if trying to contain her anger.

"She doesn't want to see you, Jack. I've already spoken to her about it. Don't make me get a barring order. You know they'll give it to me."

And I did. If she were to claim that herself or her daughter felt in danger from her murdering ex-husband, I'd be banned from anywhere within a mile or more of where they lived. Meaning any hope I had of catching Tom would go up in smoke.

"Kate... I know you don't believe me. You never did. But I haven't seen my daughter in eight years. Not once! Jesus, Kate! Would one visit in all that time have been too much to ask? Even a quick hello at Christmas? Do you know what it's like, sitting alone in a cell while everyone else is downstairs meeting their loved ones, and coming back up with gifts and presents?"

"Jack. Please!"

"Please what, Kate? Please don't tell you my life has been hell for the past eight years? Please don't tell you what it's like to have your wife and child abandon you, when you most needed their help?"

"Don't you dare, Jack! Don't you - we didn't shut you out, Jack! You shut us out! But – that's over now. The past is the past. I would have thought you'd be glad of that."

"And what the fuck is that supposed to mean? The past isn't over for me! I live it, every moment of every day. My life stopped back in October 2008. Back when I still had a family."

"You threw it away, Jack! Christ! You don't think I wanted to believe you were innocent? You don't think we wanted to visit you? It was you who wouldn't see us, remember? I tried for months to get in to Mountjoy to see you. But they kept turning me away, saying that you wouldn't see us. Can you imagine what that was like? What it was like having to tell our daughter than her daddy wouldn't see her? All the sleepless nights I had to get her through, while you were wallowing in guilt, or self-pity, or whatever fucking shit you gave in to when you were locked up? You abandoned us – not the other way around! And now, what? You think you can just waltz back into our lives, as if nothing had happened? No, Jack," she said, rising to her feet and taking her coat and bag from the back of her seat.

"We're done, now. Congratulations! We've learned to live without you, and we've moved on. Isn't that what you wanted? But – do you know what? We hadn't forgotten you. Not one night passed without my waking up imagining what was going on with you, or the terrible things that might be happening to you. And it was ten times worse for Laura!

"Do you want to know how I felt when I heard they'd let you out, Jack? Relieved. Not relieved that you'd finally be free of that place – but relief that I wouldn't have to imagine it any longer. For the first time in years, I woke up without that sick feeling in my stomach. And I'm not going back. Do you hear me, Jack? We're not going back. Enjoy your coffee, but I don't want to see you again. Just stay away from us, Jack. It's over. Are you really so blind that you can't see that?"

She eased herself through the closely packed chairs, brushing past my shoulder: before pausing and leaning down to me, hesitating for a second before putting a hand on my shoulder and giving me a quick kiss on the cheek.

"Please, Jack. Just go!"

The kiss Judas gave to Jesus was less painful than this one felt to me. There was no love in it. Just disgust, overcome for a moment by pity. I gave her a minute before walking out myself, leaving my untouched coffee behind me and turning my face up to the rain to hide the tears streaming down my face.

THIRTEEN

Kate and I met in college. She was studying Science while I was in what would prove to be my first and final year of Commerce. I was too impatient – too eager to earn money and enjoy what I imagined as a cooler lifestyle – to withstand the hardships of university life. I flunked my exams, having been chasing that lifestyle months before I could afford it.

Kate was the opposite. Studious where I was lazy. Restrained to the point of shyness where I was loud and garrulous. Which wasn't to say that she was timid, or lacking in self-confidence. Just more of an observer than a participant, perhaps already seeing through the bravado and bullshit of student life. Had I stopped for a second, I would have realised how lucky I'd been to find her.

We met in the UCD canteen, where most student romances started. The bar was too loud and drunken for anything as prosaic as an affair of the heart, and the lecture halls only allowed you to spark up a conversation if, like me, you were among those dossing their time away at the back. Most of the girls you wanted to talk to tended to be up the front, paying attention.

I overheard her telling someone at her table that she was going to get a glass of water and cheekily asked if she would get me one too, pleading the mother of all hangovers. Which wasn't far from the truth. To my surprise, she returned with two glasses, setting one down before me and offering her commiserations for my poor state of wellbeing. Too taken aback to reply – and not knowing her well enough to realise I was being made fun of - I nodded my thanks, and went back to talking to Joe Malone (another waster, who was destined to flunk out alongside me) while she rejoined her friends.

There were four of them in all gathered across from us at the long refectory table, and she was not the best looking of the group. That distinction belonged to a slim, blonde girl with a Donegal accent who I remember had been doing most of the talking. But it was the brunette with the sallow skin and dark eyes who caught my attention, as I sneaked a glance over at them every few minutes. I didn't know why - not at that stage - but there was something about her which seized my attention. Later on, I discovered that some of that attraction stemmed from the fact that she was better than me in virtually every way. I'd always been attracted to girls who were out of my league!

We started meeting for coffees. I would drag her from the library whenever boredom bit, ignoring her protestations and dragging her through October showers towards the café block. And we chatted. About college. About family. About whatever she was reading or listening to at the time – though mostly about my tastes rather than hers. Like most young men of my age I was a much better talker than a listener. We talked all the time, in stark contrast with the years following Laura's arrival, when conversation of any kind dried up.

Despite our differences, or because of them, we fitted. It made sense to neither of our families – my mother disparaging of her quietness, my father unimpressed by her learning, and Kate's parents justifiably underwhelmed by my obvious lack of ambition. But we didn't care. Within months of my leaving college and landing my first job as a copywriter for a lifestyle magazine we were engaged, and we got married the following June.

Laura's arrival two years later, after Kate had graduated, both set us backward and propelled us forward. With a baby in the house, our every minute was accounted for, distracting us from the tensions which had entered our marriage but exhausting us beyond all expectation. In truth, nothing prepares you for becoming a parent. It didn't help that Laura was a sickly child, prone to a series of ear infections and minor ailments which resulted in a reluctance or inability to sleep through the night until she was almost two. We dragged ourselves around the house like famine victims, starved of sleep and prone to become irritated at the slightest provocation. There were days when we would quite happily have murdered each other (or her). But, as is so often the case, these shared miseries ending up bringing us closer. As the unmitigated joy at having her in our lives did - this demanding, fascinating little visitor.

There were other sources of stress. We moved home twice during the first three years of Laura's life. First from our centre-city flat to a two-bed townhouse in Monkstown. And then, biting the property bullet eight months later, when we bought what would become our family home in Greystones. I would happily have rented for the following decade but Kate wanted us to put down roots, as she put it, so I overcame my terror at making any further long-term commitments and signed up for a mortgage and life in a quiet suburb, the buzz and chatter of city streets replaced by quiet laneways and village life. For me, it was a return to the town I'd grown up in, and it felt like a backwards step for someone still reeling from the long list of responsibilities which faces anyone who has sex without a condom one too many times.

From the moment we moved into our home, Tom was there. He was our babysitter, our unpaid help when we remodelled and decorated, our drinking companion when penury replaced nights on the town with evenings in front of the TV. I thought nothing of it at the time, and took gleeful advantage of his willingness to help out at the drop of a hat. And he doted on Laura. He embraced the role of uncle more fully than I'd embraced that of father, it's probably fair to say. Then again... he didn't have to do nights! His Laura was the smiling, adorable infant who gurgled at him as he pushed her buggy along the seafront. My Laura was the antichrist screaming the house down at three a.m. And three-thirty... And was generally only warming up, at that point.

By the time Laura was three we'd become used to Tom's presence about the house. If we wondered why he showed no sign of establishing his own relationship – why a man who so clearly loved family life seemed to be making no effort to start his own – we ignored it, and largely out of self-interest. Looking back, of course, his selflessness is cast in another light: less the doting uncle, than the cuckoo.

It's easy to view those years askance with the advantages of hindsight. One particular incident stands out, from the year preceding my arrest. We were having our usual Friday night movie night, which had become a staple in the calendar at that stage. A DVD and at least two bottles of wine between the three of us, once Laura was safely tucked up in bed. I can't remember what we watched, but as the choice was typically between classics (Kate's preference) or action movies (mine and Tom's) it could have been anything from 'Singing In The Rain' to 'Die Hard'. I could claim that we had Catholic tastes, but the reality was that we rarely stepped outside of our respective genres, unless Xtravision had a recent release available which we'd missed when it was in the cinema.

We'd chucked a couple of Tesco's pizzas in the oven (none of us being a fan of popcorn, particularly the microwave variety) and opened the first bottle of wine when Tom arrived - smack in the middle of a fight over some trivial matter almost certainly related to our precarious finances. As Laura got older, and more expensive, these disputes had become more frequent. I suspect Kate's irritation was due at least in part to my apparent failure to move forward in my job - prospective promotions never quite materialising and the strain on our family budget showing no sign of alleviating soon. For my part, I couldn't see why she couldn't return to work to help lift some of that burden from me, now that Laura was old enough to attend school – a proposition she was resisting partly because of a crippling fear about not being able to come directly to Laura's aid, should some illness or emergency befall her. Kate had always suffered from anxiety – even in the first months of our marriage – and our financial situation had served to exacerbate this. Which to my mind made it seem even more logical that she should resume her career. So, we were at an impasse. And an increasingly combative one.

We tried not to air our dirty linen in front of Tom, but on this occasion he walked straight into a pretty open confrontation, when we had both built up a decent head of steam. I'm reconstructing the conversation from memory, but as these tended to take much the same course my recollection is likely accurate.

Tom had let himself in the front door, which was rarely locked. Greystones was that sort of place. I remember, now - our elderly Mazda had suffered another breakdown, the bill from the garage arriving in the post that morning. And, simply put, we didn't have the money. Kate had been telling me for months we should get rid of the car while it still had some residual value, and before it started to go badly and expensively wrong - and it didn't help that she'd been proven right. A small leak in the radiator had progressed until it needed replacing, and when the garage gave the car a quick once-over, it revealed that the front brakes also needed replacing, and the bush at the driver's side wheel was worn to the point of being unsafe. All in all, we were looking at a bill of almost a grand, for a car not worth much more. And Kate was livid.

The last thing you need to hear when you already know you've fucked up, is an "I told you so". Come to think of it, there are no circumstances in which those words are welcome.

"We'll have to pay it! We have no choice!" I said.

"With what?" was her perfectly reasonable response.

I was stymied. My credit card was close to its max and our bank account was already overdrawn. I'd made the mistake of borrowing from my father once before, and he'd exacted such a price over and above the repayment that I'd resolved never to do so again. It was inevitable that we'd have to beg her parents for a hand-out, once again. Two people who already regarded me as a poor substitute for a proper son-in-law. Or more pointedly, a poor substitute for her last boyfriend who, rather than having been consigned to the distant past, they'd retained as a touchstone against which to measure my every failure. I'd never met Conor McWilliams, but I fucking hated him.

The knowledge that we'd have to go cap in hand – or rather that Kate would, given that I'd probably be turned down having been made to suffer agonies of embarrassment – added to the vehemence with which I was defending myself. I'd yet to learn the value of a simple 'mea culpa'. Which was dumb, because this always defused her anger. Admitting my guilt or stupidity – or both – always stifled her ability to lose her temper with me. When Tom arrived however I was in full justification mode, determined to blame someone or something else for my error. Which was not an easy task. Of course the car had broken down! It was a heap, and I should have gotten rid of it months ago. Which, basically, was her line of argument.

Why is it the petty things like this, that make you feel like a failure? Money plays far too large a part in the dynamics of a marriage, though that seems unavoidable, absent a large lotto win or a sudden inheritance. The second of those options would have appeared an eminently attractive one to me, at that point – whichever family furnished the corpse! Which is ironic of course, given the sudden 'good fortune' I would experience while in prison.

Tom did the two things I least needed him to – agreeing with Kate and taking some good-natured digs at the state of old 'Betsy', as we'd christened our elderly 323... And offering to front us the money to pay for the repairs. In my mind, what he'd done was underline how hopeless a provider I was. It also earned him a huge, warm embrace from Kate - which I hadn't appreciated, even then.

It's impossible to look back and not see this as an attempt to buy her affections, however ungrateful that might seem. He had developed a tendency to ride to our rescue by then - whether with last minute babysitting, or some minor bit of handiwork when my limited skills with tools of any sort led Kate to lose patience with me and call him in. I hugely resented his 'assistance'. My elder brother was far too handy for my liking, and continually showing me up like this pissed me off. I believed Kate should allow me to make a hames of things, rather than dismiss me to the sidelines in favour of my more-accomplished brother. And he was always far too willing to step in – punctuating the work with deprecating remarks about how I'd always been clumsy as a child. I wondered if he'd constructed that new sunroof himself? No doubt every screw he fitted was a reminder to Kate of how she'd traded up...

"So how the fuck was I supposed to predict that the car would break down? I didn't fuck it up on purpose!"

"The way you drive? It's amazing it lasted this long!"

So Tom had stepped in; defusing the situation, and leaving me silently seething as Kate showered him with expressions of gratitude. Even allowing him to choose the movie, despite the fact it was her turn to pick. Needless to say he chose something he knew she'd like, rather than our usual guns and bombs fest. 'Moulin Rouge' if I remember correctly. Her go-to film whenever she was feeling down, and one I'd happily have consigned to the furthest reaches of hell. My smug older brother. Mr Perfect. Showing me up, once again. It took me months to pay him back the money we owed him, which made matters even worse. As did his repeated protestations that it was fine, honestly, and that there was no hurry...

Maybe I should have been more alert to his eagerness to spend so much time in Kate's company. For her part, I'm pretty sure there was no reciprocal attraction, at that time As a couple, we were still (fiery arguments apart) both intimate and close. I think Kate saw me as a work in progress and, despite all evidence to the contrary, still regarded me as salvageable. The resentment I felt toward Tom was growing, however. And, with hindsight, it's not hard to see how my petulance and ingratitude would have fed into his hatred of me. The injustice of his hapless, ungrateful younger brother having Kate, who obviously deserved better...

Could I have done something about it? Perhaps. Maybe laughed at myself more, and taken the sting from his criticisms. Discouraged him from being at the house so often by pleading Laura's naps or the need for some time alone with Kate ("If you know what I mean?"). Perhaps finding an actual babysitter, regardless of the extra cost, and telling Kate I felt it was unfair to lean on

Tom so much. Maybe I should have tried to fix him up with one of the women at my office - all of whom seemed to be young and good looking, advertising like PR tending to attract the most confident and outgoing of the 'poplar girls at school. But I doubt it would have made a difference. He was already – despite my complete blindness to this at the time – in love with Kate. I just underestimated how far he'd go to win her.

Fourteen

Emmet McLaughlin's home was one of the ugliest I'd ever seen. A cracked driveway - sections of which had been driven upward from the pressure of the weeds beneath the concrete - led to a front door painted in flaking, army-surplus green. The walls boasted faux-stone facing to window height, yellows and browns below cream paint last touched up when The Rolling Stones were still releasing new material. There were grey stains running beneath each windowsill and tracing the line of the drainpipe, from the guttering to the porchway. The garden advertised its owner's lack of interest in horticulture by somehow being both overgrown and bare at one and the same time. It was a dump.

I'd spent the walk from the town thinking about how to approach this. The rain accompanied me all the way, leaving me sodden and crestfallen by the time I arrived at his door. The estate was deserted - chimneys trailing thin lines of grey smoke bending in the wind, a susurration of leaves audible whenever it paused. I had hoped to appear resolute but trustworthy: a look somewhat at odds with my current state.

I rang the doorbell and listened to its asthmatic wheeze in the hallway. Probably just a simple failure to replace the batteries. Something told me few visitors ever came to this door. It was three or four minutes before I heard clattering from inside, and the door creaked open.

"Yes?"

The figure emerging from the gloom wore blue twill pants unencumbered by a belt above worn brown brogues, the ensemble topped off with a threadbare purple jumper which may at one time have been cashmere. I recognised him, though it took a moment or two to place him. His hair was short but inexpertly cut, his face dominated by two outsized ears which stood almost perpendicular to his head, each sporting a crop of long grey hairs.

"Are you Mr McLaughlin?"

"Emmet McLaughlin, yes. Why?"

To the point.

"Didn't I see you in McDaid's?" I said, remembering him as one of the barflies who'd been holding up the counter the lunchtime before.

"Are McDaid's sending people to our houses now, are they? I settle every Friday, as Danny well knows! He'll get his money!"

"I'm not from McDaid's," I said. "I'm here about something else. From a few years back. May I come in?"

He gave me a look which suggested people didn't often get invited into the house, and he wasn't particularly keen on the idea today.

"It's raining," I added.

"I don't like strangers in my house," he said, using the toe of his brogue to block the base of the door.

"I understand," I said. "Maybe I could ask you a couple of quick questions here, then? I won't take up much of your time."

He thought about it, and relented, stepping back into the hallway.

"You'd better come in, I suppose."

I gave him a grateful smile and followed him through to a small kitchen at the rear of the house.

Everything I saw there indicated that there was no Mrs McLaughlin. Not that it was messy, surprisingly, given his attire. Whether there was a late or a former Mrs McLaughlin (and whether she'd left of her own account or was buried beneath the patio) this was clearly the home of a man who was used to living on his own. A copy of The Irish Times was spread across most of the pine kitchen table, with a single place setting before it - a birdshell blue plate accommodating a toast crust and what looked like egg stains, alongside a single mug of coffee. He invited me to sit down, folding the paper and placing it aside.

"Coffee or tea?" he asked.

"Em – coffee would be good."

He sighed, giving me the impression he disapproved of my choice, before opening a drawer to fetch a Nespresso capsule and inserting it into a machine to the right of the sink. He didn't ask what type of coffee

I might like (I'd heard that Nespresso machines made everything from espressos to cappuccinos) so apparently I'd be having the same as him.

"Milk?"

"No, thanks. No milk or sugar."

This seemed to cheer him up slightly and a few moments later, following some loud howls of protest from the machine, he joined me at the table, setting a plain white mug before me. As gruff as his manner may have been, it occurred to me he might well have welcomed the company.

"So. What do you want to ask me about?" he said.

"It's about the young girl who was murdered here, a few years back. Karen Williams?"

"You're the one," he said. To the point, as I should have expected.

"Which one?"

"The one that did it. You killed her."

"No – I didn't kill her! That's why I'm here. To try to figure out who did."

He thought about this for a second, an expression on his face like he'd just found shit on his shoe. I didn't take offence. I was familiar with that look.

"I know you gave a witness statement. To the guards? Shortly after it happened?"

"After you killed her, you mean? Yes – I told them."

"Told them what, can I ask?"

He sat back in his chair, eyeing me coldly and considering his options. He was a big man, with the quiet confidence that often accompanies size. I'd no doubt he'd try to physically throw me out of his house if that was the route he decided to go.

"If you came here to ask me to change my story, then you can forget it. I know what I saw. It's not the sort of thing you'd forget. Considering."

"I'm sure it's not. And I've no intention of asking you to change anything. I just want to know what it is you think you saw."

He gave this some thought.

"Why?"

"Because I know for certain that you didn't see me. Because I wasn't there."

"Wasn't where?"

"Look - please! I just want to know what you told them, so that I can understand why they thought it was me. I didn't do this, Mr McLaughlin! If I had, I'd hardly have come back here, with people looking at me the way you're looking at me now. I'd be off down the country, or in Vancouver or someplace, starting a new life."

He thought some more. If this was his usual level of discourse, it wasn't surprising Mrs McLaughlin had chosen to leave. By whatever means available to her.

"I'll tell you," he said. "But then you can leave. I don't need to be seen entertaining the likes of you."

"That's all I'm asking. And thank you!"

He harrumphed, and took another sip of his coffee.

"I contacted the guards the day after she went missing. There were all sorts of appeals on the TV and radio, and everyone was asking. I didn't think anything of it, to tell the truth. I just thought I should say."

"Say what?" I said, trying to keep the impatience from my voice. I'd no idea that he'd been interviewed in connection with anything but Tom's whereabouts.

"What I'd seen. That I'd seen you - down by the Esso station."

The Esso petrol station was on the main road out of town, at the very bottom of the Eastern slope of Matthew's Hill.

"What was I doing? And why did you think it was me?"

"I didn't think it was you. I'd never seen you before. I just told them what you looked like."

"And? Jesus, Mr McLaughlin! Can you just tell me what you said?"

He smiled, making me wonder for a second if he'd been enjoying himself by stringing me along.

"I saw a man - medium height, wearing a blue woollen coat with a grey lining, blue jeans and brown leather boots - hunting about in the field behind the station."

"And? Did you see his face?"

"No. It was too dark. But I could see he had brown hair. Not too long, not too short, with gel or something like that in it. Though it might have been the rain slicking it back, like I told them."

It was a pretty detailed description from a distance too far off to make out a face, but I said nothing. As a witness sighting it was flimsy at best, which probably explained why it had never come out at trial.

"And what did you mean, "hunting around"?"

"Like you'd lost something."

Which made sense. No wonder the guards, at least, had found his testimony compelling. It had to be me, retracing my steps and trying to find my credit card. It added up.

"So where were you, when you saw him?"

"Saw you, you mean! I was filling the car. Staring straight up at you while I was standing at the pump."

There would have been a clear line of sight from the raised dais of the petrol station to the fields behind, with nothing else around to distract his attention. Anyone filling their car at the pumps would either be staring down towards the sea, or straight up into the fields behind them. The petrol station was the only one in the area at the time, servicing a steady stream of cars entering and leaving the town.

"So you didn't see the girl?"

"No. The people I spoke to reckoned you'd already killed her at that point." For someone who apparently believed there was a murderer drinking coffee in his kitchen, he was remarkably nonplussed.

"What time was this?"

"Just after eight. I know that, because I was due in Loughlinstown to collect my mother from the hospital at eight-thirty and I was already running late because I hadn't realised the car was empty until I got in." I suspected this must have been the former Mrs McLaughlin's fault. Nothing there suggested that he was a man likely to neglect such things.

It was my turn to fall silent, as I considered what he'd told me.

"I'm going to tell people that you came here. Just so's you know."

"Feel free, Mr McLaughlin. I've nothing to hide. Whoever it was you saw at the back of that petrol station, though, it wasn't me. And it wasn't me who killed that young girl."

"Sure – what else would you say?"

He slid back his chair, making it clear that my visit had come to an end. I took a quick sip of my coffee for politeness' sake, and followed him down the hall to the front door.

He said nothing more, closing the door behind me and leaving me standing once again on the overgrown driveway. I wondered if it was poor health or lack of interest that prevented him from keeping it in the same pristine state as the kitchen. Or was it deliberate? A way of deterring burglars or other undesirables? Like me?

FIFTEEN

My visit to Tony Donald's address proved fruitless, the house silent and unlit and nobody answering my ring on the doorbell. There was a Sherry-Fitzgerald sign on the pavement outside with a 'For Sale' board across it, but I'd no way of knowing whether Donald or some subsequent occupant had placed it there. He mightn't have lived here in years. The Eircom Directory was often out of date, it being up to residents themselves to keep the details current and landlines essentially dying out anyway. I could spy some furniture in the front room - a couple of cream couches and a glass-topped coffee table - so at least I knew the current owners had yet to vacate the property.

Houses in Fosterbrook were more up-market than those in Arbour Heights. Two-storey redbricks in the main, many of them double-fronted, and on sizable lots. I'd no idea what houses in the area fetched now but this one would be close to the top of the market. It was four, maybe five-bedroomed, and about two-and-a-half thousand square feet to judge from the exterior. A big house. For people with big incomes. I thought of ringing the doorbell of the adjoining house and asking if they knew when Mr Donald would be home... but I'd noted the Neighbourhood Watch sticker in Donald's window, and knew any enquiry of that kind would be reported to the guards the moment I left.

It was half-past three now. It was unlikely anyone would be home before five-thirty, at the earliest. Resolving to return later or to call again the following morning, I turned back towards the town. Having reflected as I walked, I reckoned calling on a weekend morning would give me a better chance of finding him in, and also be less likely to arouse the suspicions of the neighbours. The hour had gone back the previous Sunday night meaning that the evenings were shorter now, and no one wants to entertain a stranger on their doorstep once it's dark outside.

It had been raining continuously all day and the trudge from McLaughlin's house did nothing to help me dry out. Looking down at my sodden trouser legs I decided to return to Cois Farraige and change, following a long, hot shower. There was nothing to be gained from catching a cold, and I had time to kill.

The walk from Fosterbrook to the harbour proved an ordeal, the wind rising and the rain increasing in malevolence, leaving my face red and raw by the time I walked into the lobby and attempted to retrieve my key from the front pocket of my jeans. My hands were clumsy with the cold, and it took several attempts before I could open the door.

I stripped the second I got into the room, gathering my clothes and depositing them in a heap on the floor of the bathroom. There was a full-length mirror on the wall opposite the door, and I took a moment to regard myself while I waited for the shower to heat up. There are no full-length mirrors in prison. No one wants to see themselves there: much less to be seen looking at themselves. I was taken by surprise the first time I saw myself on the evening I checked into the hotel in Dublin, following my release. So much about my appearance had changed in eight years. The changes to my face were familiar - but the rest of my body was alien to me. When I arrived in Mountjoy I was one-hundred-and-eighty pounds, much of that down to a growing gut, my arms and legs in contrast both skinny and underdeveloped. I knew how much my chest and arms had changed since then, having been confronted by the evidence each morning as I shaved. But the transformation of my frame, seen as a whole, was still shocking to me. Whereas before my shoulders had been slumped, my chest somewhat concave above my stomach and my legs as muscular as you'd expect of someone who spent most of their day parked in front of a desk, the line of my shoulders was straight and defined now, with muscles clearly visible across my chest and stomach, a clear line running down toward each hip and my legs firmer and fuller than I had realised. It's amazing what years of boredom-induced exercise can do for you. Though I wouldn't recommend it as a fitness regime.

I looked at my penis, flaccid and shrunken from the cold, reminded of the old joke about why the Pope wears underwear (to support the unemployed). It had been so long since I'd held someone, or been held. So many years since I'd felt myself grow and move inside Kate. It had tormented me nightly for close to a year, thinking of how he was doing that with her now. Taking my place there, as elsewhere. Thoughts like that will drive a man mad - and would have done with me, if I hadn't been able to channel them into anger. Anger which had soon found an outlet. The lean physique I saw in the mirror developed at least in part from the work to which it was put: namely hitting other men until they bled.

Shamed, I turned away and stepped into the shower, allowing the water to warm my shoulders and chest and turning around after a minute or two to let the heat spread across my back. Fifteen minutes later I was dressed and stretched out on the bed, wondering how to fill the remainder of the day. Prison is as boring as you might imagine, but it does an excellent job of parcelling up your time. There is a timetable to each day, even if largely confined to routines and obligations. Here, however... Part of me had hoped that at least one of my former friends would have gotten in contact, once they heard I was out. At this stage that news had to have reached them. I hadn't hidden away, and although I'd yet to bump into any of them I realised that this may well have been deliberate on their part. It's nigh-on impossible to avoid bumping into someone you know in a town of this size.

I was surprised to discover that I was lonely. Lonelier, somehow, than I'd been in prison, even in my most isolated periods. Perhaps it was that thing about being lonely in a crowd? Or perhaps it was the proximity to all of them. To my friends. My wife... My daughter. It was like I'd time-travelled and found myself in a world utterly alien to the one I'd left. I was in the same place, but displaced. A visitor in my own home.

I was released on October 23rd. A quiet Sunday morning, but a day of shocks and starts for me as I adjusted to finding myself back in the world. It was a few months shy of eight years since my sentencing and imprisonment, on January 23rd, 2009. By the time of the trial I'd already been remanded without bail for three months: time that was taken into account in my sentencing. Suspects in a murder case are seldom granted bail. They are regarded as too much of a danger, or as a flight risk. Had I known what awaited me inside, I might well have chosen to flee, had that option been available to me. My sentence was twelve years - meaning that I should have been released in October 2020. And I had steeled myself for that, parking hope until that magical date was in reach. Instead of which I found myself out! Though every morning since I'd had to convince myself of that fact when I awoke.

Lying on the bed now I told myself that failing to seek out my friends would be tantamount to admitting my guilt. Sure, why else would I stay away? Yes, it would be awkward for us both. But I needed it to be known that I was back, and was here as an innocent man, rather than a sinner who'd completed his penance. Perhaps a better way to think of myself, I reasoned, was as an emigrant. Someone who'd moved to the States or the like, and was back in town after a few years away. I wouldn't have had much contact: but these were my friends after all, and men pick up friendships at the point they left them, pretty much.

Like most men of my age, I hadn't had many friends to begin with. Men are generally happy with a few and are uninterested in making new ones once they pass thirty. My own little circle, prior to landing in Mountjoy, centred around three men my age who met up each Thursday night in McDaid's. John Martin, Cameron Douglas and Sean Sherriff. The football games which had originally brought us together were a distant memory, but the custom of après match pints had outlived it. We'd accepted by that stage that our chances of getting injured had increased in inverse proportion to our ability to bounce back. We had watched each other succumb in turn: a torn hamstring here, a broken collarbone there. A period of months on crutches as the prelude to another permanent absence from the line-up.

I met most of the men I knew in Greystones through those Thursday evening games. It began on the school playground, on one of those rare occasions when it was we rather than our wives picking up the kids after school. Surrounded by an almost entirely female contingent I sparked up a conversation with one of the other dads, which led to a few of us hiring a pitch in the local sports centre once a week to stage doomed attempts at recapturing our youth. The standard was abysmal, but the competition was fierce, and the after-match pints were always hard-earned.

I first met Cameron at one of those games, and he quickly became a fixture in McDaid's. As a freelance graphic designer he lived a somewhat precarious life compared to the rest of us, surviving off occasional commissions from agencies such as the one I worked for. Fortunately his wife was a software engineer, which gave them some much-needed financial security. The truth was that she earned considerably more than Cameron did – and always would, even on his best months. Which gave us a convenient stick with which to beat him whenever the opportunity arose. Cameron was Scottish, with a burr softened by years living in Ireland though still liable to re-emerge following his third pint. As a young man he'd played keyboards in an 80's punk band – more fodder for ridicule – and he still dressed a good twenty years younger than his age. He was opinionated, frequently outraged, and excellent company. I had no idea whether he'd tried to visit me in prison, but wouldn't have been too surprised if he had.

Assuming that his financial station was unlikely to have changed sufficiently to facilitate the purchase of Aston Martins and yachts, I reasoned that he probably still lived in the same semi-d as before my incarceration, and left Cois Farraige for the West of the town. I laughed when I saw the same beat-up Toyota Corolla parked in the driveway. Cameron and Orlagh, his wife, had two grown up children. Teenagers when I'd last met them - but in their middle twenties by now, I realised with a jolt. I wondered if either of them still lived at home, or if they'd left the nest by now to set up on their own?

I walked up the sloping driveway and rang the doorbell. After a few minutes of loud barking and futile pleas for quiet, the door opened.

"Jack - Jesus Christ! I wasn't expecting you!"

"Fuck off, Cameron! You must have heard that I was out."

"I'd heard rumours, of course, but – here, what are we doing talking on the doorstep? Come in, come in!"

He seemed unconcerned about inviting a murderer into his home, which was encouraging. The dog continued barking from behind the door of the kitchen, and bounded at me the second Cameron opened it - a shaggy-haired creature of uncertain parentage, which seemed to take after its master in both temperament and appearance.

"Your hair's still black I see, Cameron," I said.

'Go fuck yourself, Jack! It's not my fault my superior Scottish genes age more slowly than yours."

"Yeah, that must be it. I presume there's a bottle of 'Scottish Genes' upstairs in your bathroom?"

He walked across to the kitchen counter, turning on the kettle as he passed without bothering to ask.

'So. Jesus! When did you...?"

"Last week."

"Wow!"

There was a short pause while I watched his face assemble questions.

"Alright, Cameron. I'll tell you all about it. Just make me a coffee first. And – one more thing? In case you need to hear it?"

"Yeah?"

"I didn't do it."

"Never thought you did, mate. You're too squeamish a fucker to hit anyone, let alone strangle them!"

Not anymore, I thought, but pleased despite myself to learn there'd been someone else who'd believed in my innocence.

"I tried to see you, you know," he said.

"When?"

"A number of times. Before I gave up. They said you wouldn't see anyone. Even your own family!"

"They said right."

"You're an idiot."

"You may well be right on that one, too. But... it was hard then. At the start. And after a while... It didn't seem to matter."

"People stopped trying, I suppose. Can't blame them! It was hardly their fault you wouldn't see them."

Blunt as ever.

"I suppose you're right."

"You know I am, you stupid fuck! Seriously – what were you thinking? Sean and John tried as well - although John's wife thought you should have had your balls peeled and pickled in acid."

"I take it she wasn't inclined to give me the benefit of the doubt?"

"Far from it! You were as guilty as hell according to Claire, and the only think worse than killing that poor girl was that she'd had you in her house for dinner. The nerve of some people!"

"I can imagine it must have been very distressing for her."

"Yeah, poor Claire! Anyway - sit down! Tell me all about it!"

I sat. He made no effort to hide his fascination about my time in prison, quizzing me about 'life inside' as if these were the details of a football match he'd missed, rather than a chronicle of misery. I suspected he'd invited me in as much for the story as for the pleasure of seeing me after so many years. Three hours later, I was still there, Cameron interjecting the occasional "Holy fuck!" while I recounted the major events of those years. It occurred to me - at roughly the stage when the coffee mugs were replaced by cans of Guinness - that I'd never done this before. That I'd never told my story to anyone.

"Is this, like, therapy?" I asked him at one point, to which he'd replied, "Nah - it's entertainment!" Which seemed fair enough, given that he was supplying the beers.

He barely moved the whole time - resting his head with its shock of too-black hair on his knuckles, and watching me intently. His eyes hid an intelligence I knew well, and he would have been alert to any lie had I told one. I also knew that he'd share the results of his polygraph with the others when he next spoke to them.

"So - what now?" he asked, as I concluded with my arrival back in Greystones.

"Now? Find the fucker who killed her, and do the same to him."

I hadn't mentioned Tom. Even old friends were potential saboteurs. And Cameron was notoriously indiscrete.

"Wow! Mind you, you look like you could strangle someone now! Was that all the press-ups in your cell? Like in the movies?"

"Yeah, Cameron. Just like that. I also had a harmonica and a metal cup I used to rattle against the bars of my cage."

"In fairness, you had time enough to learn an instrument! If they'd locked me up for eight years I'd be fluent in five languages, and a dab hand at the trumpet!"

"Like fuck! You'd have spent half your time reading The Daily Star, and the rest of it playing with yourself."

He thought about this. "Fair enough," he said.

I heard the front door open as Cameron's wife Orlagh returned, her arrival proclaimed with more frantic barking. A few seconds later she walked into the kitchen, calming the dog with some scratches beneath its ears and fixing me with a wide-eyed stare.

"Jack. People told me you'd been released." Her tone of voice suggested she'd not been completely onboard with that decision.

"Hi, Orlagh. Yes, they let me out last week."

She said nothing in reply, shifting her gaze to Cameron and keeping it fixed on him until he dragged himself from his stool and started to tidy up the cans from the counter between us.

"I better be going, Cameron," I said.

"Are you sure?"

"Yeah. Things to do, and all that. Not everybody believes I've got a right to be here, for a start." Whether I meant in the town or in their house I left open to interpretation. "Maybe I'll see you in McDaid's?"

"Not a chance, mate!" he replied. "I know you didn't kill that girl, but it'd be more than my life's worth to be seen with you in public. And you know how much of a coward I am."

"It's always been one of your finer qualities."

He smiled and followed me out of the kitchen. True to his word, it would be over a month before I'd see him again.

"It was good to see you, Orlagh," I said, as I passed her. She gave me a tepid half-smile in response and I let Cameron shepherd me toward the front door, his eyes to heaven and his thoughts no doubt on the interrogation he'd face once I'd left.

"Take it easy, Jack," he said, as he closed the door on me.

"You too!" I answered.

All that awaited me was a walk in the dark: the rain having relented for the moment, but probably only catching its breath. It took me ten minutes to make my way back to Cois Farraige, and less than one to decide against returning to my empty room. I considered visiting another former friend, Sean Sherriff, but his wife tended to be even less welcoming than Orlagh, and that was before I was convicted of manslaughter. Besides. It was late. And dark. And no one wanted a killer turning up on their doorstep this close to Halloween.

With no alternative left but the pub, I went back to Molly's, hiding in the back before a giant projector screen showing a Champions League game between Arsenal and a Bulgarian team called Ludogorets. I'd supported Arsenal since childhood, but lost any interest while I was inside. Having lost interest in virtually everything else. Somehow, supporting a football team without having someone else to talk to about it, or to ridicule your choice of allegiance, took all of the fun away. It proved to be an entertaining match, the home side running out 6-0 winners – much to the chagrin of a number of the punters in Molly's, most of whom seemed to be Man United fan and therefore ill-disposed toward any rival, in the mean-spirited way of their tribe. I remembered hearing that Man United had failed to qualify for the Champions League themselves, which no doubt contributed to this. Although I had determined to fade into the background, their jeers and insults resulted in my cheering loudly each time Arsenal put the ball in the net, if only to piss them off. Which, indeed, it seemed to do.

I stayed on for a last pint (I was drinking Miller Lite following those cans in Cameron's house, mindful I could be developing a habit, given this was the fifth consecutive night I'd spent in a pub). Having drained the glass, I headed back to Cois Farraige and bed, nursing a headache, and a growing sense of despondency. I knew this feeling well. It had been my constant companion for almost three years, from the very first day of my sentence. In the end it had taken a severe beating to snap me out of it and to break that spell. But I knew to recognise the 'black dog' when he showed up.

It was a week now since I'd returned. And, in effect, nothing had changed. Yes, I'd learned a little more than I'd known previously. And had some leads to pursue, at any rate. But there was nothing there which offered me any hope of clearing my name. And no hint of a rapprochement with Kate. Or Laura.

Part of me would have gladly give up on the attempt to prove my innocence if I could just win back their trust. Maybe contrition – appearing truly repentant – would prove more effective than this futile attempt to rewrite history? But I couldn't do it. Even if they offered me their forgiveness, and a route home to my old life - I couldn't let it go. I 'd paid too high a price. Tom had to pay. And not just because justice demanded it, or because Karen Williams' family deserved it. Because I needed it. For me.

Shadows flitted across the grass outside my room. The wind had woken the trees which formed the perimeter around the car park. The slim birches still clung to their last vestiges of foliage, most of their leaves littering the lawn and the gravel pathways. I saw movement at the very edge of my vision. A shadow, moving in the opposite direction from the swaying trees. It disappeared as soon as it appeared: but there had been something there. I was sure of it.

Grabbing my jacket from the back of the chair, I ran to the hallway and out of the front entrance. I was still pulling on my jacket as I exited, struggling to get my arms through my sodden sleeves. The shape I'd spied through the window had been heading toward the car park, so I cut across the grass and made my way to the end of the boundary wall. It was about six feet high, built from breeze blocks painted cream, and topped with red bricks. I crouched down, and tried to get my bearings. The wind was rising, making it difficult to distinguish anything over the patter of the rain as it fell about me. I could hear the waves far off by the harbour, and the dulled noise of cars passing on the street beyond. My mind replayed what I'd seen when I looked out from my bedroom, and I became increasingly convinced that there'd been someone there. And just as convinced that they had been spying on me. Somehow I couldn't see the family in the neighbouring room exciting such interest.

I slowed my breathing, staying as still as I could in the conditions. But I couldn't make out anything beneath the sodium lights, which cast the ground in a soft yellow glow and highlighted the lattice of rain as it passed before them. Knowing that the best way to hear anything is to remain silent yourself, I crouched lower, and waited. Three minutes. Four. And then I heard it! A sudden disturbance of the gravel on the far side of the wall, some fifty yards away from me.

I had a choice. Wait to see if they'd reveal themselves and risk their running off – or try to grab them now, before they made their move. I took my chance, rising to my feet and sprinting toward the end of the wall closest to them.

I'd no sooner rounded the corner than I saw him. A stocky man, dressed in black pants and a black jacket, crouched low as I had been on the other side, but rising to his feet now and preparing to run. I had the advantage of momentum however and was already in motion. Within forty paces, I'd have him. Or I would have – had I not recognised his face as he turned to look back at me.

It was a face I hadn't seen since the last day of my trial. An anguished face, torn between conflicting emotions. Jubilation at the verdict – and renewed despair at the unalterable fact of his daughter's absence.

I stopped, and watched him go.

Sixteen

I awoke with a cotton-wool head and a vague sense of foreboding. Dragging myself to the nearest coffee shop - a former furniture store in an Edwardian building above the harbour - I ordered poached eggs on brown toast and tried to coax my system back into life, on what was shaping up to be another miserable autumnal day. I'd slept fitfully despite or because of the alcohol in my system and was distracted and irritable, finding it difficult to focus. I leafed disinterestedly through the pages of an abandoned Irish Independent, skimming over the trial updates and the tales of misery in Aleppo and elsewhere, too tired to berate myself for my lack of concern for those in worse straits than my own. More people had drowned off the coast of Italy while trying to make their way from a warzone to a better life. Eight children among them. Lives snuffed out by an uncaring God or welcomed into paradise, depending on your affiliations. Given that the story was buried on the inside pages, it seemed nobody really cared.

My plan was to return to Tony Donald's house around eleven, when there'd be a better chance of finding him in. The truth was that he had become the last thread in my admittedly threadbare case for the defence. I'd uncovered some inconsistencies and omissions, but nothing which might establish a case for my innocence. If this didn't pan out, then I'd seriously have to consider leaving town - perhaps returning to the city for a while, to regain my bearings. Dublin City Centre - even in October - had to be an improvement on this backwater. And at least I'd be spared the malevolent looks I was faced with each day, on these streets.

The rain had eased somewhat by ten so I decided to risk turning up a little early, and perhaps spare myself another rain-soaked walk. It turned out of course that the rain had merely been playing a trick on me - waiting till I'd left the shelter of the coffee shop before it ambushed me with renewed vigour, drenching me from head to toe long before I arrived back in Fosterbrook.

The house was as it had been the evening before, no light inside to suggest that its occupant had returned. The For Sale sign was listing slightly, having been bashed about by the wind. Catherine O'Reilly Sherry Fitzgerald. I knew Sherry Fitzgerald as one of the larger national franchises, so presumably the owners had placed it in good hands. Not that I was in a position to buy! Besides, I already had a home. I just had to evict a squatter.

I rang the doorbell, more in hope than expectation. I was surprised, therefore, to hear noise coming from the back of the house, followed by the clicking of the lock.

The man who opened the door wore a cream shirt with a green check and a pair of mustard-yellow corduroys. His resemblance to a college tutor was reinforced by a pair of thick-framed glasses and hair which was borderline foppish, worn back from his forehead and carefully coiffured. I disliked him on sight.

"Yes?"

"Mr. Donald? My name is-"

"I know who you are. Why are you on my doorstep?"

"I was hoping you could spare me a few minutes of your time."

"Well, then, you're out of luck. I have no time to spare on you. In fact I'd very much appreciate it if you got off my doorstep, out of my driveway, and somewhere far away from here. If you need some encouragement, then I'm quite happy to call the guards."

"On what grounds?" I asked.

He was taken aback for a second.

"What grounds? What grounds do I need? I have asked you to leave. And if you refuse - well, that's trespassing."

"Seems a minor enough reason to call out the guards. If you don't mind me saying."

"I do mind, thank you very much! And I mind you still being here! I have nothing to say to you."

The patience I'd stretched across the course of almost a fortnight was in danger of breaking.

"Look - all I want is to ask you a couple of questions. It's not like I'm inviting myself in! It'll take five minutes at most, and I promise you won't see me again. I'm planning on leaving town later today anyhow."

He thought about it for a moment.

"No. I don't think so. Now leave."

I cracked.

Jamming the toe of my boot in the frame to prevent him from closing the door, I gave him both barrels.

"Listen, you sanctimonious prick! I've spent eight years in prison for something I didn't do – and partly based on your testimony! The least you can do is tell me what you said. I didn't kill that girl! For all I know, you did!"

"What!" he said, outraged.

"Why not? I know *I* didn't do it - and if you lied about what you told the guards, that's as good a reason as any to suspect you!"

"I did not lie! And how is what I told them supposed to have convicted you, in any case? I never even mentioned you!"

So I'd learned that much at least. I decided to bluff the rest.

"Maybe not. But you must have said something that led them to me."

"Wrong!" he said, with a malicious grin. "They never even asked me about you."

"So why did they want to talk to you, then?"

"If you must know," he said, staring down at the foot still wedged in his doorway, "They were merely asking about our whereabouts that night."

"'Our' being you, Emmet McLaughlin and Tom Finch?"

"Your brother. Yes."

"And what did you tell them?"

He let out a sigh, resigned at having to tell me something – anything – to get me to leave.

"I told them the truth. That we'd been in The Boathouse all evening, from the time the game kicked off until closing."

"The game?"

"Munster versus Harlequins. The Heineken Cup."

"You've a good memory."

"It has been said."

"And you're saying that you were there all evening."

"Every minute."

"You must have enormous bladders."

"What?"

"To stay there in each other's sight all evening, without ever having to go for a leak."

He gave me a contemptuous look.

"Of course we used the gents! But that doesn't change the essential facts."

"Were there other people there?"

"For a Heineken Cup match? What do you think? The place was packed!"

"Do you remember anyone you were talking to, while you were there?" I asked, spying an opening.

"Vaguely. There was much drink taken."

"But there were others there? That you were talking to?"

"About the match, yes."

"At half time and so on?"

"I suppose."

"No doubt everybody had an opinion, right? A game like that, there'd be loads of Leinster supporters with divided loyalties, I'd imagine."

He snorted with disdain.

"You obviously don't know much about rugby! There may be a healthy rivalry between the provinces, but when it's an Irish team against the English there are no divided loyalties, believe me!"

"You know? I'm not sure I do," I said. "You tell me you were in a crowded pub, watching a game that had you transfixed, chatting to any number of people about what was going on – and yet you swore to the guards that you knew where my brother was for every second of the time you were there."

Donald flushed red.

"I don't think I like your tone."

"I'm sure you don't like anything about me. But that doesn't change the fact that I was locked up for eight years of my life for something I didn't do - and partly on the back of what you told them!"

"That - to be frank - is bullshit."

"Fair enough. You might not have actually put me in the frame. But you may have given the person who *was* responsible an alibi. The truth is you can't account for my brother's whereabouts for the entire time you were there – despite what you said. You lied, Donald. And I went to jail."

His sneer became a snarl.

"We're done here, Finch! But, before I call the guards, let me ask *you* a question."

"Yeah?" I answered.

"Who the fuck do you think you are?"

"Excuse me?"

"You're not a guard! You're not even a fucking journalist! What made you think we'd have to answer any of your questions?"

He smiled.

"All right then – let's suppose, shall we? You appear to like suppositions! Suppose you were right. Suppose we had lied! That I'm lying to you right now! So what? What could you do about it anyway? Nobody cares what you think, or what you believe. It doesn't matter! You don't matter. Nothing *about you* matters. Whether or not you killed that girl... nobody cares! Except maybe you and the girl's family. For everyone else, all this is ancient history. Do you think anyone in this town wants to be reminded of it? Or that they'd welcome somebody digging up those ashes? It's over, Finch. Done with, long ago. And frankly we don't care if you spent however many years it was– you see, I couldn't even be bothered to remember what you said – in jail for something that you claim you didn't do. The fact is, you can't prove your innocence! You can't. Because none of us have to tell you anything. Not. One. Damn. Thing. Now get the fuck away from my house!"

I was too shocked to react when he pulled the door open to free my foot and then pushed me backwards, sending me sprawling backwards onto the lower step.

I dragged myself upright and stood there, staring at the closed door. Spotting its opportunity, the rain resumed its onslaught, and stayed with me for the long, slow trudge back to town.

SEVENTEEN

I spent a further week looking for a flaw - an opening, any way of proving my innocence or of catching Tom in a lie. And I got nowhere. When I was in prison I'd imagined that there'd be countless ways to clear my name or to expose him once I was out. But the truth was I had nothing. Nothing to work with, and no authority to change that. He'd been too careful. Careful not to tell an outright lie when they'd interviewed him. Careful to leave no trace. His alibi was solid, because his witnesses were men willing to give him the benefit of the doubt and unwilling to admit they could be wrong. And because I'd never seen the interview transcripts, I was reduced to playing catchup and 'what ifs', and still didn't know most of what had happened, or what had been said. Or by whom.

And the evidence against me was damning! My card at the scene. Failing to admit that I'd known her. The soil on her collar....

Exposing him, I'd come to realise, would never be enough. It wouldn't matter if I proved he could have — or even did - slip away from The Boathouse that evening.

There was no finger I could point at him which would undermine any of the evidence against me. I realised proving that he could have done it, didn't matter a fuck. I would still have to account for every piece of evidence against me before they'd have any reason to look at someone else.

And I couldn't. I couldn't!

I still had no idea how my credit card came to be there. Just suspicions and conjectures. And I still had no idea how he had planned and executed it, just a theory about why. And would anyone else view that as a plausible motive? That my own brother would murder a schoolgirl, just to frame me and take up with my wife... months later? Christ!

There was only one way I could clear my name – and that was if he came forward himself. Without a confession, I was fucked. I was, and always would be, the man who murdered that child. And he would remain Katie's loving husband – and Laura's 'real' dad.

I could not bear that! To lose my chance of redemption – of getting Laura back or convincing her that the dad who read her stories at bedtime hadn't left her side to murder her babysitter...

Unless he admitted it, everything – everything that had kept me alive all these years - was gone. He'd have beaten me. Again! Humiliated me - tortured me – all over again. And this time, I knew, it would destroy me.

So I spent the next day in the pub. All of it.

Guilt, deserved or otherwise, is painful. For a long time, mine had been displaced by anger. By rage at my own situation, rather than any real concern for others. But seeing Kevin Williams had made me realise how those years must have been for them. For Karen's family. I had been separated from Laura for the same length of time - eight long years. But Laura was still alive! Still capable, however unlikely that now appeared, of returning to me. Their little girl was gone.

Not only that, but the man they believed had taken her from them was back amongst them. Walking their streets – her streets! – apparently free to come and go as he pleased. Christ! It occurred to me that Kevin Williams might not have been spying on me at all, but getting ready to do something about that. I knew what I would have done, had our situations been reversed.

Playing poker and drinking Jameson. That's what Will Keane and I had agreed. Will had been a friend of mine since college - another of those who either didn't try, or was prevented from seeing me in prison. His fault or my fault. It didn't matter. Another person I'd resolved to call on now that I was out, but hadn't.

It was a running joke between us from the moment our daughters were born, his Tess arriving ten months shy of my Laura. If anyone attacked one of them we'd track them down and then claim we'd been together all evening. Playing cards, and drinking whiskey. If you've a daughter yourself then you know the extent to which this was ever a joke. An alibi of that kind would likely have been required.

Another cold, wet day awaited me when I awoke shortly after ten. The streets bepuddled, the trees denuded, and a sky the colour of porridge. A wind with a personal grievance chilled my head and legs as I fought my way as far as Molly's and the warm welcome of a well-stocked bar. I'd stopped at the ATM en route to withdraw a hundred Euro, timing my arrival to coincide with opening time, and under no illusion about how long I'd be staying there.

At about eleven-thirty, as I cradled my second pint, I thought about visiting the Williams. They likely still lived in the area, especially given Karen's father's appearance so late the night before. Had they stayed on in the family home? Karen's bedroom just as it had been on the fateful morning when she'd left for school, never to return? Or had the passage of the years allowed them to repurpose it as a study or the like, Karen's memory better preserved in photos and drawings hung about the walls, alongside other precious keepsakes? Or had they moved away from the town, escaping the constant reminders?

It was a stupid idea, I realised. Worse: a selfish idea. What could they gain from meeting me? In what parallel universe did you invite your daughter's killer into your house and sit down together over a cup of tea? Protesting my innocence would be futile, and more likely to provoke them to anger than to lend any credence to the account I put forward. And, as I well knew, that account was at best improbable - at worst both dishonest, and cruel. My brother had killed her, I'd tell them. For no other purpose than to frame me. Their daughter just a footnote in my story and a means to somebody else's end. Karen had been taken from them, at random, to win over my wife and daughter. A girl who was now the same age as Karen had been when she died...

What solace would that provide them with, exactly? Telling them that their daughter hadn't even been the central character in her own tragedy! In their tragedy! I would be causing them pain just by being there. No. What I needed, was to prove my innocence! Which I was no closer to doing then when I'd first arrived. And the bind I now found myself in was that, if that proved impossible and I had to leave empty handed, I'd look even more guilty than before. And my coming back here would appear vindictive, even brazen. The fucker! Out, and flaunting it! Walking about on our streets, and that poor girl dead!

All this was very depressing, so I doubled down on the antidepressants. A lot of shite is talked about alcohol. I've no doubt it's true that alcohol acts as a depressant on a scientific level. But its positive, if temporary, effect on the spirits is too often overlooked, to my mind. And I had eight miserable, teetotal years to cite as evidence.

I had picked up a couple of newspapers to help me pass the time. The Irish Times and The Guardian. Both were full of Halloween ads - from pumpkin-flavoured treats, to special offers on items with only the most tenuous link to the season. Tesco were doing a special on snack-size Maltesers, Crunchies and Mars Bars. Celebrity masks were selling well, a columnist in The Times reported, Hilary Clinton proving a more popular choice this year than witches or ghouls. And, according to the back pages, Wayne Rooney hadn't "a ghost of a chance" of playing in the weekend's derby against City.

Most of the front pages and international news centred on the upcoming US presidential election. I flicked through it disinterestedly. A career politician with suspect judgement, versus a scumbag. Doubtless, given her age, Laura would prefer Bernie Saunders to either of them. Apparently his rallies were packed with people not much older than her. How different her life would have been if we'd moved over there! How different all our lives would have been! I'd have been free to watch her grow up! Change her accent! Get her first car on her fifteenth birthday (it was legal to drive from that age onward in some states - sheer fucking lunacy!). Go to her high school homecoming, and prom... all of that shit. I'd known somebody way back who'd done it. Relocated to Washington State, all fees paid by the IT company he worked for - fetching up in some dormitory town where everyone worked in the same place, the streets were always freshly swept and the only crime to speak was an occasional parking ticket. He hadn't lasted, though. Last I'd heard he was back, freshly divorced, replacing the home he'd left in Monkstown with two smaller ones in

Sallynoggin and Stepaside. A high price to pay, in the end, for lower tax rates and a good dental plan.

Despite the drink I felt restless. Your boredom threshold is set early on, they say. Mine was quite high, having had to spend long hours with fuck all to do on a daily basis. What I was really feeling was unease. The sense that there were things I should do, places I should be... instead of which I was sat in a bar getting steadily drunk while a storm raged outside. Was that a metaphor, I wondered? Did that storm out on the harbour reflect the turmoil my arrival in the town had caused? Or the tumult to come? Bollocks! It was just shite weather. Perfect weather, that is, for holing up in a pub and giving way to self-pity and despair.

Drinking brought me neither solace nor respite. Not that that stopped me. I'd walked in the door of Molly's sometime before eleven o'clock and was still there five hours later, halfway through a basket of sausage and chips (strange the things prison will give you a craving for!) and pacing myself a little more carefully. I didn't want to get messy drunk. Just to... ease things a little. To alleviate my symptoms, if you will. Despite my best intentions, however, this commitment to moderation had come a little too late. No Miller Lite for Jack today!

I was sitting in one of the refurbished armchairs (circa 1975, at a guess) which had grown noticeably more comfortable as the afternoon progressed. It was as well they had lounge service, as I doubt I'd have been able to go up and order at the bar. The seatback sagged, and I could feel the wire frame through the cushion, but it was debatable if I'd sat anywhere as pleasant in close to a decade. Though that may have been the Guinness talking.

Guinness, they say, has the "most meritorious effect upon the brain" - altering the mood in a subtle fashion compared to the sudden rush of spirits, or the flushed incoherence other beers produce. I've never felt less well-spoken as a result of drinking Guinness, and suspect it has done much to earn the Irish our reputation for eloquence. People invariably form this opinion of us when they're in a pub, so there might be something in it. I eased into a drunk like slipping into a warm bath. By the time I stood up for yet another visit to the jacks, and found my legs somewhat slow on the uptake, it was too late to do anything about it. Being pissed didn't make me blind me to the looks I was getting as the bar filled up, however. And although it might have made me more tolerant of those doing the staring, it also left me less prepared to deal with any more overt hostility. It was clearly time to leave.

Keeping my head low, I made my way to the front door and stepped out into a bitter wind, which had an immediate effect upon my stupor. Fuck, but it was cold! By the time I got back to Cois Farraige I was stone cold sober - or close enough - and shivering fitfully. My plan was to take a hot shower to ward off the chill, then spend a few hours reading the book I'd picked up in The Village Bookstore the afternoon before, the latest in the Ross

O'Carroll Kelly series. The ROCK books were witty and laugh-aloud funny, and had saved my life on a few occasions inside. When I looked for the book, however, having turned on the shower to let the water heat up, I discovered it had been moved.

It's long been true of me – and proved even more so inside, given the lack of control you have over the smallest details of your life - that I'm something of an obsessive compulsive. At least to some minor degree. Having things in just the right place is a requisite. I can't leave a knife alone if it isn't aligned parallel to the fork. Bath towels have to be folded proportionately. Books stood upright on their shelves. These are small things and not of themselves worth worrying about (or so I tell myself) but the result is that any small instance of asymmetry screams chaos at me, and is impossible to overlook.

When I'd taken the book out of its bag I had placed it at the top left corner of the desk, an equal distance between the top and spine of the book and the sides of the table. It would have been impossible for me to set it down otherwise. Now, however, it was not only in the wrong position, but at a slant. Someone had been in my room.

I thought hard, fighting the fug in my head. Who? What had they been after? Part of my brain said to inform Mick Clancy - but all it'd do would be to irritate him, and give him another excuse to pressure me into leaving town. It may indeed have been a thief - but I chose to view it instead as proof that somebody out there saw me as a danger. That despite my utter failure to make progress, someone believed I was capable of doing so. Why search my room, if not to find some evidence of my enquiries?

I checked, and found further signs of disturbance. My clothes had been moved and were no longer equidistant upon the rail inside the wardrobe. My sock and underwear drawers had been riffled, the boxers inexpertly refolded. Even my washbag had been opened, the toothpaste and shaving foam now facing in opposite directions.

Tom used to torment me for my fastidiousness when we were kids. It was easy enough to wind me up, to be fair. I was smart – but Tom was smarter. He'd always been cleverer than me ("Than I," I can hear him say.) He soon learned that all he had to do was to subtly disturb my things, and I would freak out. The changes were always so minor that it was easy for him to deny knowledge of any wrongdoing and – as the elder child – he always received the benefit of the doubt. Or perhaps my parents hoped that I'd grow out of it by having my limits tested? Whatever Tom's intentions, I'd be reduced to inarticulate rage, rendered distraught by the vindictiveness of these assaults upon order, and hurt to the quick by my parents' refusal to believe me, or to punish Tom. I was a sensitive child and easy prey for this drip-feed of torture. (And if you think that's an exaggeration, you've obviously never met anyone with OCD.)

I went into the bathroom and turned off the shower, any hope of relaxing gone. Instead I spent a further hour inspecting the bedroom, inch by inch, compiling a list of the ways and places it had been tampered with.

Whoever had been here had done a thorough job. And they'd have to know my whereabouts to have done so without fear of being disturbed. I assumed they'd have pulled the curtains while they searched, which in itself would have alerted me had I returned any earlier. Were there more than one of them, I wondered? One searching while the other kept watch? Or perhaps whoever did this had followed me to Molly's – waiting for me to order yet another pint, knowing they'd have at least thirty minutes before I finished up and left? Had there been someone there? I thought back, trying to replay scenes from the bar. But it was futile. I'd made such an effort to hide myself from view that I'd no clear recollection of anybody in the place. The cast of Riverdance could have been smacking clogs by the bar and I wouldn't have noticed.

My next concern was whether anything was missing. I never left money around. I'd none to speak of in prison, but had long had the habit of gathering my loose change at the end of the day and stacking it on my bedside locker, the largest coins at the base. Another compulsive behaviour. You couldn't depend on size mirroring value though, as I'd discovered on my first visit to the US some years before. The ten-cent coin is significantly smaller than the five-cent coin and in fact smaller than the one cent coin - an outrageous discrepancy. The coinstack from the previous day appeared intact, however. I'd made the bed that morning (housekeeping at Cois Farraige was bi-weekly) and it too appeared undisturbed, though the mattress may have been lifted to check for anything hidden beneath. The truth was that there was nothing for them to discover. Any notes I'd made were folded inside my jacket pocket as I was continuously augmenting them. They were also written in a shorthand so illegible as to prove incomprehensible to anyone else. So. No money gone. No evidence of what I was doing to be found. And no clue as to my intent.

I felt relatively safe, if angered by the intrusion. Nobody wants strange hands in their underwear (with the obvious exception). I used a trick I'd picked up in prison, balancing a coin on the upper lip of a drawer. If someone pulled the drawer out it would topple back onto the folded clothes, where I would find it next time I looked. I also reset the furniture and furnishings in line with my strictest dictates. With my room thoroughly OCD'd, I was confident I'd easily spot the evidence of any further intrusion.

Once I'd reassured myself that all was well, a wave of fuzzy wellbeing from all the beers I'd drunk washed over me, and I relaxed. I shifted the pillows against the headboard, planning to read myself into tiredness once

I'd shed my wet clothes. I realised the position I chose was the one I usually assumed in prison, where your bed is the only available place to read: alive to the irony that the only way I could get comfortable was to replicate those same conditions.

After thirty minutes, I felt sufficiently tired to turn out the light, slipping beneath the covers and drifting off to sleep content in the knowledge that nothing had been taken from the room. It was only later that I considered the possibility that somebody might break into a place not to take something, but to leave something behind.

EIGHTEEN

There was no dawn raid or anything so dramatic. When Mick came for me at lunchtime the following day I was still oblivious to the tumult raging through the town.

In retrospect, I was glad it was Mick who found me first. Middle class towns like Greystones aren't much given to lynchings, but I may well have provided the exception. I could picture it - some top-end nylon climbing rope hoisted over the 'Beware, Children Crossing' sign, and me dangling from it, my heels knocking against the pole.

Mick was standing outside Cois Farraige when I turned off the street into the courtyard, having wandered up town for a sandwich and my third coffee of the day. He was accompanied by a younger guard and a crumpled-faced sergeant who'd been a fixture at the station since I was a teenager growing up in the town. My first thought was that Donald had phoned in a complaint, and I was already cursing the prick when something in Mick's expression gave me pause.

"Mick?"

"Mr Finch. We'd be grateful if you'd accompany us to the station. We have reason to believe you can help us with our enquiries."

His face was rigid, and impossible to read. Was he warning me to take care by using this formal address? Or was his voice as cold as it sounded? I could feel sweat rise in my armpits and my face flushed, as if from a sudden shock. The past had jumped out and shouted boo! - and in that moment, I was back in prison.

"What enquiries?"

"It's with regard to an ongoing investigation."

"You wouldn't care to be a bit more specific? If it's about Karen Williams, then I'm happy to help, but if it's anything else then you'd better tell me what."

"It's best if we discuss it at the station."

"And what if I say no, and turn down your kind invitation?"

"Then we'll have no choice but to arrest you and bring you in for questioning. And I'm sure neither of us wants that."

Too right I wouldn't! News that I'd been arrested for anything from littering to loitering wouldn't be long making itself known about the town, and would make it even less likely that anyone would talk to me.

Realising I had no choice, I shrugged and followed Mick to the squad car parked at the entrance of the car park. I immediately found this odd. The station was a matter of a few hundred yards away, up on Kilmartin Drive. When we got to the car the sergeant took the passenger seat, leaving me to sit in the back with the rookie. Not a word was spoken as Mick drove up the road and parked at the rear of the station. I spent the time looking out the window at two winsome seagulls circling the harbour and disturbing the afternoon with shrill shrieks of complaint. I still regarded all this as an irritation rather than anything more serious, and quietly resolved to get Donald back at a later date. That conviction held until I was led past the front desk to a small room at the back of the station and realised that the two guards weren't following me, but hemming me in in case I tried to escape.

The room was exactly as I remembered it.

"Here, Mick? Are you serious?"

"Please take a seat, Mr Finch."

His face was like stone. The bastard! Didn't he know what this place – the very memory of it – meant to me? I'd spent the best part of three days in this tiny room with its ancient plastic chairs and beat-up desk, unable to make out anything through the high, narrow window opposite the door.

Reluctantly, I sat down, leaning back until the chair legs left the floor to make it clear that I'd come here of my own volition: not as a suspect whose guilt had already been decided by the time I was picked up. Things were different this time. Or so I thought.

They'd found her on the beach, still dressed in her school uniform. Karen Williams: but not. Dead, as she had been. Laid out, as she had been. Her heels together to make it clear that she hadn't been sexually assaulted. Her arms flat against her sides, palms upwards; like an offering to the gods. Her hair was stirring in the breeze, Mick Clancy told me. Tossed about and played with by the wind, and whipping across her face so as to give the impression of life and movement where none existed as they walked toward her across the sands.

This time there was no credit card lying around close to the scene. Nothing quite so convenient. Forensics had yet to complete their report, Mick Clancy said, as the tape whirred in the machine on the desk between us. But I was damned in any case, as the pain in my chest confirmed. Another young girl murdered, and the killer of the Williams girl back in town for little more than a week! The truth, I knew, was that they'd need little else – whatever the law might say. I'd little doubt that if the boffins failed to come up with the evidence needed to convict me there were people in this station who'd be quite happy to fabricate it, in order to ensure that I was sent down.

When Mick told me why I'd been brought in – beginning with a description of the place where the body of a young girl "as yet to be formally identified" had been found – I was unable to move. A doctor might have termed me catatonic: all I knew was that none of my limbs would agree to move when I asked them to. My arms and legs were leaden, my chair flat on the floor once more, my mouth dry and incapable of speech.

"Can you tell us of your whereabouts over the past twenty-four hours?" Mick asked, once he'd outlined the facts.

"What's going on, Mick?" I replied. Though I knew only too well.

"I'm happy to repeat the question. Can you please account for your movements over the course of the last twenty-four hours?"

"Am I under arrest?" I asked, stalling for time. Twenty-four hours? They believed she'd been killed some time since yesterday afternoon!

"You're here in a voluntary capacity, Mr. Finch, having agreed to help us with our enquiries. Do you wish to make a statement at this time?"

"The fuck I do, Mick! I had nothing to do with whatever happened to that girl - and you know full fucking well who did!"

"If you believe you have information about the person responsible for this crime, I must caution you that you are obliged to pass this information on to us or risk being charged with withholding evidence."

"My brother! Tom-fucking-Finch! The same person who killed Karen Williams! The person who's trying to frame me now. Again! Jesus..! Can't you see? He must know I've been searching for ways to link him to her death – Karen's death – and he did this to stop me!"

"You believe that a young woman was murdered, in order to frame you?" The disdain in his voice was clear. And I could understand why. What sort of egomaniac believes that the deaths of not one but two young girls is all about him?

I stopped talking.

As the silence lengthened I became aware of the humming of a small fly flitting about the room, making sudden changes of direction as it sought an exit. I knew how it felt.

"I had nothing to do with the death of this girl," I said when the silence became intolerable, the quiver in my voice undermining my resolve. "I'm happy to answer any of your questions and will not be requesting any representation at this time. I'm certain that when I've given you an account of my movements you will see fit to release me, so that you can get back to your investigations."

I was certain of no such thing. I was fairly confident that I could account for most of that time −I'd been in public for much of it. And it was unlikely that the girl would have been out and about after I'd returned to Cois Farraige. My worry was whether the witnesses I put forward to corroborate it would confirm the truth, given how our paths had crossed. A man who I'd flatly called a liar - and the father of a girl I'd been convicted of murdering, who even now had no idea that I'd recognised him hiding outside my lodgings. Would telling the truth be in their interests? No one had seen us together. Even admitting they'd met me might seem like a bad idea - especially for Kevin Williams, given what I suspected he'd been intending to do. I was even beginning to regret telling Donald what I thought of him. But I had no other choice, and no other narrative to offer.

They reminded me that the interview was being recorded and I went through the details, listing witnesses as I did so, starting with the previous morning and continuing up to the moment I arrived back at Cois Farraige to find them waiting for me. And as I did so, I became increasingly confident that the facts would bear me out. I was hardly invisible, and no doubt somebody would have spotted me walking along the road or in one of the various places I'd stopped. The Coffee Bean. Molly's. The supermarket where I'd picked up the newspapers. I went through it, hour by hour, making it clear that I was providing the details "to the best of my recollection" and stressing there could be some slight inaccuracies which should not be viewed as deliberate. I also asked that they check my story with each of the witnesses I listed as soon as possible - Donald in particular – and without revealing any details or context, so as to ensure they received an unbiased response. It was naïve to assume that news of the girl's death hadn't already circulated about the town, and it's surprising how willing people can be to readjust their memories to fit the prevailing narrative.

"And that's it, if it's all right with you? I've told you everything I know and I'm confident that the witnesses you talk to will bear me out. Now - I'd like to leave."

It was a bluff, of course. They'd no cause to hold me, but it could appear negligent at the least if they let me go. And that was ignoring the danger to my own wellbeing if I was released to the public!

"We'd prefer to continue talking with you for now, Mr Finch, if that's all right?" Mick Clancy said. "I'm sure we'll have obtained statements from the witnesses you mentioned quite quickly, and we'd only have to invite you back here again a short time later were we to... if we were to part from each other now."

I sighed, acting as if I was making a huge concession by agreeing to stay. The truth was that they might well have arrested and charged me if I'd followed through on my threat to leave.

"Sure. But can I get a coffee? Or something to eat? I missed lunch, and I'm starving!"

The young guard, who'd stayed silent throughout, raised an eyebrow. You wouldn't expect someone fresh from murdering a young girl to have much of an appetite, he must've thought. Or anyone who was even suspected of doing so. I could tell from his expression that he thought I was some kind of sociopath.

In a way, prison is like school. You learn the skills you need to face an interrogation early. Remain silent or, if you can't, then keep calm. The last thing you need to do when you're being questioned about a violent crime is to lose your temper. Getting you to do so is a slam dunk for them, however, and can save them the bother of presenting any more compelling evidence.

So I spoke little and said less for the next three hours while they asked me the same questions in twenty different ways. I was careful, but consistent. Because if anyone knew how to conduct themselves in these situations, it was me.

The last time I'd been here - following Karen Williams' death - I was flustered, panicked and overwhelmed. I found it impossible to accurately recall any of my 'movements', as they put it, during the days prior to my arrest, and would have had trouble remembering my name if they'd asked me for it after a couple of hours. But this interview room was familiar ground for me, now. Even the tactics they used – asking the same question from different angles, leaving me alone to sweat in the room while they went to 'attend to some other matter' – were familiar, and did nothing to disturb my composure. I just hoped I wouldn't have to offer up Kevin Williams. At least not yet. For any number of reasons, I'd omitted him from my list of witnesses. For both our sakes.

In the end they had no choice but to let me go. Even without a lawyer to point this out, they had no evidence on which to hold me. When they came back just after nine o'clock to deliver the news I could tell that this wasn't a popular decision. They were about to release what was essentially a serial killer into the community. If the option of stringing me up in the back yard then tossing my body into the sea had been on offer, then at least two of them would have seriously considered it, if their expressions were anything to go by. The sergeant – Kilduff - contented himself with banging his elbow into my ear as he passed the desk, disguising the blow as a stumble. I'd had worse, and I let him see that. I gave the rookie a look to warn him he would be ill-advised to follow suit, and sat there while they gathered around the door to see me out.

"I presume I'm walking back?" I said.

"No. I'll take you," Mick Clancy said, stretching his arms and gifting me a glimpse of his stomach as he did so, there being only so much cloth to go around.

He didn't speak to me again until we were in the car – the unmarked Ford, rather than the squad car – and only once I'd sat in beside him having refused to take a seat in the back.

"Mick…"

"Drop it! As far as everyone in that room is concerned, you're a double murderer… and a vicious piece of shite to boot."

"You included?" I asked.

He said nothing, easing the car through the gates and turning away from the town toward the seafront opposite the old secondary school, pulling into one of the parking bays overlooking the beach. He kept the engine idling and the heater on full, as a bulwark against the cold.

"You didn't even blink!"

"What?"

"When we gave you the details about the girl. Sharon Buckley. When we told you how Sharon Buckley had been killed, and how she'd been left there by the rocks, down on the beach. Thrown away like litter. You didn't even blink!"

"I know what was going on in there! I've been here before, remember? Of course I care that some young girl – that Sharon Buckley – was murdered! But I also know how easy it is for anything I say to be twisted into something else! I showed my concern when you dragged me in for questioning about Karen Williams - and where did that get me? Is there some reason you think the death of a girl of that particular age is a tragedy, Mr Finch? You must be feeling a lot of remorse about now, Mr Finch. No use crying about it now, Mr Finch. My arse! I'm not giving you anything you can use to stitch me up this time!"

"Stitched up? Is that what you are, Jack? "Again?""

"Why would I do it, Mick?"

"Why would anybody do it?"

"Look – you know me!" He started to reply but I cut him off. "I don't mean you know I'm not capable of it - I mean you know I'm not that stupid! And how stupid would I have to be, to do exactly what I'm supposed to have done before? Given how that turned out for me! Wouldn't I have changed things? Wouldn't I have chosen somewhere else – anywhere else – if I was going to do something like that? What sort of moron would follow exactly the same pattern that had landed him in jail the first time round? It doesn't make any sense for fuck's sake! And you know it!"

He said nothing, staring through the windscreen as two boats crawled towards each other on the far horizon, their hulls lined with sickly yellow lights. His fingers were tight on the steering wheel, his knuckles white, his face flushed as he fought with conflicting emotions. He'd sweated profusely throughout the interview in the station, and he seemed still on edge even now. I don't think I'd ever seen him so agitated.

"I can't help you," he said at last.

"I'm not asking for your help! I just need some time, so I can prove that I didn't do it."

"Yeah? And how are you going to do that then? You think you can keep wandering about the town, popping into people's houses to see what they remember? This town just lost another child, Jack! Have you forgotten what it was like after Karen Williams? How the funeral shut down the entire town? The shock and the anger that people felt? What do you think they'd do, exactly, if they spotted you walking around? Christ's sake, Jack! Wake the fuck up!"

And it was my turn to be silent.

"At least chase him," I said. "Check into his story. Don't let him go, like last time, by not following up on whatever bullshit alibi he gives you. He has to have left a hole somewhere!"

I told him about my conversations with O'Neill and Donald, and my belief that he'd had ample time to kill Karen Williams and dump the body without being noticed. "Don't let the fucker pull one over on you again! You can at least do that!"

He said nothing, continuing to stare at the distant ships as if willing them to collide, though in truth they were half a mile or more apart.

"There's enough in it, Jack. You know that. The coincidence is just too great. There probably isn't a jury in the country right now who wouldn't convict you on the basis of that alone. Regardless of what forensics throws up."

"I'm sure it will throw something up - that's his calling card. I don't know how, but he's bound to have left some trace of me on her. Like last time. I can't for the life of me think what it could be, because I've only seen him the once since I got back here. And that was from the far side of the road. But there'll be something there. You can count on it! Just... don't take things at face value, alright? If it's something as obvious as a dropped credit card again just ask yourself whether I'd have been dumb enough to make the same mistake twice. Because – Mick? If I had killed that girl? Then I'd have made certain that you'd have no way to tie me back to it."

He pulled his eyes from the sea giving me a look I was still unable to read, before leaning across me to pull the door handle open on my side.

"I changed my mind. You can walk back."

I stepped into a hostile wind which was scouring the pavement and dragging bitter needles of rain in its wake. Hunching my shoulders against the cold, I stood and watched as he reversed the car and sped away.

Nineteen

I was alone in prison. It doesn't sound much of a hardship when you say it like that. Alone. On your own. Even lonely. It all sounds... doable. Tolerable. Uncomfortable perhaps, even a little distressing at times, but the sort of thing a man can and should be able to handle. There is a moment however - and it can come at any time - when you realise just how alone you are.

Of all the things I feared about going back to prison, this was what terrified me most. Yes, I'd learned how to accommodate the intense isolation that awaits anyone convicted of a heinous crime. How it makes you a social pariah, so it's not just that no one will talk to you, or sit with you, or even greet you as you pass in the hall – but how no one will be allowed to do so. Even those with a mote of human compassion, the smallest capacity for mercy, are prohibited from breaking the silence which surrounds you. They say the cruellest punishment meted out to children in a boarding school isn't to be bullied, but to be 'sent to Coventry'. Being picked on at least means that you are seen. That you exist. At the most primal of levels that you're still in contact with other people. Being isolated, or made to feel invisible, fractures the spirit in a manner far crueller than blows. It weakens you, till you feel like you're made of glass - every gaze averted, every mouth tightly gripped adding a further crack till you walk around fragile as a rattling windowpane, not knowing if the next small fissure will cause you to collapse upon yourself in a thousand tiny shards.

But in large part my isolation in prison was self-inflicted. By denying myself visitors, I made sure there was no one who could sympathise with my plight. And I was obstinate about this. At least at first. By the time I realised I needed others, the chance had passed me by. So I had to become resilient instead. Within weeks my only human contact was via my cellmates' fists and feet. But if that was the only option, then I would make them regret it. If they wouldn't accept me, or befriend me, then they could learn to fear me. And the next time they lowered their eyes as we passed each other in the corridor, it would be for a different reason.

I remember the day when everything changed. You might say the date is etched upon my soul. The day I went from saint to sinner, as it were: from innocent victim, to something else. I can console myself by saying that I had no choice – that it really was a case of adapt or die – but that would be to justify what I became, later on. I was brought up to believe Christ's teachings about turning the other cheek, and loving my enemy. But once I understood that my suffering would provoke no such sympathy or understanding - not even pity - I began to hate my enemy. As ignorant, stupid and brutal as he was. And when I was given the chance to change things I didn't hold back.

Robbie Joyce had been persecuting me for around three weeks at this point, from the afternoon he'd first arrived in Sedgefield on foot of two assaults and a taking and driving away. He was a nasty motherfucker. Lean, around five-nine, with close-cropped hair and homemade tattoos on both forearms and a feral walk that proclaimed a grudge with the world, and an urgent need to take it out on someone else. I was ideal for his purposes. I'd been beaten up any number of times by then, though the intervals between these had grown; but he brought a new vindictiveness to it. Not just in the viciousness of the assaults, but by encouraging the same viciousness in others. He would goad those hitting or kicking me to add one final blow, and to put the full weight of their contempt for me into it. And then he'd wait. When the last of them stepped away, satiated or shamed by their own ferocity, he'd step up and take his turn. Sometimes, he'd strike the first blow - to get the party started, as he put it - then wait until everyone else had a go, before going to work on me when I was at my weakest. I'd suffered broken bones and lost teeth before - but nothing prepared me for the systematic workings of a sadist.

His speciality was the soft organs. The kidneys. The balls. The fragile column of the neck. The connective tissue about the ribs, and the ribs themselves, preferring to target these rather than break a bone or do any serious damage which might send me to the prison hospital for a period of recuperation. He didn't want me gone - he wanted me on tap. To have me around so he could indulge whatever sick compunction drove him to attack other men - or women, it transpired, when his full history leaked out - in a manner utterly bereft of pity or joy. I was just a thing to Robbie Joyce. A plaything. Had he been that way inclined – by which I mean disposed to that particular form of torture – then I'm certain he'd have added rape to his repertoire. But that crime was deemed unacceptable in most Irish jails. We were not barbarians after all...

I had been moved to Sedgefield some time before this. Freed at last from the terrible proximity of Mountjoy. The Joy was an overcrowded shithole, half of the inmates on drugs and too zoned out to pose much danger to a newbe. Although that still left the other half. Mountjoy Prison was a hundred-and-sixty year-old Victorian monument to the pillars of incarceration: namely discomfort, inhumanity, and inedible food. I use the term food lightly. Given the budgets they operated on though, it was a wonder they manged to feed us at all. Over seven hundred people in a prison built for a maximum of five hundred and fifty, with most of the supposedly single cells housing two, sometimes three inmates in the same ten by twelve room. My abiding memory of the place was of people tortured into submission by simple things like a cellmate's incessant drumming of a pen on their newspaper, or the continual clearing of their throat. Of the piss pots and buckets which took the place of toilets in the cells. (Inmates who couldn't wait till the door was unlocked in the morning would often take a shit in a piece of newspaper and throw it out the window, rather than stink out the cell and risk the wrath of their cellmates.) Of the stench of urine which seeped out of the bricks, and burnt the back of your throat.

And the ritual. The same soul-crushing schedule, each and every day. The hour's exercise or 'educational training' after breakfast. Dinner at twelve-fifteen, eaten in your cell because there is no canteen. Then lockup time again until five-thirty, followed by two more hours of what they laughably termed recreation. Lights out at ten o'clock and, for me, another long night of suffering. Time to dwell on what I'd lost and what form of recreation my fellow inmates might pursue the following day. Mountjoy is a dump in the truest sense of that word - a place where people regarded as having no value are fucked away. I couldn't wait to see the back of it when, after the three longest months of my life, I was ferried off one morning in the back of a white transit van to Sedgefield, to what would become my new 'home' for the best part of a decade.

Sedgefield was at least more modern, having been built at the end of the previous century rather than midway through the one before. Though the palette was restricted to greys, white and black (and an occasional splash of shitty brown) the corridors and cells were more spacious, and the guards less worn down by the hopelessness of their task. There were basic steel toilets in the cells, most of which held the regulation two inmates. Still cramped: but nothing compared to the hell that was Mountjoy. And, inside every cell, a device which did more to save lives and reduce the incidence of self-harm than any amount of counselling or supervision - a television. People unfamiliar with the relentless boredom which accompanies a custodial sentence cannot imagine what it means to have some form of escape, however vicarious, or some source of conversation outside the minutiae of prison life itself. So much of your time is spent in your cell. For someone like me who was often 'on protective', it could be as much as twenty-three hours a day. Even for ordinary prisoners, having to eat your meals in your cell (that refractory canteen you know from the movies where riots invariably break out does not exist) means you are stuck in a small room from six or seven each night till the following morning. And normally with somebody else. Sartre was wrong about many things - but he was on the money when he said that "Hell is other people".

And Sedgefield had classes! Training in the most basic of trades - but times you could look forward to nevertheless which would occupy your hands, as well as your head. I learnt plastering and bricklaying while I was inside, and though I may never employ those skills outside of assembling a backyard barbeque, those classes helped to keep me sane. I made headstones in engraving class, sold on to people unable to afford the expensive monuments flogged by the funeral homes. I spent long hours carving sad, simple verses into modest slabs of granite and slate. I took whatever was going, and fabricated a working day for myself in Sedgefield (mornings from nine to twelve, afternoons from two to four) and felt blessed for it. It would have been great if my fellow inmates sought similar forms of release from their boredom. But they did not.

I cracked on a Thursday. Thursday October 27th, to be exact. I'd been practicing my striking and pointing – the art of adding mortar to the space between bricks to repair a joint, or add an extra layer of protection against the elements. I'd become quite handy with a trowel: though I made a mistake I wouldn't repeat by laying it down when Robbie Joyce and three of his friends approached me. Never give up a weapon, regardless how small or unpromising it may seem. A set of car keys will disable a man as effectively as a crowbar, if you know what to do with it.

"Finch!" he shouted. I didn't bother to reply. I knew the drill by then. Robbie wasn't given to lengthy conversations. He just wanted me to look at him before he started. To see the fear in my face before he smashed it in.

For a man like me – brought up with no exposure to violence, and in a culture which abhors it – it requires an effort of will to act contrary to your instinct. What my instinct told me was to flee. Or plead for mercy. But there was no escape route from that corner of the yard, and begging would just give him the added satisfaction of watching me squirm. And besides... he had underestimated me. Firstly, because his threats carried less weight, now that I'd proven to myself I was capable of taking a beating. It wasn't as if I'd become immune to the pain. But I knew that I could take it. And the chances were that, whatever he tried, I'd have had worse.

And secondly because I was going to kill him. Perhaps not literally: though I'd by no means ruled it out. In that moment, as he called out my name, I decided to strike first. And to use the element of surprise to fuck him up in ways he couldn't imagine.

You need to understand where I was at that time. There's a point you reach after repeated beatings when you either give up, and surrender to life lived as a punchbag, or arrive at such a place of desperation that you decide to resist. And that's a decision which precludes any notion of restraint. When I decided that this would be the last time Robbie Joyce kicked me in the kidneys while I was whimpering on the floor, I did so in the certain knowledge that I'd have to do more than just stop him. Self-defence is a meaningless term in a situation like this. Defending yourself – to be quite clear about this – means hurting someone else. As badly as you possibly can.

I held my hands out in front of me, palms up, elbows tucked in. A stance which seems to say "Please, no, stay back!" but in Krav Maga is so much more. Keeping your arms out before you means that you can hit first and hit fast, while keeping your palms open means you are equally prepared to block, punch or strike.

I kept it simple for Robbie. Which seemed only fitting.

As he walked toward me - a smile on his face like an undertaker's cat - I stepped forward and landed a punch to the socket of his left eye. I did what the book said and twisted my fist as the last moment, to ensure maximum impact. The blow rocked him backward, but I was already moving. I hit him with a jab to follow my cross. Then I rotated my right elbow, extending it and snapping the ball of the joint into his left cheekbone, sending him reeling. I didn't hesitate. Grabbing the back of his neck, with the line of my palm pressed against his jaw so that my forearm pinned him down and away from me, I held his head down and hit him with two massive knee strikes - one to his jaw, one to the centre of his ribcage - and kept repeating these till I felt him give way and slump to the floor. Your instinct at this point is to stop. But you do not stop. You only stop when there's no longer the danger of your opponent recovering and coming at you. And there was no way I was allowing Robbie Joyce to do that. That day or any other. He was bent double at this stage, his hands up to his ruined nose and face. So I took a step backward and launched a kick directly at his head, sending him sideways to collide against the wall with my foot propelling him into the concrete.

And then I stopped.

In all, this took about ten seconds. I raised my hands again and tensed, waiting for the inevitable response from his friends, preparing myself for a beating at least the equal of any I'd received before. But I wouldn't go down easily. My quarrel was with Joyce but I'd no problem doling out a similar measure to whoever went for me first. I'd be overpowered of course, but at least one of them would be joining Joyce in a bloody heap by the time they took me down.

Apparently, they were thinking the same thing. And as the seconds passed, it became obvious that no one wanted to make that first move. Joyce was keening quietly, half-conscious, a wide smear of blood running from where his head had hit the wall to where he lay, his breathing loud and laboured through his broken nose. I felt bile rising in my throat, but choked it back. I couldn't quite believe what I'd done. Or how easy it had been to do it... Months later, I would ask myself if this was the point at which I changed - the moment when what you do becomes who you are.

And by and large, that was it for me. Word spreads fast in a jail, and there's a ready supply of soft targets available for those whose inclinations tend that way. And it changed surprisingly little about my life inside. Yes, the beatings and the minor stabbings I'd been subjected to (one to my back, one to my left buttock) ceased. But everything else – the isolation, the despair at the long years ahead of me – remained the same. For year, after year.

The contempt I saw on the faces of my fellow inmates was replaced sometimes by fear, or caution, but I was still ostracized. And looking back I'm not sure that I would have lasted my sentence had a chronic overcrowding problem not led to my premature release.

By the end of 2015 Ireland's prisons were filled beyond capacity. Almost five thousand prisoners were incarcerated, in facilities intended to house no more than three thousand. In Mountjoy - the first and often the last port of call for those with shorter sentences - prisoners were sleeping in shower stalls and on floors. Conscious that numbers traditionally spiked in the run-up to Christmas (for all the reasons you'd expect) the Minister for Justice requested that accelerated release be considered for any qualifying prisoner.

You wouldn't imagine that someone sentenced for killing a young girl could qualify. But this was the moment when my solicitor - a flamboyantly gay man with the improbable moniker of John Wayne – had proved his value. At my trial, given the absence of any evidence of sexual assault or violence to the person outside of the strangling, and given the circumstantial nature of the evidence against me, he had successfully argued that I should be charged with manslaughter rather than murder, on the basis that I'd agree not to contest the charge.

Pleading guilty, he had convinced me, was the almost impossibly difficult, but logical choice. It was clear that the evidence they'd gathered would result in a conviction - Mr Wayne had been explicit in this regard - and all that could be gained from a long court battle was a legal bill Kate was ill-equipped to pay, and abject misery and exposure for both herself and Laura while things dragged through the press. So I admitted to a crime I did not commit: in return sparing them that ordeal, and earning myself a twelve-year stretch, rather than a life sentence. I'd lost whole days since, ruminating over that choice, and berating myself for having agreed to plead guilty. But whether it was karma or blind luck, it had paid off in the end. I was here. I was out! Though that was unlikely to be the case for long. Because I now had to prove my innocence not only of Karen William's murder, but of this second girl's as well! Which was a challenge made even greater by who that second girl was. Because - contrary to what I'd told the guards during my questioning - I knew her.

TWENTY

They had only mentioned her name a couple of times at that point, but the truth was that Sharon Buckley and I had already rubbed shoulders. And not in a manner which reflected well on me. She may have spat in my face - but her sneering taunts in front of a bunch of other teenagers about 'an older man hassling an innocent young girl' had significantly greater import now that she was dead.

I hadn't told Mick Clancy about our encounter yet - but I realised I'd have to when I saw her face emblazoned across the front page of the Irish Daily Mail in the reception area of Cois Farraige the following morning. There was no mistaking her. Although the photo showed a smiling, friendly teen - rather than the vicious little bitch I watched tormenting a classmate - it was her, all right. And everyone who'd gathered in the church carpark to enjoy that spectacle was now a potential witness against me.

Prison gives you the resilience to cope with anything life might throw at you - except a return to prison. And it was clear now that I had a limited amount of time to prevent that from happening. I had to act quickly, or it would seem like I'd been hiding things. I could reasonably claim not to have recognised the name when they'd first mentioned it, but now that her photo was out I could no longer rely on that excuse. Marching into the station asking to see Mick Clancy wouldn't work either. They'd have me back in that interview room with the tape rolling before the lobby door closed behind me. So I staked him out instead.

In movies or on TV a stakeout is always portrayed as a long period of boredom with an inevitable payoff. You never see the detective give up and go home. Invariably their quarry will emerge from hiding, or provide them with a clue of some kind to follow. The reality is different in every respect. Aside from the boredom, I also lacked the advantage of a warm car or van to sit in while I waited. Instead I was huddled, shivering, around the corner from the Garda Station, a cold wind stretching its fingers toward me from a steel grey sea, pricking its way through the folds of my clothes and penetrating my bones. The bay was ruffled like an unmade bed, small waves moving left to right along the shoreline, with an occasional gull hovering transfixed in the wind, screeching complaints about the absence of prey.

I needed a warm coat - not the trendy leather jacket I'd picked up the day after my release, in my rush to buy clothes which differed from the regulation jeans and sweatshirt of the incarcerated. I'd dropped close to a grand in Massimo Dutti on Grafton Street, adding trousers and shirts to the brown jacket, along with socks, underwear and two crewneck jumpers in black and navy. I was a relatively fashionable ex-con, if such a thing exists, but utterly unprepared for standing about in the full force of a winter gale. I was about to give up to the promise of a hot shower, followed by a pint in a warm bar, when I saw Mick emerge from the door of the station and pull it closed behind him against the best efforts of the wind.

I caught up with him as he crossed to the narrow pathway tracing the shore.

"Mick!"

He stopped and smiled at me, though there was little warmth in it.

"I thought you'd give up."

"What?"

"I saw you, you moron! I figured you'd chuck it in within an hour, but you surprised me!"

"You saw me standing out here, and just ignored it?"

"No less than you deserve."

"I didn't do it, Mick!"

"I know." He sighed. "Only a feckin' retard would commit the same crime in the same town and expect to get away with it. It doesn't matter, though."

"They'll still crucify me for it?"

"Like Christ himself!"

"So – what can I do?"

He appeared to give it some thought, though I suspect he'd considered his answer long before he'd emerged from the station.

"Pray that your luck holds up better than last time. It's not looking so good for you."

"What have they got on me?"

He grimaced.

"I can't tell you that, Jack. As well you know."

"Jesus, Mick!"

"They're going through your room right now. I just hope you remembered to hide your porn."

I glared at him, and his expression softened.

"If someone is out to get you, Jack, I reckon they're more than likely to succeed. You've no friends hereabouts, not really, and you haven't exactly been making any efforts to change that."

"The barman in Molly's likes me," I said.

"Barmen like everyone, providin' they pay for their drink and don't start a riot on the premises."

He was right of course. Since arriving in town I could count at least four people who'd be more than happy to testify that I was an aggressive, even violent, bollocks.

"So what do I do? Run?"

"No point. And I couldn't let you, in any case. If it came out that I'd been talking to you and you'd legged it afterwards..."

I understood. Then he'd be in deep shit. And right now Mick Clancy was the only ally I had.

"I'd say you've a couple of hours at most before word gets around about Sharon Buckley's death. And about a millisecond more before people start looking for a rope and a tree."

"Would I be better off somewhere else? Back up in Dublin, maybe? Providing I told you where I was?"

He considered this.

"Mightn't be a bad idea. And, if I were you, I'd be heading to the DART Station right about now, before a posse starts to gather in front of the saloon."

I gave him the number of the cheap phone I'd picked up in Tesco's a few days beforehand, and told him that I'd come back to Greystones whenever he called me.

"Please, Mick!" I said, before I left him. "Look closer. Whatever they find, whatever they say they have on me - look again. Whatever it is that Tom has planted - "

"Ah, for fuck's..."

"Whatever he's planted, don't take it at face value. Look deeper! He has to have made a mistake! Whatever the evidence might seem to say."

He said nothing, then nodded once and wheeled about to return to the station, leaving me standing there, wondering what convenient clues they'd find this time to send them after me.

In the event I never made it to the DART station. Deciding a change of clothes was a more urgent priority, I made my way back to Cois Farraige to find a Garda car in the carpark – and my daughter waiting for me outside the lobby.

"Laura! What –"

She cut me off.

"We heard about Sharon Buckley. She was in my friend Molly's class!"

"Laura, I swear to God! I had nothing to do with that!"

She stared at me for a few moments, before appearing to come to some sort of decision.

"Mum and Tom said you're sick. That you'd get put away for good this time, and that I'd never see you again. Like it was a good thing!"

I said nothing.

"Did you kill Karen Williams?" she asked, holding her breath while she awaited my reply.

"No! I swear to God!"

"Stop swearing, for fuck's sake! If you didn't do it – then why wouldn't you see us, when you were in prison? I'm your daughter! Do you know what it was like? Never seeing your Dad again? Having everyone say... hearing all those things about you? If you didn't do it, then why didn't you tell us that?"

"Your mum wouldn't have believed me."

"I would've! You're my Dad!"

I felt my heart break at the word.

"Come on," I said. "We can't stay here. The guards will be going through my room and if they spot me out here they may well take me back in."

I turned back towards the sea, my sodden clothes forgotten at the prospect of a first conversation with my daughter in almost eight years. A first conversation full stop, really. Because this fifteen-year-old girl bore no resemblance to the seven-year-old kid I'd abandoned, all that time ago.

"You have to understand, Laura. I didn't refuse to see you because I was guilty - but because your mother thought I was. I couldn't bear to see it in her eyes. She'd never have taken you with her, anyhow. Not when she thought that way about me."

She considered this for a second.

"How do you know?"

And it was my turn to pause.

"You're right. Maybe I was wrong. About all of it. But I couldn't bear the idea of you seeing me like that... Your mum either. Things happened in there, Laura. Awful things. I - I wasn't someone you'd want to see back then. Not how I was. And by the time I'd learned how to cope... Well. I thought it was too late."

"For your own daughter! Fuck you, Dad! I needed you!"

I felt tears prick at my eyes.

"You're right. I'm sorry! I was just so full of anger, you know? And self-pity. And so... lost. I thought it was better to keep everyone away from me. You can't imagine what it was like! But - you're right. I should have thought of you first."

This seemed to satisfy her, as her expression softened. Though she still couldn't look me directly in the eye.

"What are you going to do?"

What could I tell her? That there was nothing I could do now, apparently, but pray? Or that the man she was living with - her new 'dad' - was behind everything that had happened? That he was a vicious, conscienceless killer? And how would I do that without tipping him off, or having her dismiss everything I'd said as fantasy? Not that it would matter anyway, unless I got myself out of this.

"I don't know, pet," I said, using the term of endearment I'd used when I tucked her in each night, after her bedtime story.

"But believe me, Laura – whatever you hear – I did not kill Karen Williams. And I am not responsible for Sharon Buckley's death. I think this happened because I was getting close to proving my innocence and the person responsible got worried, and is trying to frame me again to keep me from discovering the truth."

She stared at me, looking straight into my eyes this time as if the truth might be found there.

"Christ, Laura...! I'm sorry! I really am. But I've got to concentrate on this right now. If I can't prove I didn't do this, then your mother is right, and I might never see you again."

"I'd visit. I'd always have visited!"

"I know."

Her head dropped for a second, then she stepped forward, wrapping her arms awkwardly about me and telling me in a muffled voice to be careful.

"I will," I replied, choking back sobs and promising myself that whatever happened this would not be the last time I held my daughter. Whatever came next, I'd make sure of that.

Twenty-one

Reckoning that it made no sense at that juncture to go into Dublin, I walked to Molly's instead, willing to risk whatever awaited me once news of Sharon Buckley's death got out in return for one last pint in freedom. There was just no time. It was ten-thirty by now – meaning the guards had had at least an hour to go through my room. And I was certain it wouldn't be something they found on Sharon's body that would damn me this time. Tom and I had had virtually no contact since I arrived back in Greystones, so it would have been difficult if not impossible to engineer such a simple way of placing me in the frame. And it would have been way too much of a coincidence in any case for something of mine to have shown up again beside the body. Whatever stood to deprive me of my liberty this time would have had to travel in the opposite direction. From the body to me. Or to my room, to be exact.

It made sense. It'd be so much easier to get into my room in the deserted boarding house and leave something there than to steal something from me. When you first realise that someone has been in your home, your instinct is to check whether anything is missing. Not to look for something which hadn't been there before. Whether it turned out to be a keepsake or (God forbid!) a piece of her clothing, I'd no doubt the Guards would turn up something in the search of my room that would land me straight back in the shit, as deep or even deeper than the last time. If I right, then I was fucked! So I might as well go for a pint and let my clothes dry out before they came for me.

"Jack, isn't it?" Len the barman greeted me as I walked in, standing up from where he'd been crouching to restock his shelves, putting a hand on his back as he did so. Given that he was well over six foot tall he must have found bending over in the narrow space behind the counter more than a little uncomfortable. The bar was about a quarter full, a low murmur of conversation audible above the music playing through the speakers in the alcoves. Sixties lounge music. The tempo slow, as befitted a weekday evening.

"A pint of Guinness, please!" I said, shrugging off my jacket and hanging it across the back of a stool. I wanted to be ready when they came for me, and an upright stool at the bar seemed a better choice than one of the low armchairs. But I would have my second surprise of the day first when the door opened, and it was my brother rather than Mick Clancy who walked in. I stared at him, my brain whirling feverishly. Had Donald called him? Did he know I'd met Laura? Could he have heard I'd fingered him for Karen Williams' death, while I was being interrogated in the Garda Station? What was he after?

"Jack."

I said nothing, and awaited his next move.

He hesitated for a moment, then pulled out the stool to my right, placing his jacket on the next one in line and sitting down beside me.

"I don't know what to say to you," he began.

"I'll bet!" I said.

"This other girl..." His voice trailed off.

"I heard. But you know that it wasn't me."

"Do I? How am I supposed to know that, Jack? For fuck's sake..! Why did you come back? For that? Don't you know what this will do to them? To Laura and Kate? Laura believed in you! In spite of everything!"

"And she still does!" I said, watching as a look of puzzlement worked its way across his face.

"They'll never let you out. You'll be in prison for the rest of your life!"

"Good to see that you still believe in me, brother! Or are you just so damn sure that they'll find some 'proof' I was responsible? I wouldn't bet on that, though. Not this time around!"

"What are you saying, Jack? That you did it - but you hid the evidence?"

"Give me a fucking break Tom! I had nothing to do with that girl's death - and you know it!"

"I know it? How would I know it?"

It was all I could do not to blurt it out, to scream it right in his face. But my intuition told me to hold my peace.

"Isn't that something a brother would know? Surely you know me well enough to know that I'd be incapable of such a thing? Sure - isn't that what brothers do? Take each other's side? Have each other's back?"

"I tried that last time, Jack. I really did! But the evidence..."

"Was it "overwhelming"? Was that it? That was how they put it, wasn't it? And were you "overwhelmed" Tom? Is that why you never took my side? Never gave me the benefit of the doubt? Or were you too busy working your way into his wife's knickers to spare a thought for your younger brother?"

He was fast. I barely saw him drop his shoulder before the punch connected on the side of my jaw, twisting my head toward the bar.

"That's more like it," I said, nursing my chin. It stung like a bastard. "That's the big brother I remember! Never could resist an opportunity to get a dig in, could you? Although you surpassed yourself this time."

"You deserved it!"

"Oh, I don't mean the punch, Tom. Frankly, I've had worse! And from far bigger fuckheads than you."

"Don't push me, Jack! I'm doing you a favour just by being here."

"Yeah? And how do you reckon that? Or are you just hoping to be here when they take me in? Go on, then.

Order yourself a pint. It shouldn't be long. Not with what they'll have on me, I'll bet. Another open and closed case, no doubt about it!"

"You're sick, Jack."

"Obviously! I'd have to be, wouldn't I? I mean - what man in his right mind would kill not one, but two girls? And for what? Eh? What motive could a man possibly have to sacrifice two lives, just to get what he wants. Or to hold on to it!"

He held my stare, unblinking.

"Why are you here, Tom?" I asked.

"No - why are you here? Why did you come back? What did you expect would happen? I mean - all that was over, now. It was done with! Kate and Laura... They're happy. Settled. Or at least they were! I understood you wanting to see Laura – but you must know what she thinks of you."

"Enlighten me."

"You almost ruined her fucking life! Christ – can you imagine what it's been like for her? Having a convicted murderer for a father? Growing up around here with everyone knowing that?"

"Although I'm not quite her father now, am I?"

He paused, shifting on his stool and staring down at his fist. I noticed his nails were trimmed almost to the quick, the merest line of white visible at their tip. They'd never have found traces of compost on his hands.

"Look. You've been gone eight years. That's an eternity for a kid of Laura's age! Of the age she was when you… They may not have moved on, exactly – but they've learnt to cope. Without you! And your coming back here…"

"Coming back to see my wife and child?"

"Not your wife! Not any longer. And that's your fault, not mine. Jesus! You wouldn't even see her! What did you expect?"

"I'll ask you again, Tom. Why are you here?"

"Because I needed to see you. To see if it could be true. What they're saying. I don't want to believe it, but…"

"But you've always known I was capable of it? Is that it? Is that the story? Good old, honest Tom! Prepared to say the unspeakable – even about his own brother! And all in the interests of truth! I know what you said to the guards after Karen Williams' death, by the way. You couldn't have stitched me up any tighter if you'd held me down and put the cuffs on yourself!"

"I didn't tell them anything that wasn't true."

"That's not quite the truth, though, is it? And it was never about what you said to them – but what you didn't say. I would never have touched that girl, or any other girl of that age… and well you knew it! The only person I'd ever hit in anger was you, big brother. And you gave me more than enough reasons for it."

"Where is this going, Jack?"

"Going? Where I'm going – it looks like – is back to jail. Framed, for a second time! What is it they say? Shame on me? I suppose I should have seen it coming! I just never thought... Well. Things aren't always as they seem, Tom. You of all people should know that."

I stood up as I spoke, having seen the front door open a few moments before - the same young cop who'd accompanied Mick Clancy to Cois Farraige poking his head in and spotting me before retreating to get reinforcements.

"They're going to take me in now, Tom. But make sure you remember to tell Kate and Laura that I told you I didn't do it. And don't forget, mind. Or try to twist my words into something else. Because I will hear back. Do you understand? I've spoken to them both already. You didn't know, right? They're not under your control anymore, brother. And when all of this is over? I'll have them back! Both of them! Mark my words."

I brushed past him and made for the door, determined to get to the welcoming committee before they stormed in to take me away. Being led off to a garda car was one thing - being placed in handcuffs in your local is quite another.

Twenty-two

It was a wristband. One of those stretchy, silicon ones they hand out for good causes, with some meaningless phrase or aphorism embedded in the design. Be Strong! Fight For Right! That sort of thing. This one, ironically, was for an anti-bullying campaign. Speak Up! Speak Out! ran the legend. Clearly Sharon Buckley had a sense of humour.

They showed it to me when they sat me down at that same small table. This time, though, there was no pretence at civility. The band was orange, the colour vibrant through the plastic evidence bag.

"Recognise this?" asked a thin man in an ill-fitting blue suit. He looked like a teenager who'd borrowed his dad's work clothes. If his arms hadn't been in the sleeves he could have turned full circle without disturbing the fabric. I said nothing for a second, trying to get a read on him. He was clearly in charge here – Mick Clancy was standing back against the wall alongside the young guard – and, given his age, doubtless some kind of hotshot. Or a relative of someone higher up the totem pole. His eyes beneath a long fringe were a piercing blue, his mouth the sort of thin line a child might draw, curled up on one side in what was intended as a look of contempt.

"No. But I imagine you think I should."

"This is the same wristband Sharon Buckley was wearing when she disappeared. When you murdered her!"

"Wrong. I didn't murder her, or anyone else. And did you mean the same sort of wristband she was wearing – or have you confirmed that this particular wristband was hers?"

I knew there hadn't been time for the detailed forensic tests necessary to identify its owner.

"Don't play semantics with me! It's the same thing!"

"It's hardly semantics. And it's very much not the same thing – unless you're intending to haul in anyone who owns a Volkswagen Golf every time one is involved in an accident on the dual carriageway?"

He scowled at me.

"You've been read your rights, correct?"

I said nothing, knowing that it would infuriate him. The tape machine hissed quietly in the absence of a response.

In the end the young guard spoke up, confirming that he'd read me my rights when arresting me on the street in front of Molly's: and earning himself a withering look for the interruption.

"Is that correct, Mr Finch?"

"I'm sure that we can trust the guard to have performed his duties correctly," I replied.

"I'll take that as a Yes. Now, why don't you explain to us how Sharon Buckley's wristband came to be found in your hotel room?"

"Again - you need to confirm for me that this is actually Sharon Buckley's. And as to how it was found, I would presume that it was discovered by your men in the course of their search. Or did you mean to ask me how it *got* there, rather than how it was found?"

"I don't think you understand the gravity of your situation, Mr Finch!"

"Oh, but I do! Which makes it even more important, wouldn't you say, that you ask me accurate questions, rather than trying to mislead me? Come to think of it, I'm not even sure who you are? For all I know, you could be some Transition Year student Detective Sergeant Clancy took in on work experience. In which case I'd be aiming at a B grade at best if I were you, based on your performance so far."

For a second I thought he was going to take a swing at me. Mick Clancy apparently thought so too, as he suddenly stepped forward between us.

"This is Detective Inspector Brady," he said. "From Harcourt Street. He has taken charge of the Sharon Buckley case."

"I suppose that makes sense," I replied. "After all, he is closer to her age."

Mick stifled a grin, and stepped back.

"I don't think you get it, Mister Finch. We've got you! Once we prove that wristband belonged to Sharon Buckley – and we will prove it – then you're fucked. Pardon my French."

"Anglo-Saxon," I said.

"What?" he asked, increasingly exasperated.

"Anglo-Saxon. Not French. Like most so-called curse words we've inherited. Like prick. Or shite. Or fuckwit." I gave emphasis to each word, staring him straight in the eye.

He stood up and sent his chair flying behind him.

"Don't fuck with me, Finch! You killed that girl - and we're going to prove it! I hope you enjoyed your time in that pub - because the next time you set foot outside prison, they'll be carrying you out in a box!"

"Wow. I don't think that one even needs correcting. But let me ask you a question, Detective Brady. Do I seem like a moron to you? Oh, I'm sure you could think of several other adjectives to describe me - but I'm clearly not a fool. And that, supposedly, is what you're going to prove. That a man who was convicted of one murder, because he left a vital piece of evidence behind, would do exactly the same thing again. Whatever 'evidence' you think you turned up, it was planted. I guarantee there'll be no fingerprints of mine on that wristband - or on anything else you might have found - because whatever it is, I'll never have been anywhere near it. And before you tell me I could have wiped my fingerprints off afterwards, ask yourself why I'd wipe my fingerprints off something I'd then leave lying around for you to find? This is bullshit! And if you took your head out of your arse for long enough you'd know it."

"I know what the evidence says - and that's all I need to worry about. Unlike you, Mr Finch. You should have plenty to worry about! Not least what sort of greeting someone who killed not one but two young girls will get, when he finds himself back in The 'Joy! In fact, I might well let the authorities know you're coming so they can arrange for a proper welcome! We wouldn't want you ending up in the wrong cell now, would we?" He gave a leery grin, exposing two lines of small, yellow teeth.

"You should chuck the cigarettes, Detective Brady. Girls tend not to like it. Boys either, I dare say." I was no homophobe, but suspected he might well be.

I heard the young guard cough as he tried to disguise a laugh.

"I don't think you'll have to worry about what women want any more, Mr Finch. It's hardly going to be a problem for you."

With this, he stood up, sweeping the evidence bag from the table in front of me and waving it in my face.

"Why don't we take a break there, and start again after we've confirmed this wristband as belonging to Sharon Buckley? Interview adjourned at eleven forty-nine pm."

They took me to a cell at the rear of the building where, true to what Brady had said, I spent a sleepless night imagining what would await me, if I got sent down again and found myself back among the sadists and scumbags in Mountjoy. Before they locked me up, however, I gave them his details and asked them to inform my counsel of my arrest - hoping against hope that John Wayne might be willing, once again, to ride to my rescue.

Twenty-three

Word had clearly gotten around.

Greystones is not a place you'd associate with angry mobs, but one appeared to have gathered in the car park outside the station. There was at least fifty of them by the sounds of it, and the number appeared to be growing. And I was scared. More than that – I was terrified.

Hearing your name chanted aloud, attached to violent epithets, is a pretty chilling experience. That there were people only yards from where I sat who'd happily rip me to shreds, given the chance, induced a numbness that extended from the surface of my skin through to my bones. I knew that I was safe, of course – for now at least. Nobody out there would be given access to the station, despite their repeated threats to storm the building... but there was precious little goodwill on this side of the walls among those responsible for shielding me. I hadn't set out to antagonize Brady – but I hadn't been able to resist it either. The pestilent little fuck! I'd met his type before, the last time I was processed through the system. Everybody he met was either an aid or a barrier to his personal advancement, and he would treat junior colleagues little better than the criminals they dealt with. But I needed him!

If he didn't look beyond the surface.... I was dependent on Brady doing his job, a thought which gave me pause and some minor cause for regret. Perhaps I shouldn't have baited him? Fuck! If he wasn't prepared to look past the supposed 'evidence' of the wristband, then what hope had I of their ever unmasking the real culprit? I needed them to be... What? Professional. Thorough. Maybe not geniuses, like the detectives on TV, but competent. Determined. Dogged in pursuit of the truth. Which was something of a forlorn hope, I knew.

There was a shorter, easier route for them – and I knew how quickly that could become the first and only choice. Why bother looking any further? Here they were, with a convicted murderer whose profile, and the profile of the victim, matched perfectly with his previous M.O.. Not only that but they had an article of the girl's clothing, in the shape of that wristband, found hidden in his hotel room. The fact there was pretty much unrestricted access to Cois Farraige would count for nothing when set against my record. And despite what I'd said during the interview, I had little doubt that they'd link the wristband to Sharon Buckley.

And Mick was right, of course. It took a major stretch of the imagination to accept that anyone would murder a young girl just to stop his brother making enquiries about him. The truth was, that you couldn't believe that - unless you also prepared to believe that Tom was responsible for the first murder. It was the only way it made sense... My hope was that they'd catch Tom for Sharon Buckley's death, and prove me innocent of Karen Williams' by default. But my fate hung between those two extremes. I'd either be found innocent of two murders: or convicted of both.

The cell they'd stuck me in was a sorry affair. A tiny box room I suspected was more typically used to store files, barely six feet wide and eight feet long. There was one rectangular window, high on the wall opposite the door, the glass obscured by a peeling adhesive decal. The walls were the yellow of day-old egg stains and the floor was covered in an olive-green linoleum. At least it was warm, though, courtesy of an ancient Victorian radiator almost a foot thick which gurgled and clanged as hot water was fed through its coils. The door was a metal blank with a spyhole about a foot from the top. The cover on the far side of the spyhole seemed to be missing, allowing me a fisheye view of the corridor outside, which seemed deserted for now. It at least made the space seem a little less claustrophobic. And it also gave me something to do - rising from the cot beneath the window every few minutes to check for signs of someone outside.

It would be the following morning before anybody appeared. I was woken from a fitful sleep by a sergeant I hadn't met before carrying in a tray with triangles of buttered toast and a stainless-steel pot of dank tea. I remembered being served the same meal in the National

Maternity Hospital on the morning Laura was born. I'd barely polished off the toast – having given the tea a wide berth – when I heard footsteps outside and spied the sergeant returning, accompanied this time by my brief.

John Wayne was wearing a pinstriped suit that nobody outside of the legal profession could hope to get away with. The stripes were almost as wide as a pencil - cream against navy – with a vermillion tie secured in a Full-Windsor completing the ensemble. His shoes were highly polished Oxford brogues; regulation black, rather than brown. John Wayne was the sort of man who'd regard the wearing of brown shoes with a blue suit as an unforgivable crime. Considering that he happily represented murderers and rapists this said much about his attitude to personal grooming.

He got straight to work.

"I understand that you wish to retain me as your counsel, Mr Finch."

"I do indeed, John."

"Mr Wayne. Good. Then that's settled. Run along, guard. I need some time alone with my client."

He opened his briefcase and removed a leather-bound notepad, fishing a pen from his inside pocket. No doubt it was a Mont Blanc, or some even more exclusive brand I'd never heard of.

"To paraphrase the bold Oscar, Mr Finch - to be accused of killing one young lady is a misfortune. To be accused of killing two looks like carelessness."

"That's exactly what I'm hoping you will prove."

"How so?"

"Because it would have been the height of carelessness if I'd left any evidence behind me, after killing this girl. Given how I was convicted of killing the first one. Mr Wayne – I did not do this."

"I take it you hold the erstwhile Cain to your Abel responsible for your present misfortunes?"

"My brother? Yes. I don't know how - but it's almost certainly got to do with stuff I uncovered about his alibi for Karen Williams' death."

"Pray tell! Do I detect the whiff of a mistrial? That would be a most excellent diversion!"

"Let's concentrate on this one for the moment, can we? I need you fully focused on this. You're going to have to be at your very best to get me out of this. And your record's not exactly brilliant, in that respect."

"I cannot keep apologizing for my failure Mr Finch. I have far too many cases to administer to even consider such redundant behaviour. Besides - I think you'll admit that you did not prove your own best counsel on that first occasion."

"I don't remember you *ever* apologizing, to be fair! I don't think we exchanged one word from the moment they led me from the dock till you walked in that door two minutes ago."

"You appear to be overlooking the fact that you pleaded guilty, if my recollection is correct?"

He relented.

"Well. Be that as it may. Tell me the worst! Gory details excepted, of course."

I spent the next hour recounting the details of my arrest the evening before and outlining the particulars of the case against me, based on what I'd managed to glean during my interviews. It's fair to say that he didn't look very encouraged by what I told him. He wrote on his notepad throughout, circling certain passages with a flourish. When I finished, he sat and looked at me for a long moment before speaking.

"You, Mr Finch, are – and I believe this may well be the correct legal term – up the Khyber! There isn't a jury in the land who wouldn't send you down in the interval between elevenses and lunch."

"You're not being very reassuring, Mr Wayne."

"Reassurance is of no use to you in the present circumstances. Well," he continued with a sigh. "Let's look at what we've got."

He leafed through his notes, flipping over the pages and studying his notations with close attention. With his head bowed a fringe of curly white hair swept across his left eyebrow. The term Fop might have been coined for him, despite the irony of his name.

"So! We have your protestations of a superior intellect to plead, in mitigation of the evidence of the wristband. Ergo: my client says he is too clever to have left it there. And so conveniently left at that! Hardly a robust defence though, is it Mr Finch? And – begging your pardon, etcetera - your intelligence might be somewhat difficult to prove. What else? We have the possibility you may have been spotted walking about the environs of the town at the time of the murder, by person or persons unknown. Not something upon which I would stake my own freedom. Any character witnesses you might propose are likely to prove of equal value. Though we may be able to keep mention of your previous transgression from the jury, on the basis that it could prejudice a fair trial. Your history is a matter of public record, however, and we'd have to find twelve men and women who never read the newspaper or watch the television. Then again, that may well be the only cohort willing to accept your claims of intellectual prowess... We have your protestations of innocence... naturally. And – to be frank – little else!"

"But doesn't the fact that the wristband was found somewhere which could be accessed by any number of other people – anyone who worked in the hotel, or anyone lurking about, like Karen Williams's dad – introduce reasonable doubt?"

"Introduce?" He gave me a patronizing smile. "Well... Perhaps in other circumstances."

"What sort of "other circumstances"?"

"Circumstances in which the accused was not already a convicted killer. Those circumstances."

I put my head in my hands.

"So what are you saying? Are you even going to take my case?"

"Why on God's earth would I take on a case I am almost certain – nay certain – to lose? What's in it for me, dear boy? Excuse the shameless self-interest but, as you know, I care little for anybody else."

"There's still the forensics to come. That has to give us something. Providing they dig deep enough!"

"I seem to recall that the forensics did little to strengthen your case in the previous instance. What reason have you to believe they will prove otherwise, on this occasion?"

"They have to have made some progress since then! I'll bet they could uncover several more layers of evidence now, with the new tools at their disposal. And he won't know that! He'll think he can use the same ways to hide any evidence that he was there as he did before."

It sounded weak even to me. He looked sceptical.

"I'll tell you what, Mr Finch. Let's wait for the forensics report, as you suggested. If they uncover anything to alleviate the odds of a humiliating loss, then I'll consider taking your case. In the meantime, you may continue to cite me as your counsel and I will provide you with the requisite advice and protection. Beginning with this – stop talking. I don't know what you hoped to achieve by spending several hours in an interview room with the investigating officers in my absence – but that behaviour stops now. Fashioning a rope with which to hang yourself is not what might be termed wise. I recall you said you intended to cite evidence of your intelligence as a factor in your defence? Intelligence is a difficult thing to argue at the best of times – it is even harder to establish in its absence."

I knew he was right. But I also knew that if I just sat back, hoping something would happen to clear my name, then I was screwed. I had to push Brady – and hopefully Mick Clancy as well – to dig deeper.

I nodded my assent, and remained silent while he packed up his briefcase and waited for the guard to come in answer to his holler of "Service!"

Once he'd gone, I settled in for a long day of waiting. Mr Wayne had told me that he'd apply for bail but I shouldn't hold out hope of it being granted. Which meant that - unless there was some dramatic last-minute development, such as my brother turning up at the station to confess – I would be heading back to Mountjoy to await a hearing.

If they were to formally charge me, then it had to be done before the end of the following day. Which, in turn, would result in my being remanded in custody... which meant the 'Joy. Or if I got lucky, Shelton Abbey in Arklow, if Mr Wayne could make a compelling case based on the fact that I'd been taken into custody in County Wicklow, rather than County Dublin. I'd push him to cite the danger to my person if I were to be returned to Mountjoy: an argument with a significant basis in fact. Given recidivism rates in Ireland, I was likely to cross paths with at least one or two 'old friends' there. And reunions of that kind were seldom happy occasions.

To stave off the anxiety all this induced, I spent the next hour or two practicing Krav take-downs in the cell. Which must have been a strange sight for the guard who brought my lunch and evening meal. And not one likely to provoke his sympathies. Still: it kept me busy.

I was already thinking in terms of prison life. It was as if my brain and body had already shrugged off hope of avoiding a return. Knowing how to deal with boredom there is an essential skill: the alternative being insanity. Genuinely.

I'd always been the restless type - a foot-tapper and fidgeter since I was a child – and I'd found the inertia and stasis of prison life difficult to bear. You can only pace around your cell so many times before you either drive your cellmate mad, or go mad yourself. I remember watching a tiger in Dublin Zoo striding back and forth in his cage, wide-eyed and restless, learning from a keeper it was because captivity had driven him insane. So, when evening came, I sat down on the blue plastic mattress and played the games I'd developed over long years to keep my brain in check. Memory games in the main. The exact sequence of events in all twenty scenes of the five acts of Hamlet, and the twenty-seven scenes of King Lear. The first choice line-up of the Arsenal 'Invincibles' team, and the Italia 90 Republic of Ireland squad. The lyrics to all sixty lines of Dylan's 'Desolation Row'. Anything to distract and occupy my mind. When I finally made an attempt to get some sleep,

I did so in the certain knowledge that my days as a free man were over. For the present – if not for good.

TWENTY-FOUR

Lego makes an excellent killing machine.

I'm not sure why I awoke with this thought. I'd been lost in a dream of childhood - myself and Tom in the family home in Glasthule, our mother and father there as well but shadowy presences, memories of them having faded over time. Tom was building one of his signature Lego constructions. There was no Star Wars or Harry Potter Lego then - no curved or tailored blocks, nothing but single or double-width blocks of two, four, eight or twenty studs. There were red-framed windows which you could insert into a wall, but little in the way of decorative features. I'd heard it argued that this created a better environment to stretch a child's imagination, but people supporting this claim were also inclined to advocate for a diet of red lemonade and fishfingers, on the basis that if it was good enough for them, etc.

Tom would spend hours building tunnels – the walls five or six bricks high, with windows at regular intervals to allow him to peer inside. He'd create huge structures with multiple tunnels running from a central chamber, a flat plate connected to a short column of bricks acting as both a handle and a lid. Inside this chamber he would place wasps he'd captured in a jam-jar, the sweet conserve lining the sides irresistible to the insects, but sticky enough to trap those who didn't fall into the water beneath. He'd use a tweezers to pick up a wasp and drop it inside, replacing the lid and lying down to watch as it buzzed about in an angry panic and tried to escape from its brick-lined prison. Tom usually had five or more tunnels radiating from the main chamber, many of them with sharp turns and changes in direction – and only one of them with an opening to the air outside. All of the other tunnels were bricked up at their extremity, forcing the increasingly desperate wasp to turn about each time it reached an impasse.

Sometimes the wasps would grow despondent, or exhausted, and curl in on themselves to die. When this happened Tom would tap his finger against the sides of the chamber to rouse them, or even lift that section and shake it to stir the insect back into life. But this was not the extent of his cruelty. The final section of roof at the end of the open tunnel had another lid, with a thick handle of bricks above it. When the wasp spotted its escape – its buzzing always increasing in volume as it grew nearer – Tom would wait, his hand poised on the handle, before smashing the lid down on the hapless prisoner just as he opened his wings to take flight. I can still remember the crisp crunch as he compressed it against the base plate – its tiny body reduced to a mangled, hairy carapace and the lacy filigree of its wings.

He would spend hours watching his captives fight their way toward the promise of freedom before growing bored and walking away, abandoning the others to a watery death in the jam jar.

I resisted the urge to compare my lot with Tom's hapless victims. I had no intention of allowing myself to be manipulated again. No doubt he was already dusting off his performance as the concerned brother. Despairing of his younger sibling's 'troubles'. The illness which had driven him to kill again. I could picture him before me – his sympathetic, tear-strewn face, vouching unwavering support for his wayward brother. Fuck him! And – if they fell for it again – fuck them all!

The day passed without further interruption. Unlike the last time I'd found myself behind bars, I would have welcomed visitors. I needed to see Kate and Laura, and assure them that I was innocent! And I wanted to see Tom, although he was unlikely to expose himself in that way. It was late evening by the time John Wayne returned, followed into my cell by Brady and Mick Clancy. They led me to the interview room where I was formally charged with the murder of Sharon Buckley – Brady telling me with undisguised glee that the wristband had been "categorically" identified as belonging to the dead girl. I was informed I would be brought before a judge the following morning in the district court in Bray (across the county line in Dublin South, removing any chance I had of being remanded to Shelton Abbey) and then left alone with my counsel.

Everything he said to me was a blur - even my own answers immediately passing from memory, as the enormity of the situation crashed over me. By this time tomorrow, I would be back in Mountjoy. Locked up once more with an even bigger target on my back, and a guarantee that I'd receive no sympathy from inmate or guard alike. And if someone took it upon themselves to exact retribution for the two girls I'd murdered...

Krav or no Krav, I didn't know if I could face it again. The tiny room. The smells. The beatings. The complete isolation, which would offer me the greatest chance of survival, and my greatest source of despair. For a moment I cursed the fact of my release - these few, short days outside having proved just long enough to underline the horrors of incarceration. I'd be tormented anew, now that I knew what it was like to walk along a seafront, have a pint in a pub, eat at a time other than twelve or five.... And talk face to face with my daughter and my wife.

From this moment on, it was just a matter of time. There would be the period on remand. Then the trial: with my face - and their names - emblazoned across the pages of the press for days, or even weeks. Although a lengthy trial seemed unlikely... And then the inevitable sentencing, and life in a cage. Any application for early release in the future would be immediately rejected. There was doubtless a world of trouble awaiting whoever had signed off on my release this time as it was - they wouldn't risk making the same mistake again. And anyway, I realised with a jolt, that option would never be available to me. I might have been able to plead down from murder to manslaughter the last time – but this time? I would get life. The statuary sentence. And life meaning life.

I was young enough now, perhaps, to survive the treatment awaiting me inside. But what about when I got older? How would I defend myself then? I knew with certainty that when that day came I would choose my own exit. I could never submit to a life spent as a punching bag. Far better to take your own life, than to allow yourself to become that. To be their creature, forever.

I tried to convince myself that for now at least there was hope - however dim. If they wouldn't dig deep enough of their own accord, couldn't Mr Wayne compel them to? And if they wanted to present a watertight prosecution, wouldn't they *want* to check and double-check the results of the forensic examination? Because therein lay my only hope – challenge the initial forensic report, and hope that a subsequent investigation uncovered something which, even if it didn't prove my innocence, at least identified the presence of some other party. A second person, at the scene of the murder. Either leading them directly to Tom or producing sufficient uncertainty to compel a jury to return a verdict of reasonable doubt.

When I put this to him, and asked how long it would take for a privately funded examination of the forensics to take place, Mr Wayne made it clear that we were talking weeks not days. He was still non-committal about representing me at trial, but agreed to send the report to a service he regularly used when seeking to undermine state's evidence. Once I had reminded him that I had the money to cover the cost... And the cost of his referral.

Either way, I now had to steel myself for a return to Mountjoy. And all that this would entail.

I've never taken pleasure in violence. Yes, there had been a period – given the treatment I'd endured up till then - when I'd revelled in my new-found prowess. And in taking revenge on my tormentors. But I had never enjoyed the violence itself. Never felt the thrill of landing a blow, or smashing a foot, hand or knee into another's body. It's said that the playwright Sean O'Casey became physically ill at the thought of violence - and I understood something of this. Violence is not as you see it on the screen. It is brutal. Primal. When you hit someone, you feel your flesh - your bones - connect with those of another. And it damages both of you. You cannot punch someone in the face and not hurt your knuckles, and expose them to further pain with every subsequent blow. You cannot feel your fist connect with the narrow bone on the side of someone's jaw without wincing, as you feel it give way. When you grip someone's neck, you feel their skin and sweat against your fingers, and feel that skin graze and bruise as you apply pressure to it. When you bend someone over and launch your knee into their head, chest or groin, you feel those parts against your own skin, and sense the harm you are doing to them. There is nothing balletic or artful about a fight. And - to win one - you have to embrace this. Of necessity violence turns you into someone else. And, if you're lucky, you won't like him.

Sometimes, however, violence is necessary. I had no illusions about what I'd do – or become – if I had to go back. This time, however, it would be different. In the past I'd resorted to violence to stay alive and to remain sane, in preparation for my release. All my thoughts were focused on the future. This time though there would be no future to look forward to. No justification for what I did, other than self-preservation. And what would that make of me?

The night passed. And on the following morning events took care of themselves. The early morning wake-up, and the same meagre breakfast. The visit from Mr Wayne to prepare me for my court appearance. The transfer to Bray Courthouse in the back of a Garda van. The photographers and journalists waiting for us in the car park, shouting questions and grabbing snaps while the young guard – Something Duffy from Leitrim - attempted to cover my head with a jacket he'd taken from the back of the van. I'd shrugged it from my head, determined not to hide - attempting an expression of resolve and allowing them to lead me through the courthouse doors, and down to the holding cell.

There was one other person there when they closed the door on me. A young man of nineteen or twenty, sweat beading on bad skin. I wondered whether this was from worry or withdrawal, but avoided eye contact, taking a seat on the far side of the cell while I waited to be taken up.

After a wait of about ninety minutes it was me – as the main event - who was summoned first, two guards I hadn't seen before flanking me as I was led up the stairs to the dock at the rear of the courtroom.

Bray District Court is a relatively new building, all glass and polished cement, and the courtroom mirrored this aesthetic. Two lines of dark wooden benches faced a raised dais holding the judge's chair and, a foot or two lower down, three seats to accommodate the court secretaries. The wall behind the dais ran upward to a long, rectangular window, the ceiling higher than at the rear of the courtroom, where the dock stood: a plain, open space with low sides, in the same dark wood as the benches. The walls to left and right were panelled with sheets of light wood – varnished pine I thought - the other walls painted matt white, with the exception of an eight-foot-square section in buttercup yellow directly behind the judge's chair. The other officials' chairs were upholstered in the same industrial grey as the ribbed carpet on the floor.

As a contrast with the Central Criminal Court, where I was arraigned after Karen Williams's death, it was stark. Everyone was so much closer - the court reporters barely a few feet from me as the charges were read and the rituals observed, culminating with my being remanded to Mountjoy to await trial (Sedgefield was never an option as I'd yet to be convicted of a crime and Cloverhill – where the majority of prisoners on remand are housed – immediately ruled out due to the nature of the crime).

Given the perennial backlog of cases before the courts, remand doubtless meant months. For innocent men and women being placed on remand essentially amounts to a prison sentence for a crime they didn't commit. Even if their innocence is proven five minutes after their trial eventually commences - or the charges are thrown out, as so often happens, on the steps of the courthouse. Imagine spending six months locked away from your children - almost certainly losing your job – quite literally for nothing. That half a year of your life is not returned to you along with your liberty. Nor, sometimes, is your family.

My young cell mate wasn't having any better a day, and rejoined me in the basement within forty minutes of Mr Wayne's fleeting appearance in my cell. I wouldn't see my counsel again until a trial date had been set. But in truth I needed Bruce Wayne not John Wayne, given what I was facing. Ignoring my cellmate and staring steadfastly at my feet, I cursed myself for not running when I could have, between when they'd first questioned me and when they returned to arrest me at

Cois Farraige. How valuable would those few hours seem, a few years from now?

The journey to Mountjoy took about an hour and passed in silence. Two more guards accompanied us, probably pulled from Bray station, one sitting on either side of the van, its caged windows offering a restricted view of the world as I passed from it. The young man sobbed quietly throughout, snuffling fitfully until one of the guards fetched a tissue from deep within his pocket and instructed him to blow his fucking nose. There was some minor note of sympathy in his voice I thought, though nothing of that sort came my way. The looks they gave me were of barely restrained malice. I would have few friends among the prison staff, I knew. Whatever about the rest of the prison population... no doubt some of whom were already eagerly awaiting my return.

It was early afternoon by the time we were processed and admitted, meaning that we'd missed lunch. I fought the urge to scream as they led me to my cell along those same Victorian corridors, misery, self-pity and rage oozing from every doorway. Once they locked the cell with that impossibly loud clang, however, I could hold it back no longer - cradling my head in my hands, silent shrieks rocking my chest and shoulders.

Those outside of prison are probably unaware of a silent scream − of the release it both provides and denies you. This is no place to show weakness or to expose your emotions. My status as a remand prisoner - and the nature of the crime I'd been accused of - meant that I had been allocated my own cell, one of the few inmates on that wing to enjoy this privilege. Which left me alone. For now.

I had been given time. Time to prepare. Time to adjust, as best I could. I reckoned they'd keep a close eye on me for a day or two, as they always did with new prisoners, till boredom or laziness led them to turn their attentions elsewhere. I'd discover who was awaiting that moment well before then. People are seldom assaulted without warning in a prison. There's always a taster, or a threat. A promise of what's to come. I wondered if the reputation I'd earned in Sedgefield had travelled with me, or I was viewed as new fish? I hoped that it hadn't. It could prove the difference between being attacked by one or two of them, and an assault by more of them than I could defend myself against.

My options, in either case, were the same. Did I take the beating - or fight back? The fact that I was on remand made this an even harder decision. The last time I'd been in this position I was easy meat and the thought of striking back hadn't even occurred to me. Not that it would have done me any good, then. Now, however, getting into a fight would reflect on me and any such incidents would doubtless be referenced when I came to trial.

In the end that choice was made for me. I'd barely left my cell, once the doors were opened for prisoners to wander down and collect their evening meal, when a pair of short-haired goons in regulation loose-fitting jogging pants and tee-shirts approached me on the corridor, the rolling swagger of their walk a clear statement of intent. The front one had his chin thrust forward, his pursed mouth a harbinger of malice. He let his friend walk to the back of me before sticking a hand in my chest in preparation for delivering whatever little speech he'd been rehearsing while they planned my welcome. I didn't wait to hear it. I grabbed his middle and ring fingers with my left hand and bent them sharply back, turning sideways as I did so to direct an elbow into the nose of his companion, just as he was pulling back a fist to punch me in the kidneys. Unlike in the movies, where one blow of this kind suffices, I knew better than to leave it at that and added a second and third strike to his blood-filled face. All the while I kept leveraging the first one's fingers backward till the knuckles faced the ground, forcing him onto his knees. One of the guards had spotted what was going on, and was advancing on us from his station by the lunch counter, so I finished up. I broke both his fingers and hit him square on the temple with the same elbow I'd used a second before, smearing his face with his friend's blood, and dropping him like a stone. I then held up my hands and waited for the inevitable takedown (not as rough as I'd anticipated) and for the handcuffs to be fitted behind my back. Two other guards had joined their colleague by now, grabbing me beneath the arms to march me off. I had been in Mountjoy for about three hours, and had yet to speak a word.

Twenty-five

Contrary to popular belief, there are no gangs as such in Irish prisons. There are loose alliances, and small groups of friends, but no tightknit system binding one inmate to another. Which meant there was little effort made to exact revenge for what I'd done to Toner and Murray, whose names I'd learned when they brought me in front of the warden. I was back in that same office three days later, after which I was left alone. Total damage – one broken nose, two broken fingers, a dislocated elbow and some cracked ribs.

None of them mine.

Time moved on. You don't adjust, but you make accommodations. The routine impinges. The fires of hope are tamped down. As Beckett puts it, you go on. I was there for three weeks when I had an unexpected visitor, and my hopes rose once again.

Mick Clancy looked strangely out of place in a prison. You would have thought as a law enforcement officer he'd have fitted right in – maybe not as part of the furniture, but at least as part of the general ambiance. Instead he looked manifestly uncomfortable, as he took a seat at one of the low tables in the visiting room. He was sweating, I noted, running a finger beneath the collar of a white-to-yellow shirt as if to emphasize the point.

"Jack."

"Mick."

"So. How are they treating you?"

"Like a criminal."

He smiled.

"A lot of that about, I'd reckon."

"True. So - what brings you here? You'd clearly rather be somewhere else."

"I fucking hate these places! Excusing present company, but they have the smell of desperation to them! Like the tissues in a teenager's bedroom. I don't know how anyone works here - it'd send me round the bend!"

"I can't see you as a screw somehow, Mick. You're not cut out for it."

"Thank Jaysus for that!"

The visiting room was empty apart from ourselves. They mustn't have had an office available elsewhere, and had opened this place especially for the interview.

"Should I have asked my counsel to be here?" I asked as he rearranged his arse on the chair, the former considerably larger than the latter.

"Nah. I suppose it's up to you, though. D'you want him here?"

"No, I'm good. I don't think I have the five hundred quid it'd cost for him to sit here for fifteen minutes anyway."

"That's lawyers for you! Send you a Christmas card in December and bill you for the correspondence in January."

"He's not the worst, in fairness."

He gave me a look suggesting he regarded this as a subtle distinction.

"I hear you've been in a spot of bother," he said.

"Yeah?"

"One of the lads told me. Bit of a disagreement with a fellow prisoner. Or three."

I said nothing.

"Anyhows - that's not why I'm here."

"And what is, Mick?"

"You, ye fecker!" He shifted uncomfortably once more. "I haven't been able to square things, and it bothers me."

"Square things how?"

"You and the girl. Sharon Buckley."

My heart gave a small leap.

"So... you still don't think I did it."

"That's about the size of it. Feck ye! It'd be a lot easier if I did. The prevailing view is that we have our man. And as far as I can tell, no one else is looking to upset that apple cart."

"Least of all Detective Inspector Brady."

"Least of all him."

"So what made you become the odd man out? Your conscience get at you, did it?"

"Conscience my arse! I just don't like it when things don't fit together."

I'd been counting on this! I leaned forward, eager to draw him out.

"Like - what you said about not leaving evidence behind? Like the first time? I had to agree — reluctantly, mind - that you're not a fucking idiot. So..."

"So it had to be someone else! And you know what that means don't you? If I didn't do it this time, then I have to be innocent of Karen Williams's death too!"

"Hold on there now, Jack. One step at a time, if you don't mind. I'll admit, if they discover this one wasn't kosher-"

"Then they *have* to reopen the other one! He did it, Mick! And you can't let the fucker get away with it twice! Did you hear anything back from the forensics?"

"Ah, for feck's sake! You know I can't discuss that stuff with you, Jack. I shouldn't even be here!"

I relented.

"I know. And I appreciate it! You don't know what it's like. Locked in here, not knowing what's going on outside. For all I know, they've all given up and settled for keeping me in this hole forever - guilty or otherwise."

"They're still looking, put it that way. These things move slowly."

"Tell me about it!" I changed tack. "Do you know how Laura and Kate are doing?"

"They haven't been in to see you, then?"

"I'm sure the pair of them have Laura on lockdown. There's no way they'd let her in to see me now. Tom won't want me talking to either of them, that's for sure."

"Does he know? That you think he's behind... You know, all of it?"

"No. At least, I don't think so."

I thought back to my conversations with Emmet McLaughlin and Tony Donald.

"Although he might. But, either way, he won't want me protesting my innocence to Kate or Laura. There's no good in it for him if they start asking questions, or digging around on my behalf."

He paused for a moment, looking thoughtful but downcast.

"You realize you're stuck here one way or the other? Until they find something. Or not!"

"The thought had crossed my mind."

"It could take months."

"Is there nothing you can do? To speed things up?"

"Who the fuck do you think I am, Jack? Sure I'm just some gombeen from Wicklow! Those boys don't pay attention to the likes of me."

"They'd listen to Brady though, wouldn't they? Any chance you can get him to put a rush on? Seriously, Mick. I'm not sure how long I can last in here!"

"Not while you're so busy making friends."

"Keeping a low profile isn't exactly an option for me, Mick. Not considering what I'm in for. The fact that my face is still all over the papers isn't helping. People in here can read, you know."

"I thought it was illiteracy that turned people into criminals. Or are all those sociologists wrong?"

"They can still look at the pictures... and this is no laughing matter, Mick. I'm a marked man in here."

"I'll see what I can do. The man has an ego like Ron Jeremy's dick. Though as for his dick... Maybe I can convince him it'd get him his conviction earlier."

"Whatever works! If this goes all the way to trial, then I'm fucked. And you know it."

He looked at me for a long moment, then asked me the question I'd been waiting for.

"And what is it you expect them to find?"

"I don't know," I said. "But it's my only hope. Forensics have advanced a lot, I have to believe, over the last eight years. They must have new ways of uncovering evidence. Of getting beyond the obvious, and finding what lies underneath. I can't imagine Tom knows about all of them, so I'm trusting that he has left something behind. Some small clue that will prove I didn't do it."

"That's a lot of 'ifs', Jack."

"I know. But I can't see any other way out. Please, Mick! I don't want them to rush it, because that'd be even worse! But I need to get out of here!"

"From what I've been hearing, you can take care of yourself. Bit of a change, all in all, from the fella I knew back in 2008!"

"Needs must, Mick."

He nodded understandingly.

"Be careful, though. You could end up getting off on the murder, and stuck inside on some other charge."

"It's hard to make those judgement calls when someone's trying to stab you, and they've brought their mates along to help them out."

"Yeah. I reckon it must be! Well. Still and all, Jack."

"Yeah. I get it."

"Look - I'll keep you posted, okay?" he said, rising from a grateful chair and taking his ancient raincoat from its neighbour. If furniture could sigh with relief...

"I'm making no promises, mind! I'll work on Brady, and see if I can get him to hurry things along. But don't be holding out any hopes, alright?"

"I get it, Mick. And thanks for trying! And if you happen to see Kate or Laura..."

"I'll make a point of it. There's no law says I can't give the family of an accused man an update. And I'd quite like to take a look inside that house anyway, so as to check out that brother of yours. Given your no doubt crazy theory about him."

"It's not crazy, Mick! And don't let him fool you. He's an accomplished actor at this stage. After all - he's gotten away with murder for the best part of a decade!"

"Let's hope he won't be doing so for the next decade, eh? Or the few after!"

"If I'm going to get out of here, I'm going to need a lot more than hope."

He nodded and turned to leave, the prison guard returning as he exited and accompanying me back to my cell. My home, if Mick Clancy failed to unearth something, until my untimely death.

Twenty-six

In the end they botched it. I got the news from John Wayne ten days after I'd been remanded. And that was that. All hope gone.

What forensics found was the following: death was caused by asphyxiation. The perpetrator wore gloves of some nature, judging by the absence of sub-cutaneous marks or surface indicators (which, I'd learned, sometimes included fingerprints recorded in the oils on the skin). Bruising to the victim's neck was consistent with a heavy restraint, perhaps of a leather or leatherette material. There was similar bruising to the right upper arm, consistent with the victim having been dragged or held tightly, perhaps in order to subdue her. There was no evidence of further injury to the body. There was no indication of sexual assault. Fibres discovered on the victim's clothing are currently the subject of matching efforts with the victim's home and environs. No foreign bodies or DNA trace evidence were located on the body, or on any item of clothing. Death would have been instantaneous following the breaking of the carotid bone, but the assault could have been prolonged in nature. [Results in this respect are inconclusive.]

The report took another twenty pages to say much the same things, detailing the tests that had been carried out and the procedures followed. In short, they hadn't managed to find anything! And I'd been absolutely certain that they would.

The result of this was that there were no further barriers to proceeding with the prosecution, and a petition was already before the courts to set a date for my trial. I was in prison now, and I would be in prison afterwards. There was no other likely outcome, and Mr Wayne knew it.

"I fear that may be that, old chap! I know I'm not telling you anything you don't already know. It's damage limitation from here on in, I'm afraid."

Which brought us to the matter of my plea.

"You know 'the score', as they have it, Mr Finch. Though I have to warn you, in present circumstances we cannot rely on a judge to impose a reduced sentence should you choose to plead guilty to the charges."

"I will not be pleading guilty! Reduced sentence or not!"

I didn't bother assuring him that I hadn't done it. No one ever does. In fact - as a lawyer will explain within minutes of meeting you - confirming your guilt to counsel will immediately require them to recuse themselves from your case. As a result defence lawyers exclusively represent innocent men.

What I'd hoped would be a conversation about a petition for release in advance of trial on the basis of new evidence uncovered by forensics, or a petition to dismiss all charges, continued in this vein instead. I would not see Mr Wayne again until the trial date was set... and more than likely not until the day of the trial itself. And that was if he didn't make his excuses and quietly drop me, as he'd made it clear from the start he was quite prepared to do.

I was alone, now. When they came to take me back to my cell I was in a state of utter despair.

Twenty-seven

It's the little things you have to adjust to in prison. And it's the same when you get out. Things like opening a door - something you never do inside. The door to your cell, and the doors leading anywhere else in the prison are locked and unlocked by a guard. When you get up, when you sleep, when you eat - even when you can go to the toilet - are all controlled by a schedule you cannot alter. Some of the cells in Mountjoy have toilets: but that is even worse. In a shared cell you're in that toilet every time someone gets up off their cot to take a piss or a shit. There in that same small room, nothing but a low partition separating you from the noise and the smell.

There is constant intimidation, even for those locked up for much less heinous offences than mine. Walk out on the corridor as a new prisoner and listen to the threats shouted out for the "new fish". The gestures. The promises of "a good ride". What makes it worse – intolerably tense - is the presence of blades. Only a week before my arrival an inmate had been snatched on the corridor, a shoelace thrown about his neck to hold him as he was dragged into a shower and a blade taken to his face resulting in his requiring over 120 stitches, and changing his appearance for life. The face is the favoured target here. And there is thought put into it. The predominant weapon is a double-bladed shiv, made by embedding two shaving blades a quarter inch apart in a toothbrush head. Two blades rather than one, with a gap between them, so as to make it more difficult to stitch the resulting wound.

The threat of assault without warning is a constant for all prisoners, and even greater for those in single cells, who lack even the minimal protection offered, if reluctantly, by those you live alongside. Although there are set periods throughout the day when prisoners are free to leave their cells many never do so: and for this reason. Instead, they spend twenty-three and a half hours every day banged up. Hiding out, and knuckling down. Serving their time. This was my life, once more. And would be as far out as I could see.

For the following month, I did my best to get by. To get through each day. When what lies ahead of you is a life sentence however you are denied even the comfort of marking it down as one more struck from your stretch. Whereas other inmates could cross out a date on their calendar, and had a release date to aim at, even if it was subject to change, the sentence I'd receive would have no end. A life sentence means exactly that. Even if your status changes and you do qualify for early release at some far-off point in time, your chances of being granted it are slim at best; and in truth closer to emaciated. For a lifer, each day is simply one more in an unending sequence.

I spent my days in a state of hyper-vigilance, waiting for someone to attack. Just as junkies need a fix – and there are enough of those here to fill two hospitals, let alone one prison – those who delight in assaulting others need an outlet for their cravings.

It was a shock, then, when I was told I was to have a cell mate. This was not standard policy. Particularly for prisoners being held on remand for violent offences. But Mountjoy was once again so overcrowded (the run-up to Christmas being as busy a time for criminals as for the retailers from whom they stole) that every spare cot was needed. Many of the cells already had a third occupant, a mattress stood against a wall and taken down each night and placed in the space between the bunk beds and the narrow countertop used to hold the ashtray, TV and kettle. Some inmates preferred it that way. More people to talk to, in the interminable periods of lockup. More people to keep an eye out for you on the corridors. At least I had the consolation of knowing I'd be given my own cell once I was convicted. Lifers always get their own cell, regardless of their crime.

Anthony Murphy was a gormless young man from Coolock, on the city's Northside. A doe-eyed, slow-speaking youngfella with a mess of tousled blonde hair and a raised mole in the dead centre of his chin. He was taller than me at a little over six foot, and thinner than an anorexic greyhound. If he'd tried, he could have made his escape through the letterbox in the front gate. The thought of being locked in with him for most of the day – and night – filled me with abject dread.

Privacy is something you learn to take for granted. Even if you've shared a bedroom as a kid, having your own space – and the option of escaping to it – is something we all come to regard as a necessity. I think this is even truer for men – though the fact that we are happier in our own company is doubtless evidence of some deep-rooted social deficiency.

So we nodded hellos and I pretended to be engrossed in a book, while he unpacked the plastic bag they'd given him to transport his belongings from his previous cell to this one. I slept in the upper bunk, the lower one having served me as a sofa during the day. Gone, now. As I listened to him humming to himself – part habit, part nervousness – I counted the ways in which my life had taken a turn for the worse. Apart from the loss of privacy, there was the simple presence of somebody else in that small space. Their breathing. Their farts and coughs. Their tics and peculiarities. All of which would have to be endured.

And there was the TV. I had used mine sparingly, having inherited a small bargain-basement flatscreen when I was assigned to the cell. I could count the shows I watched on one hand, and there were days when it stayed off entirely. I knew that would change, now. Which was something of a mixed blessing. On the one hand I would likely be subjected to an endless stream of drivel, from early-morning chat shows to soap operas in the evening. On the other hand, the noise would do something to mask his presence. I heard a rasping sound, and figured out it was Anthony sellotaping pictures over his bed. I knew without looking that this would be a collage made up of photos of his family, and semi-pornographic pictures snipped from newspapers and magazines. No overtly pornographic images were allowed (topless was fine but no full-frontal nudity) although interpretation of this rule varied from guard to guard. And they only saw the ones pinned up in view, not those hidden beneath mattresses as engines of minor consolation. Oh, dear God.

Anthony had been escorted to my cell by a guard named Doyle, a squat Biffo with a shaven head beneath his cap who'd already made it clear he'd no intention of adding me to his Christmas list. For now, his hostility was held in check. But whether he was aware of my history in Sedgefield, or just waiting for my sentence to be confirmed, I knew from experience that he'd avail of any opportunity to make it plain. Whether this involved more zeal than necessary when subduing me in the aftermath of a fight, or outright persecution, he'd be pretty much free to do as he wanted. Whatever you did inside, you never hit a guard. Not, that is, if you could help it. In Doyle's case, that remained to be seen.

Anthony, it transpired, was considerably more and less than he appeared. Though still in his early twenties, he already had two children - both girls - and a girlfriend who berated him at full volume for the duration of each of his thirty-minute evening calls.

"I've only meself to blame," he'd tell me in the aftermath of the latest bollocking. "Sure, they have it harder than we do!"

His magnanimity was accompanied by a quiet stoicism. As cellmates went, he certainly wasn't the worst I could have ended up with. And I knew that a taciturn, reputedly dangerous cellmate couldn't have been top of his wish list either.

I learned that Anthony was inside for burglary: a nine-month sentence almost certain to be commuted to three or four at most, due to overcrowding. Providing that he kept his nose clean. He spoke of his profession as of any job, and displayed neither the hope nor the inclination to change his vocation. Prison inmates have a surprising degree of self-knowledge. A prisoner usually knows what, and who, he is. He taught me some interesting things. A word to the wise - keep a television on when you are out of the house. It is the single biggest deterrent for someone choosing whether to break into your house or your neighbour's.

I didn't volunteer my own history, simply stating that I was on remand. I was under no illusion though. He would have known the facts within minutes of being told he was changing cell. Such things are deliberately disregarded in a prison, however. If you have to work shoulder to shoulder with someone in the canteen or laundry, it doesn't do you any good knowing they're inside for rape, or for assaulting a pensioner. Life is only bearable in prison while such things remain hidden: or at the least unspoken.

Within a few days I had adjusted to Anthony's presence. He was more perceptive than I'd given him credit for, and seemed to instinctively know when to remain silent and when to spark up a conversation. He had no disturbing habits I'd been able to identify, and apart from an addiction to 'EastEnders' and 'Downton Abbey' he didn't abuse the television overly. I failed to understand his devotion to the latter, particularly given the running commentary he provided slagging off everything from the snobbishness of the central characters to the inaccuracies of the period details (he may or may not have been right on these). Till I realised that he was watching the show in synch with his girlfriend, so they could chat about it later in their evening call. Through such small things are vital bonds maintained.

When Anthony asked me about my own family I was circumspect with the truth, telling him I had a wife and one child, a daughter of fifteen. The last part, of course, was true. Why I claimed Kate as my wife... that might be hard to explain, but the reality is that she had never ceased to be that, for me. Though the pain of seeing her with Tom had cut deep, and particularly with the child they'd had together (whose name I'd learned was Julia, after our grandmother) it still felt like she had always been my wife. Then and now. This was the station she'd occupied in my life and in my heart when I was first committed, and on through the years of my sentence (the divorce papers I had ignored and discounted). I had continued to see her as my wife through the simple expedient of never seeing her at all. We'd only become estranged, in my eyes, during the short time I'd spent outside. And as I planned to win her back – though Christ knew how – that didn't count. She was my wife. I'd made a vow, and I had never broken it. She and Laura were mine, whatever might have happened while I was away. And as for the little girl, Julia...

But this was delusional bollocks! The simple fact of seeing him with his arm around her that first day back made concrete all the fears and agonies I'd suffered at the thought of her sleeping with someone else. Unless you've experienced or suspected an infidelity, you can't imagine the torture it causes you, the damage it does to every facet of your existence. You can't sleep. You're unable to banish images of them together from your head. You are literally overwhelmed: by feelings of hurt, of anger, of despair. Of self-loathing. It's no wonder that it has always provided the material for tragedy, or that it drove Othello mad.

When you can't even hate the person who betrayed you, it's even worse. If you can convince yourself they are worthless or cruel, you can at least endure, and tell yourself you're better off without them. I had never had that luxury. I knew Kate hadn't betrayed me. Not really. She was just another victim of Tom's treachery. Like me.

Their marriage was built on lies from the moment he first planned on getting me out of his way. It was an unholy thing, with Karen Williams' blood on it. No, Kate was not to blame, and I'd no doubt that if I hadn't been taken from her - from Laura – we would still be together now. And we *would* be together again! Somehow. Once he'd been exposed. If I could just get out of here...!

"Does she have a fella, your Laura?" Anthony asked me one afternoon, as we vegged out in front of a Christmas movie. "Ben Hur" I think, or "El Cid". Something heroic and overly long with Charlton Heston.

"I don't know," I said. Which was true. I knew almost nothing about Laura's life.

"She's wha'? Sixteen?"

"Fifteen."

"Well, then."

He left me to dwell on this.

I'd already done Anthony a favour, by twice extending his span of life. Within ten minutes of his arrival I'd suggested that he should put his health first and make an immediate and positive change, by giving up cigarettes. He wasn't keen on the idea, I knew - but after much soul-searching, he decided to acquiesce. Of course, it's possible that the nature of my crimes and the fact that I'd made this suggestion while standing approximately one inch from his face may have played some part in his decision, but I preferred to view it as an act of mature reflection. I understood why men smoked in here - to relieve the boredom and to mark intervals of time in an otherwise formless day – but I couldn't tolerate the idea of the air in my cell being filled with a fug of smoke. His offer to smoke 'out the window' was swiftly rebuffed, given that the window opened less than three inches and was as likely to admit a gale as to permit the smoke to exit. I consoled myself with the belief that he now regarded himself as better off both financially and constitutionally as a result of my intervention. Rather than that he wanted to kill me in my sleep.

Anthony's mood (some minor withdrawal symptoms apart) remained remarkably constant, other than in the aftermath of the weekly visits from his girlfriend and his kids. He would return to the cell after these morose, and uncommunicative. I let him be on those occasions. If he wanted to talk, he would.

"What's the plan then, Jack? For when you get out?"

We'd maintained the fiction that my trial would lead to my immediate release.

"Oh, I don't know. The usual? A huge steak in an expensive restaurant, then off to a swanky hotel for a threesome with a masseuse, a nurse and an air hostess! A typical Friday night."

"Yeah, I'll bet! More like fries and a burger and back to the missus for a quickie. You hope!"

"I hope!" My lack of visitors hadn't escaped his notice.

"What about you?"

"Ah - probably head out somewhere with the kids. Sure, they'll be dying to see me. Maybe take them off somewhere! My mam's family has a 'van in Wexford. Near Courtown? It'll be cold as fuck down there but the kids love it, what with the beach and the amusements, and all."

"Sounds like a plan!"

He smiled. He had dazzlingly white teeth, maintained with the aid of the dental strips his girlfriend dropped into him at every visit along with a supply of pot noodles and some chocolate bars and crisps. He always offered to share these treats but I reckoned his need was greater than mine, and always declined.

"And after that?" I asked.

"Ah, sure. You never know."

But we both knew. The chances of Anthony staying on the straight and narrow were lower than a snail's testicles, apart from the short interval of good intentions and heartfelt promises which would proceed his release. His best hope of avoiding a return to jail – as always – was not to get caught.

The days leading up to my second effort to extend Anthony's life passed like this. Chatter. Routine. The occasional threat of violence. Crappy food. Boredom. Sleep. But nothing stays the same indefinitely.

One man's fight is not another's inside. The first thing cellmates usually agree when they're thrown together is not to back each other up, but to keep their quarrels separate. I'm not taking any hits for you and you're not taking any hits for me, as the parlance has it. A P19 for causing trouble for an officer is nothing compared to pissing your cellmate off by dragging him into aggro he's got nothing to do with. Regardless - when the time comes – you're faced with a choice which will alter that relationship one way or the other. It's one thing to watch your cellmate return to the space you share following a beating. It's another thing entirely to see someone batter him right in front of your eyes.

Anthony's 'crime' was to have gone out with another inmate's girlfriend, back when they were teenagers. But to be honest, the pretext for rivalries or enmities like these was usually so slight as to be negligible. An excuse was all. Some form of justification for what was already planned.

Unfortunately, it was Nelius Byrne who had it in for Anthony. 'Byrner' to those who knew him. Which given that one of his many convictions had been for arson was somewhat ironic.

Byrner wasn't a slicer. Which was good. But he was a hard chaw - squat and powerful, pumped up in the prison gym and keen to parade his brawn whenever the occasion presented itself. His dispute with Anthony, like most such disputes, had begun outside; but feuds were carried into prison more often than they emerged there. And larger wars sometimes transcended the borders marked out by the prison walls, so at times it felt to other prisoners like they were living in some urban battlefield as old scores were settled, or rivalries renewed. At its worst – I remember one November in Sedgefield – not a single day would pass without someone getting slashed.

It's a common misconception that prisons breed violence. In most cases, the culture here reflects life outside. Only the choice – or availability – of weapons varies. Life is red of tooth and claw in many of the communities these prisoners come from and the practices, like the feuds themselves, come in with them.

The sensible thing for me to do when I heard of the beef between Anthony and Byrner was to avoid them both. Of the many people you don't want to fall out with, you never cross someone who is part of a crew. Numbers count. Sure: you might get away with taking on one of them. Or even a couple. But they will eventually find a way to corner you. And I had no wish to return to the outside world – whenever that might be – with scars that would cause even those who knew me to look away and wince.

The truth was that if Byrner and his brethren wanted to get Anthony, there was nothing I could do to protect him. Not unless I was stupid beyond belief!

How stupid?

That stupid.

TWENTY-EIGHT

Being imprisoned is torture. In part, it's the torture of being a useless man. A man who cannot protect or provide. Who can do nothing to help the family he left outside. There's no way to earn money beyond pocket change. No way to respond, if there's a problem or an emergency. No way to offer solace to your kids outside of a weekly visit filled with desperation and shame. No way to avoid the look in the eyes of your wife, girlfriend or mother which tells you, despite their effort to disguise it, how much trouble your absence is causing for them. And all of it because of something that you did.

I'd grown fond of Anthony – but more than anything else, I pitied him. The likelihood was that he would spend a good portion of his life inside. And although that might well be as a result of his own actions, the fact remained that he would miss much of his children's growing up. Their birthdays and Christmases. Even their marriages, and the births of their children. And choosing 'a life of crime' is only partly a choice. The reality for Anthony was that he had no possibility of earning more than minimum wage, or the dole, unless he pursued other options. Had he stayed in school perhaps, things might have been different. If there were more employers out there prepared to offer a second chance to those who'd served a sentence, then maybe there'd be another way out. But the reality is that recidivism is directed linked to education - and with fuck all qualifications and a prison record, the odds were stacked against him.

Maybe this was just bleeding-heart thinking, a throw-back to my student ideologies. A rare enough thing in here! Most inmates claim to be socialists, but outside of their passionate defence of a welfare state they tend to be more right-wing in their views than the editor of The Daily Express. Which is not to say that I didn't pity myself, too. I did. Being put in prison for something I didn't do was hardship enough for one life - but to find yourself back there...

Anger and self-loathing tend to accompany pity. And violence provides an outlet. Maybe I was no different to any of the men who turned to violence for some form of release, because I'll admit that I welcomed the opportunity to vent my feelings when the chance presented itself. Even if it was ostensibly in defence of somebody else.

I was out of the cell for one of my rare visits from Mr Wayne when they came for him. Our meeting hadn't lasted long. There'd been another change to the provisional date for my trial. To June this time. A delay of a further two months. Although, as my chances of winning the case were slim to non-existent, this wasn't in itself a bad thing. Nothing new had happened. Mr Wayne's request for an independent review of the forensics was still pending. If we could establish the time of death more clearly – which was a key focus of the independent review we'd requested – then there was at least an off-chance that someone might have spotted me at roughly the right time, providing me with some sort of... maybe not an alibi as such - but something we could use to weaken the prosecution's case. But no new witnesses had come forward

Anthony had received better news – he had been granted early release. And word had travelled fast. He'd already spent two weekends on temporary release, and had kept religiously to the conditions. In all, he'd served four-and-a-half months of his sentence. Exactly half, give or take a day. A good result for him. And a final chance for those who had it in for him to make their move.

Up to this point, I'd won all of the fights I'd been involved in during my second stint in Mountjoy, using a mixture of surprise, speed and a focus on ending things quickly which bordered on the vicious. This was blitzkrieg fighting - hard and fast, and totally committed. I'd picked up my share of injuries along the way, but they were rare and typically minor. My opponent seldom got a chance to respond before I ended the fight, and always leaving them in no position to resume it.

This time, however, I lost.

There are obvious problems associated with fighting four people in a confined space. Primary among them being that there are four people. Which is how many people I found in my cell when I returned from the meeting with Mr Wayne. Five, including Anthony - but he didn't really count, given that he was in a headlock. Which left me with three to deal with on my own, unless the one holding Anthony decided to relinquish his grip so as to make it four. Which he did.

"Lads?" I started.

"Fuck off out!" replied Byrner. "This has nothin' to do with you."

Which was of course what I should have done. And I probably would have, if all they'd planned to do was give him a bit of a beating. And if Charlie Ahearne hadn't been there.

Charlie was a lifer. This means several things. For one, it meant that he had killed someone. On your first meeting with Charlie you'd find this easy to believe. Tall and well-built, with a permanent five o'clock-shadow extending to his shaven head, Charlie was malevolence made flesh. A scowling, hostile beast of a man, the milk of human kindness having spoilt many years before leaving behind something rank, and bitter. Stevie Wonder had more chance of locating the Higgs Boson than you or I had of finding Charlie's better qualities. Rumour had it the person he killed was already comatose on the ground when Charlie stabbed him. Repeatedly. Up to eight times, depending on whose version of events you heard.

The chances of Charlie being granted early release were exactly nil, a status guaranteed by the role he had undertaken in prison. Charlie was a gun for hire. With nothing to lose from the addition of extra time to his sentence, he was the 'go to' guy if you needed some dirty work done without any repercussions for yourself. A new mobile phone, or some drugs or cigarettes, were usually enough to purchase his services. Because the fact was that Charlie liked his work, and might well have done these 'favours' in return for a simple please and thank you. Which may not have been a problem in itself, had he and Byrner not differed in one key respect. Charlie liked blades. In fact, when I walked into the cell, he was standing at the back with what looked very much like the handle of a shiv in his right fist.

There's nothing brave about acting to protect someone else in a situation like this. Normally, such things are done without thinking. As an instinctive response rather than as a conscious decision. I was calm, however, and under no illusions. If I took Charlie on, then the chances were that I would lose. If not to him then to the combined weight of those with him. And might well end up on the business end of that shiv myself. I gambled that those with Byrner shared the same misgivings - or would be wary of slicing me in case they suffered for it later - and hit Charlie a massive blow to the temple, reaching past him and trying to fold his hand back upon his wrist so as to dislodge the blade.

You can't go into a knife fight without getting cut. This is an established fact. If there is a knife in your opponent's hand, then any attempt to take it from him will result in an injury. The only question is how severe. As I twisted Charlie's hand upwards against the inside of his wrist, he rotated his forearm and slashed me at the point where my thumb met my palm. I felt the blade cut into my tendon, the pain indescribably bright. The thing about pain, though, is that it breeds anger. I hit him again, smashing my right fist into the side of his head and following it with punch after punch to his face. I'm not sure how much effect I had on him, but his grasp on the shiv loosened sufficiently for me to shake it from his grip, and to kick it beneath the bunk once it hit the ground. Folding his wrist all the way back now, till his fingers met his arm, I heard the bone crack and drew a grunt of pain from him. I didn't stop though, knowing I had to put him completely out of action to have any chance of avoiding serious injury, or worse. I rotated his hand still further, driving him to his knees in his attempt to minimise the damage, and bringing his head in range of my knee. I got two quick blows in before I was seized from behind. I had the satisfaction of seeing Charlie fold and drop to the floor, before the first of what would be many well-placed punches landed in the small of my back. They spun me around and started to choose their spots, while I alternated between trying to block them, and hitting back. I caught one of them a decent blow on the jaw, sending him lurching backwards, but the sheer weight of numbers meant there could only be one outcome. Soon enough they had me curled up on the floor, attempting to shield my head while they rained kicks at me. During a momentary pause I peeked out between my fingers to see Charlie lying prone in the narrow space between bunk and desk, and smashed my heel into the top of his head to make sure he stayed there.

The whole thing – from my arrival back in the cell to the guards bursting in in response to Anthony's screams – couldn't have been more than a couple of minutes. But the repercussions would last much longer. I will live the rest of my life in fear of someone stepping out of the shadows and pulling a double-edged blade across my face before I have the time to react. If I was ever to be released, I'd still have to rely on the penal system to ensure that Charlie would remain banged up, till he was a very old man. Stuck inside, I'd have to pray for a transfer out of The Joy and hope that someday, before our paths crossed again, he'd make the mistake of taking on someone faster and harder than he was. Someone who'd finish the job in a way that I could not or would not.

The confines of the cell saved me from serious damage, having restricted my attackers' ability to pull back their feet to deliver more powerful kicks to my head and body. In this respect it was just as well that there were three of them, all fighting for space to attack me. Regardless, they did a pretty thorough job. On me. The irony being that Anthony had escaped virtually unscathed! More than that - on account of the obvious threat to his safety his release was moved up - and he was out, and free, before I left the hospital.

I lay on a gurney that evening, one wrist handcuffed to the side, a bored guard dozing on a chair beside me, and counted my injuries. The worst of them wasn't the broken ribs, which grated against the bandages they'd used to strap up my chest - there being no other remedy for an injury like this than to bind them and give them time to heel - but the damage to my reputation. I would be fair game, now. Now that it was clear that I could be taken down, as long as enough bodies were involved in the attempt. Now that it was clear that doing me over would meet with others' approval. My only hope was that I had done enough damage to Byrner's friends to dissuade any of them from volunteering to be first in line.

Above all, though, I was afraid of Charlie Ahearne. Like me, he would recover. And when he did... he had the rest of our lives to get even.

Twenty-nine

They brought me back to Mountjoy the following morning, but it was a different place to the one I'd left. I was no longer safe there. If I ever had been. There was a clock ticking whose beats I heard in every footfall on the corridor outside my cell.

Prison feuds are sorrily predictable. If you asked anyone on the wing what would happen next the accounts would vary little, other than in the timelines and the exact nature of the injuries to be inflicted. Charlie would come after me. He would not come alone. And the outcome of that would be – at best – permanent disfigurement. At worst... blinding - cuts to the face often resulted in the loss of sight in one or both eyes - or some other disability I would carry with me for the remainder of my sentence. Meaning I would become easy prey for anybody else wishing to register their protest about the killing of two young girls. Things would be like they'd been when I was first imprisoned, eight years ago. Only worse.

The only alternative was just as stark. In essence, it meant giving up any hope of freedom in return for my safety. Some might argue, in return for my soul. Because there was only one way to stop Charlie Ahearne: and that was to stop him for good. I could employ whatever euphemisms I wanted, but it came down to this. I didn't think Charlie would kill me, at least not intentionally, because there's a scale which regulates such things in prison and my breaking his wrist only legitimised a cutting or an assault similar to, or one step up from what I'd done to him. But if I was to prevent that - and the likelihood of some life-changing injury - then I would have to kill him.

I couldn't wait for him to come at me either. When he made his move, he'd come at me in numbers - and the chance would disappear faster than my good looks. So instead, I would have to be the hunter. Which last time I'd looked it up was pretty much the dictionary definition of 'premediated'.

Whichever way I looked at it, I was fucked.

It wasn't fear which kept me from sleeping that night, however. It was despair. Despite everything I'd done, everything I'd sacrificed, I would be spending the rest of my life in prison. The best I could hope for was transfer to a less secure unit, at some distant point in my old age. I'd have no chance of getting further than Sedgefield for decades, given my crimes. Those committed both inside and out. And I had to accept the likelihood that I'd be dependent on maintaining a similar disposition for many years to come. I would become the man I'd been accused of being, all that time ago.

For most people, the line between causing an injury and committing a murder (unless we act instinctively, or in the heat of the moment) is an obvious one. Perhaps despite ourselves, we are not killers. Taking a life is ultimately inconceivable for most of us, regardless of our moral or religious beliefs. But I knew which choice I'd make, if it came to it. Which forced me to recognize something I'd always denied of myself despite how brutalised I'd been by eight years in the system.

I had thought – despite everything – to have retained my humanity. Maybe, looking back, this was what Kate had always seen in me. This capacity. That was why she'd been so quick to believe that I had killed Karen Williams - because I was the sort of man who'd be capable of such a thing. Even my own wife – the mother of our daughter – believed that to be true. I might have been innocent of Karen's death but, in some primal sense, I was still a killer. A man who would weigh his own safety or his own interests above the life of another.

Would a jury see that when they looked at me? Even if we managed to challenge the forensic evidence, or to sow sufficient doubt about the details of the case against me, would they still look in my eyes and see that kind of man? Someone whose nature if not his actions made him guilty? All of which would be moot, of course. Even if I got off on that charge – even if they vindicated me in Karen Williams' murder as well as Sharon Buckley's – dealing with Charlie Ahearne would guarantee my imprisonment. Regardless. Ultimately, it wouldn't matter who I had or hadn't killed, or whether it took place inside or out. The verdict, and the punishment, would be the same. I would be that man. And they would never let me go.

My cell was empty when they brought me back. Anthony had even taken his pictures from the wall above his bed. I suspected they would be slow to replace him. What occurred might have been on the back of an attack on Anthony, not me, but they would view proximity to me now as a danger in itself. Which suited me fine. I'd miss Anthony — difficult as that would have been to imagine on that first day, when he'd turned up with his belongings in a plastic sack — but I needed to rely on myself from now on. And, contrary to what they might think of me, I had no wish to place anyone else in the firing line, when the time came. I didn't need a companion. Or an accomplice.

Word of the previous day's events had circulated, and a number of those passing my door shouted remarks in at me. Most of them prophesying what was in store for me - though there were some congratulatory ones too from those with good reason to rejoice in Charlie's misfortunes. For now, my reputation was enhanced. But I was a marked man.

I wasn't afraid of Byrner or his cohort. They'd won after all, and there was nothing to be gained from giving me another beating other than the likelihood of landing a P17. Anthony was gone, and Charlie would sort me out himself. Until he was back, then, I could be ignored. Tick, tock.

"Finch?" Malone, one of the older guards on the wing, poked his head around the door.

"Yes?" I remained where I was on the upper bunk, my knees tucked under my chin.

"You're to see the governor. His office, five minutes!"

And with that he left, leaving me to stretch painfully and spend a couple of minutes trying to wrestle my beat-up features into some semblance of a presentable appearance. Christ knew what sort of bawling out I was going to receive, but the summons was hardly unexpected.

It seemed things were even worse than I'd thought when I arrived at the governor's office to find John Wayne sitting there, his burgundy leather briefcase balanced on his knees and a stony expression on his face. Christ! Were they going to charge me now? Even before I went to trial for Sharon Buckley's murder?

Mr Wayne had the expressionless look a man might wear if he'd farted in the presence of the queen. The man was harder to read than a wet paperback.

"Sit down, Finch," the governor said, without looking up from the yellow college-lined notepad he'd balanced between the desk and his knee. He was busily scribbling notes to himself, though it was impossible to know whether these related to me or a previous meeting.

I sat and waited. After all, I thought ruefully, I had nothing but time.

The governor, Mr Clarke, was a moustachioed man in his mid-forties. Young to hold such a senior position and regarded by the prison population as hard, but fair. Hard if you got on the wrong side of him: fair if you managed to get away with whatever infraction had brought you to his office. An ever-present pair of glasses were lodged above his forehead in his close-cropped, greying hair. I'd heard of his appointment back when I was in Sedgefield, but met him for the first time the day I arrived back in Mountjoy. I reckoned he'd been promoted to just about the worst management job in Ireland.

At least five minutes passed before he lifted his head, Mr Wayne retaining an impassive expression throughout, not even offering me a sideways glance. He was either mightily pissed off with me, or would rather not acknowledge me as his client at all. I wondered how he'd react when they brought him back here to tell him what I'd done to Charlie Ahearne. There can't be many barristers asked to represent the same man for three separate murders. No doubt I'd make for an interesting chapter in his memoirs.

"I've been filling Mr Wayne in on the details of your most recent spot of bother, Finch," Clarke said at last. "He was naturally very concerned about your welfare." He gave a little smile.

"As I understand it, Mr. Clarke," Mr Wayne began, "My client was the victim of an unprovoked attack and guilty of nothing more than defending himself against a knife attack by a violent prisoner. A convicted murderer, no less! I would remind you that he is detained in these august premises on remand, and as thus is regarded as an innocent party under the law. There is nothing I've heard about that incident which should in any way affect the matter before us. You are of course free to pursue your investigations following Mr Finch's release, but that may appear a somewhat redundant exercise... given your no doubt onerous workload."

Clarke raised an eyebrow in reply, and returned to his notes.

"Your client put two men in hospital."

"On the contrary, Governor Clarke. They put themselves there! That is the only reasonable reading of those events. And let us not forget the injuries done to my client whilst under your protection. Is it deemed acceptable, now, for prisoners on remand to be assaulted beneath the very eyes of your staff? My understanding is that this altercation, as you described it to me earlier – and my congratulations on your choice of euphemism - went on for several minutes without the intervention of the guards! How can this be, I wonder? I'm certain the courts would look most unfavourably at such a demonstrable failure to guarantee the safety of any individual who might suffer the same misfortune. Innocent of any offence - yet apparently at the mercy of some form of summary justice in advance of his trial!

Should he live that long, that is, in this apparently lawless institution!"

Clarke looked up again, nonplussed. Doubtless an ability to keep your cool is a necessary attribute for someone running a prison. And outraged lawyers were probably way down his list of irritants.

"Your client doesn't appear too concerned about his safety."

"You're fucking kidding me!" I said - earning myself a dirty look from both simultaneously. I decided to keep my mouth shut. There was clearly something going on here that I didn't understand.

Clarke sighed.

"We take the safety of all our inmates extremely seriously, Mr Wayne. And if, indeed, it does turn out that your client was the innocent party in this... incident," he gave me a look suggesting he regarded this as highly unlikely, "Then action will be taken against those responsible."

"I assure you that will be the case! Such a serious assault must have consequences, if anarchy is not to become the status quo!"

Having ensured that I'd escape any repercussions from my encounter with Charlie Ahearne and his mates – from the prison authorities, at any rate - Mr Wayne changed gears.

"It seems to me, Governor Clarke, that we can essentially view that matter as moot. Given the papers before you - and the certainty that my client will be found innocent in due course of all charges relating to the matter which placed him in your care - I think we can safely close the book on this one. That would appear to be the most expedient course of action, wouldn't you agree?"

Clarke said nothing. He hadn't reacted to the dripping sarcasm which accompanied Mr Wayne's use of the word "care"; and whatever papers were before him he seemed unperturbed. But it was an obvious win-win. If he let the matter drop, then both he and I would avoid any blowback from the altercation in my cell. Not that Charlie Ahearne would see it that way.

"Mr Finch," he said, looking to me. "It appears you and I will be saved the bother of a difficult conversation. We don't treat broken bones – of any inmate under our 'care' – as something to take lightly. In the circumstances, however.... you can return to your cell, and pack your belongings."

He waved a pre-emptive hand towards Mr Wayne. "And I will instruct a guard to accompany you, for safety. Though I'm not entirely sure whose."

I stared at him in disbelief. Was I being moved? The prospect that they'd transfer me from Mountjoy to Sedgefield to head off any further trouble should of course have occurred to me. But I'd thought they wouldn't accept remand prisoners there.

"And where am I going, if I may ask?"

"You're going out, Jack!" he said, using my Christian name for the first time. "And I pray God Mr

Wayne is right, and we never have the pleasure of your company again. I'll give you two a minute to consult together while I get myself a much-needed coffee, and then a guard will come to take you to your cell."

I sat there, dumbstruck.

I was out!

THIRTY

It was the wristband. The real wristband this time. Sharon Buckley's mother had found it looped around a toothbrush holder behind the bathroom sink two days beforehand, and after agonising about it for twenty-four hours finally rang the garda station, where word of its discovery reached Mick Clancy.

From there, the dominos tumbled in a neat line.

The wristband found in my room in Cois Farraige was not, in fact, Sharron Buckley's. Which raised the question of whose it was, and what it was doing there. My protestations that it had been planted now had some credence. Which, in turn, removed any barriers to Mr Wayne's request for a more detailed forensic examination of the crime scene and Sharon Buckley's clothes and body. In the circumstances, they initiated this immediately and made sure it was as thorough as possible given the scrutiny being placed upon the whole investigation. It transpired that there was more to uncover than just the different provenance of the wristbands. DNA samples had been requested in the original examination, but when those found on the wristband from my room didn't match Sharon's, it was assumed that the traces must have come from one or other of her friends who could have tried on the band while they were with her. The absence of Sharon's own DNA was conveniently ignored.

The DNA they'd recovered was never identified, other than to rule Sharon and myself, and the tests had been shelved given that they added nothing useful to support the central case against me. Her parents had already identified the wristband found in my room as belonging to Sharon – it matched the one she'd been wearing the day she was last seen alive – and they saw nothing to gain from confusing the issue.

With their key piece of evidence discredited however, the argument for keeping me in prison when my safety was already under threat collapsed. And by eight o'clock that evening I was back in Cois Farraige, word already circulating around town that the guards had been forced to release me.

But Mick Clancy was a tenacious fucker, bless him – and he wasn't done yet. He ensured that detailed tests were conducted over the following days to identify everyone whose DNA had been found on that first band, instructing his men to collect samples from all of the girls in Sharon's class, and any other kids who knew her. It took nearly a week – time I spent holed up in my room, on Mick's advice, given the widespread outrage both locally and in the press at the decision to release me. But the results, when they came, shocked everyone.

Four separate students' DNA were identified. As expected, three of them came from people in her school. But the dominant sample came from Laura. My Laura! Someone who attended a different school altogether, outside of the town, and who insisted she'd had no contact with Sharon Buckley, and had certainly never had an opportunity to wear her wristband!

Things moved quickly from there.

I met with Mick and the now somewhat subdued Brady twice more, going over every detail of my story and this time (this time!) being listened to when I voiced my belief that Tom was behind this murder - just as he'd been behind Karen Williams'. Using the wristband – almost certainly Laura's, as now seemed clear – as a basis for probable cause, the guards obtained a search warrant for Tom and Kate's home and went through the place with a fine-tooth comb. Which was when another failing of the original forensics examination was discovered. And one more piece of the puzzle fell into place.

Some fibres had been found on Sharon Buckley's skirt. Two separate samples, each from a different fabric. As with the DNA evidence, the only focus of investigation was in the context of the case against me. They'd tried therefore to tie the fibres to any of the places I had been. From Cois Farraige, to the coffee shops and pubs I had been seen in, to the hotel room in Dublin where I'd spent those first nights prior to coming to Greystones. All these tests proved negative. These were minute samples, in any case. Traces which might have gone undetected even a few years beforehand. Thank fuck for the relentless march of science!

When they conducted the same tests in Tom and Kate's house, they found a match. The first of the two samples was a match to the living room sofa - part of a three-piece suite they'd bought in a furniture store in the Powerscourt demesne less than six months before. The second sample – much more damning – came from their bedsheets.

There were some people who suspected Laura of being involved, at least for a short time. Feuds between girls are always capable of escalating, whatever natural aversion we have to believing girls capable of violence. Sharon Buckley herself was proof of that capacity - as I'd witnessed in the church car park the day our paths crossed so portentously.

And it was a reasonable enough conjecture, that hesitation excepted. It was Laura's wristband after all which the guards had found during their investigation (nobody knew at this point where the wristband had been discovered). The teenagers had fallen out. Perhaps over a boy. Laura had confronted her or the other way around, and the dispute had escalated, resulting in the accidental death of Sharon. Plausible, if unlikely.

But two things immediately contradicted that version of events - and gave rise to even more important questions. The first, and most important, was the fact that the murder was identical in all the essential details to that of Karen Williams. When Laura was seven years old. And the second brought us back to the second sample. While Laura could reasonably be expected to carry and transfer fibres from the downstairs furniture in her home, how likely was it that she – or any of the other suspects whose names were randomly thrown into the mix - could transfer fibres from her parents' bedroom sheets? Such a transfer would most likely have originated from someone sitting on the unmade bed to pull on their clothes prior to the murder. And that pointed in one of only two directions. To Tom, or to Kate.

Or to Kate. Was that possible? Had Laura been asking herself the same question? Had her mother been capable not only of murdering a girl of Laura's age -of two girls, it now seemed likely – but of framing her dad? Did this explain her apparent willingness to accept my guilt and her subsequent refusal to testify on my behalf? Could she have held Karen Williams down, and squeezed the breath from her body... and for what? To be with Tom?

Who was to say they hadn't already been together – furtively meeting up behind my back while we still shared a home? Strangling was apparently more typical of women than stabbings, or attacks with other types of weapon. Karen was a fairly slight girl in my memory of her - probably less than a hundred pounds in weight, and only five-three or four in height. Kate was five-eight and strong, despite her slim build. She'd attended the gym religiously that last year, at least twice every week and sometimes as often as five times if her schedule allowed it. Could she? Was it possible?

I was sitting on my bed in the upstairs room they'd allocated to me in Cois Farraige, while these thoughts played around in my head. Outside the rain had been joined by a chill wind, and the room didn't seem to retain heat as well as the previous one. I had my knees tucked up before me, a cup of instant coffee cupped between my hands, trying to absorb its warmth.

The logic unfolded itself. A girl of Karen's age would be much more likely to follow a woman to some out of the way place than a man. Could she have lured her away under some pretext, then grabbed her and stifled her cries? How hard would it have been to slip the credit card from my wallet on our bedside table? Or to take some soil from the bag of fertilizer in her own garden?

And there was the third possibility - that they had killed Karen Williams together. That they had schemed and planned, ensuring each had an alibi, joining Tom's strength to Kate's... what? Cunning? There was no evidence of that in her. At no stage in our marriage had I seen any indication of such a quality. Kate was open. Honest. As far from capable of murder as Laura had been at that time. No. Nobody would believe that. Either working alone, or in concert with Tom, she simply couldn't have done it. Let alone have done it twice.

There had been nothing to stop her from separating from me back in 2008, if that was what she wanted. She would probably have gotten the house in the settlement anyway. And how would it serve her financially to have me in prison, rather than on the outside earning a salary - a large portion of which would go to herself and Laura following a separation or divorce? She would have had to hate me, to consider such a course of action. Not loving me any longer wouldn't have been enough.

I was starving! I'd ventured out once before, as far as the minimart at the petrol station further up towards the town, but pot noodles and packets of biscuits will only get you so far. The pot noodle – chicken curry flavour, supposedly – was a mess of stodge and MSG and about as tasty as the cardboard wrapper it came in. The biscuits – fig rolls, and McVitie's digestives I'd livened up by adding some cheese slices – were better, but would do nothing to replace the twelve pounds I'd dropped since being taken back to Mountjoy. I'd lost the weight through a combination of exercise and anxiety, stress being the larger factor by far.

The relief I experienced on being released was impossible to calculate. The discovery of Sharon's wristband had literally saved my life. But why had it taken so long? Perhaps it had been found days before, I reasoned, but Sharon Buckley's mother hadn't wanted to accept what it meant. They had her daughter's killer in jail, after all. The guards had told them the case against him was sound. He'd done the same thing before, for God's sake! So why rock the boat? Why cast doubt on everything? I knew how I would have felt in the same situation. But in the end, it seemed, her conscience got the better of her. And thank Christ for that!

I had always been confident that a second, more detailed forensics examination would throw up more evidence, and the abject failure of the first examination had shocked me. But without the wristband it would have been difficult if not impossible to bring the various strands together, and cast suspicion on Tom. Would Mick Clancy really have had all the DNA traces tested in its absence? How would they have matched the fibres they found to the items of furniture in his house, if he had never been placed under suspicion? Would Laura even have been questioned, or have identified the wristband as her own? The best I could reasonably have hoped for was that sufficient doubt would have been cast upon my guilt to make a conviction unsafe – or at least difficult to obtain. Whereas now...!

I was restless, writhing with conflicting emotions and finding it impossible to sit still. I felt as if I was still in my cell, unable to move beyond the bedroom. I was so on edge that when the knock came on the door, it startled me.

"Jack?"

"Mick?"

"Who the fuck do ye think it is? C'mon, open up."

I slipped the lock and pulled the door back to let him in. His hair was plastered to his head, a scattering of raindrops across the front of his grey slacks making it look like he'd pissed himself after one too many pints. A happenstance you could never rule out.

"An inspector calls!" I said.

"And a good one at that! Grab your coat - we're heading to McDaid's."

"Are you sure it's safe?" I asked. "Wasn't I supposed to keep my head down? In case of lynch mobs, or the like?"

"You'll be all right with me. If anyone asks I'll tell them I'm conducting an interrogation, and to piss off!"

"Do the guards usually give their suspects pints on those occasions?"

"Sure! Helps to loosen them up. And anyway, who said I'd be giving you drink? As far as I'm aware, you'll be the one buying!"

I couldn't argue with that.

"What's been going on? I can't keep track of things, stuck away in here."

"Leave it till we're there, all right? Don't worry - I'll soon have you up to speed."

I took my jacket from the back of the chair and followed him out the door, struggling to keep up with him as he strode from the building towards the pub.

I spotted her the second we walked through the entrance of McDaid's. She was sitting at a table at the back, head down, her hands in her lap and her back hunched as if trying to avoid people's notice. I looked across at Mick, and he gave me a little wink.

"Thought you might want to catch up with someone!" he said.

I rushed over to the table as Laura stood up. We hugged for what seemed like minutes, while Mick stood by awkwardly, rocking back and forth on his heels in embarrassed silence.

"I – eh - think I'll go interrogate the barman about how long he's left it since the beer lines were cleaned. Talk to you in a few minutes. Depending on how negligent he's been. And I may need to demand proof."

I smiled at him, and sat down with Laura.

"I can't believe you're out, Dad!" she began, still a little breathless.

"Nor can I!" I said. "What did Mick Clancy tell you?"

"Just that they'd found new evidence, and it meant they had to release you!"

"That's about the size of it. I told you I didn't do any of this, Laura. All this time..." I swallowed hard at the thought of the lost years between us. "All this time, I was innocent. Just like I told you."

"I know, Dad. I believe you!"

She reached across the table and gave me another hug. When she sat back she had tears in her eyes, one of them escaping and drawing a slow trail across the perfect skin of her cheek. My beautiful daughter!

"How's your mum?"

"Oh my God! I don't think she knows what to think. It's been mad at our house – the cops have been right through it, and Tom has been in with them twice, talking about what has happened. Why are they talking to him, do you know? He doesn't know any more about what happened to Sharon Buckley than I do."

"I'm sure they have their reasons," I replied, resisting the urge to tell her anything further. She'd find out soon enough. They both would.

"Does she know you're here?"

"No," she replied. "I only met Mr Clancy by chance, when I was downtown with Eve and Molly."

I had no idea who these friends were - who any of her friends were – but I let it pass. There'd be opportunity enough to learn these things in the future.

"He asked me if I wanted to see you, and I said yes, then he brought me here and left me, while he went to get you."

I nodded, unable to stop smiling. No doubt I looked like an idiot.

"What has your mother heard? About me?"

"Just that you'd been released, and that there was a rumour going around that they had proof you didn't do it!"

I could thank Mick Clancy for that rumour, I reckoned. No doubt this was why he'd felt it safe to take me out of Cois Farraige.

"Is she okay?"

"Mum? I... I don't think so. She keeps crying. And she won't tell me why."

"And Julia?" I asked, hesitantly.

"She's fine. A bit confused. She doesn't really understand what's going on."

I felt for Laura. The poor girl had had more than her fair share of parental problems to deal with over the years. Her father's arrest and imprisonment. The divorce, and her mother remarrying. Having to get used to Uncle Tom acting like something else. The arrival of a new baby... Her father's continued absence from her life. Well, all that'd come to an end, now. I'd make certain of it. Looking at her, I realised at that moment how much I loved her, and how wrong I'd been in refusing to see her for all those years.

"I'm so sorry, Laura! For everything. You shouldn't have to go through all of this."

"It's all right, Dad. You're out, and that's all that matters!"

I paused for a second, thinking what else she'd have to go through before all this was over. Of what Kate and Julia would have to go through, too.

"Has Tom talked to you?"

"No. He's... he's all in a panic, Dad. He won't say anything to either of us, just keeps pacing around the house and checking things, like he's trying to clean up after the search they did, or something."

I'll bet he is, I thought. But it's too late to close the stable door now, brother of mine. It doesn't do to underestimate science.

"Sorry, pet!" Mick said, suddenly hovering over the table like a particularly scruffy harbinger of doom.

"I'm afraid I'm going to need your father back for a few minutes."

"It's okay Mr Clancy!" she said, rising from the chair and gathering a rucksack from by her feet. "Will I see you soon, Dad?" she asked.

"Of course you will, Laura! I'm back for good this time. You'll soon be sick of the sight of me!" I gave her a kiss and watched her out of the door, heading back to a house overflowing with tension and fevered desperation. I didn't envy her. It would be a different place soon enough.

"You don't think it's a bit early to be making promises like that?" Mick asked, dropping himself into the chair Laura had vacated and placing two pints on the table before us. Both glasses were full, I noted. Meaning Mick had probably had another one at the bar while I was talking to Laura. Quality control, no doubt.

"So. What's going on?" I said, the minute he'd taken a first sip.

"Jaysus! Give a man a chance!" he took another, longer swallow. I couldn't be certain, but I suspected that he was deliberately prolonging my agony. I supposed the fucker had every right to, in the circumstances.

"I owe you, Mick. I mean it. If you hadn't followed up..."

"You told me not to take things at face value. Remember? And the whole thing felt wonky to me from the start. Like you said – what sort of moron would make the same mistakes twice, or kill two girls in the same way, in the same town?"

I smiled.

"There's more though, isn't there? I can see it in your face."

"Nothing that we've found. 'Least, not yet. But let's just say that they're looking at the Karen Williams case again, and at the evidence against you."

It made sense. If they believed Tom could have been responsible for Sharon Buckley's death, then finding my credit card and the traces of fertilizer by Karen Williams's body became easier to explain. It wouldn't have been difficult for my own brother to get hold of those. He'd have had countless opportunities to steal my credit card. And he had free run of my garden every time that he called. If they really had linked him to Sharon Buckley's death, then –

"I think it's over, Jack. Not yet. But soon as the dust settles. We're looking at charging your brother tomorrow morning, if our guy in the DPP feels he can make a case. And it's looking that way right now. Whichever way things fall, there'll likely be enough doubt about your conviction in the Karen Williams case to get it overturned."

I couldn't believe it. Was this true? *Could* it be? After all this time, the idea that I could be free! Not just now - not just for Sharon Buckley's murder - but from all of it! Free of the stigma of guilt from Karen's murder as well, and justice finally done for her... I remembered the look on her father's face when I'd spotted him lurking outside Cois Farraige. The night when the idea had first begun to form.

A sense of calm slowly began to descend on me. The truth was that I was exhausted. Eight years of it. Over! All that fear. The pain, physical and otherwise. All that violence! The violence I'd done, as well as the violence done to me. Over! All that damage...

Although, maybe not. I would never be truly free of it, I knew. What had happened to me had shaped me – made me into someone, and something different. I would do everything in my power to change that. To try to go back to being the man I'd been before. To the father I'd once been. To the husband, if I could convince her to take me back. I would do whatever it took, to regain a normal life.

I could get a job! I'd likely be in line for some sort of settlement according to what Mr Wayne had told me – but either way I had enough left over from my dad's inheritance to keep me afloat while I looked around. Maybe I could sell my story to the newspapers? Or find someone to ghost-write a book? There had to be something!

Because I'd be a different man now, to the outside world. Not a convicted murderer: but someone with a fascinating story to tell. The innocent victim of a terrible, and ingenious crime. Somebody who'd displayed remarkable courage and determination, qualities that you'd think would have to have currency for some future employer. To have overcome so much..!

Finally – after all these years – the man who'd really murdered Karen Williams would be exposed and convicted, and my name and record would be cleared. It was over! And we could all start over once again.

I raised my glass to Mick Clancy – everything I wanted to say to him communicated in that gesture. He met my eye and nodded, and smiled back.

Thirty-one

I met Mick Clancy again a couple of months later. I'd taken a by-the-month let in a sprawling development of apartments and townhouses on the outskirts of the town, still within walking distance of the town centre and the various amenities. And Laura. I'd spent the morning walking the harbour wall, standing still and silent at the end of the western pier and gazing out toward Howth across the expanse of Dublin Bay. Watching cormorants hunt across the ribbed surface of the water and listening to the shouts and laughter from the construction workers further down the coast on the far side of the harbour. They'd taken the hoardings down the week before, and work was progressing on the first line of houses by the new marina.

I moved on after a few minutes, walking up to the main street and making my way through the town, counting off the businesses. Café, Coffee Shop, Optician's, Pharmacy. Fish and Chip Shop, Restaurant, Cycle Shop, Off Licence. Restaurant, Gallery, Restaurant, Coffee Shop. Laundrette, Food Hall, Travel Agency, Coffee Shop. Bank, Boutique, DART Station. Constituency Office, Coffee Shop,

Restaurant, Estate Agent. Library, Coffee Shop. Boutique, Dry Cleaner's. Take Away, Coffee Shop, St Vincent de Paul, Carpet Store and Skateboard Shop. As many of the restaurants also served coffee this meant that there were nine such establishments on the main street. On one side alone. Nobody in Greystones would ever be stuck for somewhere to host a coffee-morning!

It had become something of a ritual for Mick and I to meet each Friday afternoon, at the end of the working week. Occasionally Cameron Douglas would join us, the three of us occupying the same table at the back of Molly's. I'd yet to find a job, but I'd had a few interviews, and there were some reasonably promising prospects. It was still difficult to explain away an eight-year gap in your CV, but I'd gotten better at handling those questions. As uncomfortable as it was, I'd learned that it was easier to deal with these head-on. People would find out once I was hired anyway - and did I really want to work for someone who'd view me with suspicion, even after I'd been cleared of all charges? For some, my involvement in those events was enough of a deterrent. And I got it. They could do without the disruption.

Closing the case hadn't done Mick's reputation any harm, though. Not just around the town, but professionally. It was a given that I always paid for the pints, whenever we met up. I suppose I owed him that much. And he supposed so, too.

He was missing from his usual spot by the bar when I walked into Molly's. A game he wanted to watch was about to start on the TV, and he'd taken up residence at a high table further in where he had an uninterrupted view of the screen, his coat thrown across a stool to his left to hold a place for me. I noticed there was no glass in front of him. The mean git. He'd rather go thirsty than risk a breach of the usual practice.

I caught Len the barman's eye, and he replied with a wink. He knew our order at this stage and two pints of Guinness arrived a minute or two later, carried over to our table by a lounge girl of about Laura's age. Laura was in Dundrum doing some New Year's shopping with her Mum. I'd spoken to Kate twice since my release. The conversations had been strained, but cordial. I suppose the truth was that neither of us knew how to treat the other, given everything that had happened. Still. Things would get easier, in time.

I'd barely exchanged greetings with Mick before the game kicked off, and I settled back in my seat knowing there'd be no more chat until half time. I'd little interest in a premiership match between Norwich and West Brom, so I sat back and allowed my mind to wander. I'd learned to relish such moments, given everything that had come before.

Tom was in Mountjoy, on remand for the murder of Sharon Buckley. They'd never be able to prosecute him for Karen Williams' death, but it probably wouldn't matter when it came to sentencing. The charge was one of murder, not manslaughter. Given the circumstances, there was no way he could argue that the act hadn't been premeditated. With both Donald and McLaughlin revising their testimonies – no doubt an attempt to save face in the golf club - enough suspicion had fallen on Tom for Karen Williams' murder for my own conviction to appear unsafe... and for it to be quashed a few weeks later, after a grandstand performance before the court of appeal by John Wayne. Meanwhile the town was still in mourning for the lost girls, memories of Karen Williams' death as fresh now as they had been in the weeks following her death. Two angels taken from us, as the narrative went. Though the truth was that Sharon Buckley had been anything but.

I had been justified in the faith I'd placed in Mick Clancy. I'd had to depend on his looking past those first indications of my guilt, and searching for the things which remained hidden. And he had not let me down. He was a relentless fucker, and I'd been right to believe in him. He might be a cranky bastard, and lacking in the most rudimentary of social skills, but he was also, as was now generally accepted, a great detective.

It was the wristband, of course. When I first met Laura and recognised the luminous orange strap on her wrist as identical to the one Sharon Buckley'd been wearing during our confrontation at the church - when she'd raised her hands to either side of her face to launch a globule of spit at my face - everything snapped into place. It was a matter of a moment to slip it from Laura's wrist when I met her outside Cois Farraige and took her hands in mine, imploring her to believe me when I told her I was innocent of Karen William's death. As, indeed, I am. I'd only touched the outer side and edges of the band, but I cleaned those down later that evening using an alcohol-based spray, which evaporated along with any traces of me before I placed it carefully on top of the wardrobe in my room. Sometimes people break in not to take things, but to leave them behind. I knew that they'd concentrate on the band when looking for DNA. If they'd only done their job right the first time, I'd have been spared the horror of Mountjoy - but I suppose that I couldn't complain, in the end. Although Charlie Ahearne might beg to differ! On reflection, I reckoned it might be a good thing for Tom to keep his relationship with me quiet, when he was inside.

The fibres were easy to obtain. After all, how difficult can it be to break into your own home? I knew every inch of that house, including where Kate kept the spare key, and all it took was forty minutes waiting around for Kate to leave one weekday morning, and five minutes inside with a piece of adhesive tape to grab some trace samples from the sofa and the bedsheets. And transferring them to Sharon Buckley's clothes was just as simple.

I look across at Mick now, and resist the urge to consider him a fool. After all, what he did was truly exceptional detective work. He hadn't accepted things at face value (although with much prompting from me). He had followed the evidence where it led, relentlessly. He'd uncovered truths and made connections in a manner that inferior policemen – that wanker Brady included – would never have done. And he could be justifiably satisfied with the outcome.

When it comes to justice, as in war, there are compromises to be made. In order to right a wrong - to ensure that a murderer was brought to justice, and received his due punishment – somebody had to pay a price. I regret that, and I wish that it could have been otherwise. But the greater good was served. Whether that means I was justified (like those drone-strike commanders who talk about 'collateral damage') or am now myself some kind of devil, is for others to judge. Or for no one, rather, because the truth will never be known. The girl was a bitch, she did not suffer, and my conscience is clear.

Epilogue

The truth was that it could have been anyone. Had he not seen Finch emerging from the garden centre that morning with that bag of fertilizer then it might well have been someone else! But something sparked in his memory about the unique properties of different soil types, and Finch's fate was sealed. He bought the next bag from the same pallet, and had all that he needed. All he had to do then was bring a zip-lock bag of the stuff with him when he went to examine the body, and to smear some on her shirt when he knelt down to check her injuries. And as for the credit card... it had been a matter of a moment to slip it from his wallet when he saw Finch heading to the toilets in McDaid's, having followed him there that same evening. He'd watched him drop the wallet on the table after he paid for his round, and when he stood up to go to the gents Clancy simply sat down in his place to say hello to the two friends Finch was drinking with, palming the wallet as he did so. He'd seen Finch pay for the drinks with a debit card, entering his pin on the little portable terminal the bar staff used and getting some cash back, and correctly assumed that a credit card would be unlikely to be missed. It was probably maxed out, like his own! When he went to the toilets in his turn, taking the wallet with him, he pulled a Visa Card from the back of the wallet and slipped the wallet into Finch's jacket on the back of his chair when he returned. All he had to do then was to drop the card in the grass and tread it into the cud as they began their search of the area around the body the following morning, leaving it for one of the others to 'discover'. He was safe at that point, in any case. Having already spent several minutes traipsing about he'd ensured that any trace of his footprints from the day before could be explained. Same shoes, same prints. Who'd bother looking to see if they'd been made at different times, if that was even possible?

It was simple. As simple as keeping Finch from the truth had been, once it became obvious that he wasn't going to let it go. That he would forever worry at the thread of events, and keep pulling, unless he was directed toward another.

It was all so... easy.

But the girl! It could all have been avoided. Just a simple misunderstanding!

He hadn't meant anything by the comment – it was a joke, really. And she'd acted like she was... not interested, obviously - that was the wrong word - but, the signals! The vibe she had given out, encouraging him to talk to her like that! It was no wonder he'd thought he could say it to her - that she'd see the joke, and respond in kind. And then to react like that! With horror, or the like, instead! Like she was disgusted... Leaving him exposed like that! His job – his reputation – put at risk! And all for a simple misunderstanding! Taking offence like that, when she'd been laughing right up to the moment he'd said it! He could not allow it! Nobody would understand.

And he had let her be, hadn't he? If he'd really been interested in her, like that, wouldn't he have... once he'd quietened her? He hadn't even looked – had resisted the idea of undressing her, even though that would have been better in some ways. Would have thrown them further from the scent, by giving them a clear motive. In a way he still wished that he had, so Finch couldn't have gotten away with that bullshit plea of manslaughter.

He looked across at Finch, his smug face tilted back as he drained the last of the Guinness from his glass. Finch was no danger to him. The search of his hotel room had turned up nothing, but whatever suspicions Clancy had about how Tom Finch came into the frame for the murder of the second girl – Sharon Buckley – it didn't matter. Not now.

"Another pint?" Finch asked, rising from his seat.

"Why not?" Clancy replied.

He watched the match, comfortably settled in his seat. Finch joined him in due course, placing two fresh pints on the table before them. Two ordinary men, living ordinary, boring lives in a small coastal town, enjoying a quiet afternoon in the pub.

It was done, now. All the loose ends tidied away. Put to rest. Like his conscience.

Also by Steven Duggan

Virgins

The Dead Dane

The Elder Terror

The Loss of Ordinary Plenty

To contact the author email

stevenduggan@hotmail.com

Steven is represented by

Phil Patterson at

Marjacq Scripts

www.Marjacq.com